One Hundred Days

One Hundred Days

Donna Sage

Matador
Unit E2 Airfield Business Park,
Harrison Road, Market Harborough,
Leicestershire. LE16 7UL
Tel: 0116 2792299
Email: books@troubador.co.uk
Web: www.troubador.co.uk/matador
Twitter: @matadorbooks

ISBN 978 1803135 830

British Library Cataloguing in Publication Data.
A catalogue record for this book is available from the British Library.

Printed and bound in Great Britain by 4edge Limited
Typeset in 11pt Minion Pro by Troubador Publishing Ltd, Leicester, UK

Matador is an imprint of Troubador Publishing Ltd

FRIDAY

Mary began to make her way home through the cold, dark evening.

She stood at the bus stop doubled up, recovering her breath. She had a stitch in her side, everything in her bag was jumbled up, and for what?

"He could have waited, he must have seen me," she thought resentfully.

Oh well, only fifteen minutes to the next one. But that was all it took; her toes were ice, her ears hurt and she could feel her nose swelling.

The bus came round the corner, warm and welcoming, a puddle of light spilling out all around it. The doors closed behind her like comforting arms and for a few minutes, Mary just sat. As the warmth slowly seeped into her, she began to take an interest in her surroundings: a man she recognised as a regular sat opposite politely ignoring his neighbour crowding him with shopping bags; a young girl chatted on her mobile phone; an older woman was giving instructions down hers as to how to cook fish. A little boy about two years old further down the bus wriggled in his seat. He drummed his feet against the seat in front.

"No," said the middle-aged man next to him sternly.

Mary became aware of the man opposite again; he had gone white and was staring towards the end of the bus.

"Are you all right?" she asked the man. He nodded; he was fine, thank you.

SATURDAY

Another rejection letter landed on the mat.

"That one was my best hope," Mary muttered to herself bitterly. "If this goes on much longer, I won't stand a chance of getting back into research work."

She dropped the letter in the bin.

As she wandered round the flat doing the weekend chores, Mary's dissatisfied state coloured everything she touched but:"I will not give up. I will look for a more interesting temp job than the one I have. And I will move out of this dingy flat," she vowed defiantly.

Going through the advertisements occupied a few hours but did not yield results, so Mary posted a CV online and settled down to wait for her friend Gemma to arrive. They had planned to go bowling or out for a run but Gemma had caught her heel in an uneven paving slab and sprained her ankle so Mary suggested they order a take-away and have a night in.

"You can put your foot up and rest," she advised.

Mary soon recovered her usual good humour as she and Gemma sat putting the world to rights over a glass of wine although, as always, Gemma was less concerned than Mary whether the world was right or not. Gemma found her friend's chatter interesting since she never listened to the news herself but tonight her foot hurt and she was tired. The doorbell rang, the food was here and Gemma was eager to eat. Mary tipped it onto plates and for a while all was quiet.

"How's Max?" Mary inquired.

"Fine, fine. You can ask him yourself when he comes to pick me up." Gemma looked thoughtful then added: "Speaking of boyfriends, there's a new intern starting at work tomorrow."

"Oh no, don't start that again." Mary's tone was decisive.

"I've met him before," Gemma continued. "He's a friend of Max's. He wants to get some experience of book-keeping and tax and so on before going into business for himself. His name is Ben. He's cute…. and rich."

"Oh, for goodness' sake!"

But Mary knew there was no stopping Gemma once she had made up her mind so she determined to look on the bright side; someone new at work might relieve the boredom. Especially if he upset Gary.

SUNDAY
DAY 1

Mary was feeling lazy. She stretched out her hand and her fingers connected with her book. She drew it towards her being careful not to knock out the bookmark and positioned it half under the bedclothes then lying on her side, she began to read.

A cup of tea would be nice but she was nearing the exciting bit. She flicked through the pages to see how many there were to go. Quite a few. Tea it was then. And then back to bed to finish the book.

By the time Mary finally got up, it was nearly lunch time. It was easy to waste the afternoon and by dinner time Mary was even feeling optimistic about the impending week at work bearing in mind the entertainment possibilities presented by a newbie falling foul of Gary's little ways.

She settled down in the chair and turned on the television. Flicking through the channels she came across a newsflash; a little boy – Jared Parker – had been kidnapped. As soon as they put up a photograph, Mary let out a gasp. It was the little boy she had seen on the bus.

She replayed the scene in her head; the boy being told off for kicking the seat, the man sitting opposite her watching and turning white…. was it something to do with the little boy or coincidence? The man was looking along the bus but he might not have been looking at the little boy and anyway, even if he was watching him, so what? She had been watching him herself. Anybody would. His antics made it impossible not to.

She must put it out of her head. But stories like that always bothered Mary; the poor little boy, his poor family. Mary knew only too well the disbelief stabbed through by the underlying knowledge of indisputable fact, the hope that sprang eternal that a loved one would somehow come back.

Mrs Parker's exhausted state would not be enough to make her sleep tonight.

Mary picked up her phone and dialled the number given at the end of the broadcast.

"I saw a man watching Jared Parker on the bus," she informed the constable at the other end. He noted the circumstances and took a description.

"We'll be in touch if we need to talk to you again," he said.

"And that's the last I'll hear of it," thought Mary.

She cut herself a slice of cake, made a mug of coffee and found a film to watch. Gradually, she became engrossed in the story then the moment the titles had finished she made another cup of coffee and headed for bed. It was getting late.

* * *

The door banged shut shaking the musty wooden shed and Mary was alone in the dark. She reached out her hand and met dirty sacking, cold and slimy to her touch. She withdrew it, knocking a rake from the wall. It clattered down missing her head by inches and she sat, frightened, on the damp floor, breathing hard and wondering what to do. She *must* think. Now: the door is over there. She crawled to it and tried to tug it open but her childish strength could not make it budge. All was quiet. Mary waited and listened. Where was Ellen? He had Ellen. Mary had watched him tuck Ellen under his arm and carry her away. She slumped against the wall. A spider crawled across her face and she screamed in terror. She beat on the door until she was exhausted then lay on the floor in despair, her dress dirty and torn. In spite of the cold (or perhaps because of it) she began to doze. Suddenly, there were voices. They were coming her way. She shouted and shouted…. until she woke herself up dripping with sweat and shaking all over.

Stupid, stupid dream. It was always the same; it had not changed down all the years.

She pushed back the bedcover and sat on the edge of the bed cooling down, then she gulped some water from a bottle she always kept on the bedside cupboard. She opened the drawer and took out a photograph of Ellen. Not that Mary needed a photograph; she could remember every detail of what her friend looked like. They had been inseparable. In her memory it was always summer and they always had fun. The picture did not show two little girls running through the long grass, holding hands and spinning round until they were giddy, but as Mary looked at it, she could still hear Ellen laughing.

She put the photograph back in the drawer, blowing her friend a kiss as she did so. It was long ago when she had stopped expecting Ellen to walk back through the door, had accepted it would not happen.

"I'll never forget you."

Mary lay down. It was rare for her to dream about the shed any more. It was that missing child that had set it off; well, once they found him, the dreams would recede again. She drifted into a fitful sleep. She had work in the morning.

MONDAY
DAY 2

Mary woke early. She turned on the television news hoping to hear that the little boy had been found. No such luck.

"I hope the police have some leads they're not telling us about," she muttered. "Otherwise…." Mary shuddered. Otherwise help would be needed on a supernatural scale for there to be a happy ending.

"Gosh, look at the time." Mary shoved her sandwiches into her bag, put on her coat and ran for the bus.

Arriving at work, she discovered that Gary had allocated Ben a desk right in her line of sight. She studied him critically. Gemma was right, he was cute. In fact, he was film-star good-looking and demonstrated impeccable taste in his choice of shirt and jacket. The only thing out of place was his thick, unruly hair but that merely added a boyish charm.

Gary's voice broke into her reverie.

"Mary, this is an A-5-73 document so why did you file it

under A-5-74?" It wasn't a rhetorical question. Gary clearly expected an answer.

"Sorry."

What else was there to say? Mary had made a mistake as everyone does from time to time and Gary was making her feel like a child being told off by teacher for some misdemeanour. He picked up the report and strode back to his desk. Mary imagined him adding a point against her name to a tally in his head and sighed.

Gary's desk was in the far corner and from this vantage point he could see the whole office whilst retaining a high degree of privacy himself. Not, however, total privacy and as she observed out of the corner of her eye, Mary saw something move next to him. Or she thought she did. Part of the ever-present shadow in the corner behind him detached itself – a man was standing there.

Gary continued to concentrate on his report, unaware of the visitor. He raised his coffee mug to his lips and as Mary watched, the figure stepped forward and applied a skilful tweak so the mug slipped in Gary's grasp. It hung at an angle of forty-five degrees and as though in slow motion, a gloop of coffee splodged out onto his tie, fallout drops spattering his shirt. He brushed ineffectually at his clothes and looked around to see if anyone had witnessed the accident. Mary became conscious she was staring and looked away just in time, suppressing her smile of pleasure at justice done. Gary would never believe that it was not just the satisfying spectacle of him looking an idiot that held her attention, it was also the handsome man he seemed completely unaware of standing next to him, smiling and signalling to her: "Got him."

Gary marched past her and headed out of the door and down to the car park to his car. Free to direct her attention to her mystery friend, she turned her gaze in the direction of Gary's desk once again. He was backing into the shadow, finger to his lips in a silent "Shh…." Then he was gone.

Mary shuffled the papers on her desk, selected one and walked over to Gary's desk. As she went to put the paper down, she looked at it, clicked her tongue and turned on her heel as though she had been about to leave it but had spotted an error and changed her mind. But the real purpose of her little walk had been to give her the chance to closely examine the corner of the room. There was nothing there.

Mary returned to her own desk and sat down. Of course, there was nothing there. Gary had spilt his coffee, pure and simple. Ghosts aren't real. Pity, though: he had summed up the situation in the office and cheered her up by quietly taking His Self-Satisfied Pomposity down a peg or two, no harm done.

But he *had* been there: she had seen him. She wasn't crazy and her eyes hadn't deceived her. And why shouldn't he be there? Who says there's no such thing as a ghost?

Instantly, Mary answered her own question: "My mother. My school teachers."

A miserable child stood before her accused of lying, her resentful reaction echoing down the years: "How would they know, anyway?"

But the child was a child no more. She was sensible, balanced and not at all impressionable. Light plays tricks. The brain plays tricks, especially when tired. Mary had not seen a ghost in years and the reason was simple: her mother was right. Ghosts do not exist. Only children yearn for a playmate and invent what is not there.

Cora had seemed so real Mary still found it hard to believe she had been a figment of her imagination but: "I have a vivid imagination. I desperately wanted a friend my own age so I made one up. I got older and I grew out of it. Ghosts do not exist."

Gary returned wearing a bright golfing jumper over his now open-necked shirt and flung open the window. Mary was a little cold but it was a small price to pay.

Come lunchtime, there was one obvious topic of conversation: Ben the ideal boyfriend who, Mary noted a little sourly, had managed to navigate Gary's moods and foibles perfectly that morning, unlike herself. Give him time.

Of course, Gemma had made up her mind before he even arrived and Vicky, Mary's other friend in the office, did not take much convincing to agree that Ben and Mary would make a lovely couple.

"He's nice," they said and Mary could not deny it. He was good-humoured and patient to a fault, acting as though he did not even notice Gary's habitual sarcasm and cheerfully carrying out whatever he had been asked to do as if Gary were the politest individual in the universe.

"Give him a chance. If he asks you out: go. It's only a date, it'd be good for you."

"*If* he asks me," thought Mary. Like they weren't plotting something.

And sure enough, the moment she was alone, Ben came over and asked her out. Apparently, he had happened upon this quaint little pub and thought perhaps they might stop by after work before it got too busy.

Ben found them a table and went to the bar. Mary studied him like a specimen in a jar. Some indefinable quality made the barman notice him, made the jostling crowd part to let him through with the drinks. Mary was glad of his old-fashioned attitude; she had not wanted to join him in the crush.

"Cheers."

Deflecting questions about the unsatisfactory mess which was her own life, Mary turned the conversation to Ben. He used to be in insurance – Mary pulled a face – but Ben explained: "Actually, it was fun. You get to talk to lots of different people and listen to stories all day. You call them and all you need to know is the extent of the damage and its cause but they say 'Well, I was having my tea and I heard this crash so I went outside….'"

Ben chatted on affectionately about the resourcefulness of some of the people he talked to, climbing up in the loft at the age of eighty-six and saying 'The assessor can come any time except it's Silver Choir on a Tuesday and I go dancing on Wednesdays' compared to others who sat in a heap and expected everything to be done for them.

All the time Ben was talking, his eyes were glued to Mary's face. The intensity of his attention unsettled her even though he was clearly trying to be amusing.

Self-conscious, Mary looked down. Her face was obscured by her golden-brown hair. She composed herself and looked up again, smiling that funny, crooked smile where one corner of her mouth turned up and the other turned down with the smile in between. The effect was like the sun coming out from behind the clouds. Ben sat basking in its warmth.

But by now the pub was filling up.

"Time to go," said Mary looking around.

"We must do it again," suggested Ben, and Mary smiled and agreed that that would be lovely.

Gratefully, she accepted a lift home in Ben's sports car, waved 'goodbye' and let herself into her flat.

TUESDAY
DAY 3

In the morning at the bus stop, Mary stood thinking about Ben and how annoyingly perfect he was. Charming, amusing and even good at attracting the attention of barmen. And avoiding pitfalls at work. Work. As a picture of the office formed in her mind, she remembered the ghost.

It was a shame he was not real. He had brightened a day that had been rapidly spiralling from mundane to depressing.

On entering the office, Mary looked surreptitiously around. Her heart was beating faster although she would not have admitted it. Which in no way explained the sense of relief which equalled her sense of disappointment to find he was not there.

Vicky and Gemma, however, were lying in wait. "Well?"

"Well, what?"

"Well Ben, of course! Did he meet your exacting standards?"

"He's a bit intense but he's nice. We'll see."

"Does that mean you're going out again?"

When Mary admitted they were, Vicky let out a whoop and started fanning herself with a report.

"Kindly put that down, Miss Burwood. And try to learn the difference between desks and chairs. It is the latter which are for sitting on."

Gary had arrived and the day had begun.

Mary sat down. She opened a spread sheet and started trawling through the numbers but all the while she kept peeping towards the corner: nothing. It had been a trick of the light.

At lunchtime, the others went to Mario's for coffee and doughnuts but Mary excused herself on the grounds that she had work to finish. Which was true enough.

Alone in the room, her computer screen glowing with menace, the words in front of Mary streamed to her eyes, passed down through her arms and out through fingers that flew across the keyboard. But for all she made it look easy, it was draining. Twenty minutes passed. A long, loud sigh escaped. Mary needed a break.

She woke up the internet and searched the news channels for a report on the hunt for the little boy. 'It is now forty-eight hours since toddler Jared Parker was snatched from outside a newsagent's in Reyswood….'

That alone was enough to make Mary shiver. But the shiver that passed through her was a different sort of shiver. A breeze ruffled her hair. There was a presence in the room.

Mary sat still, listening; not a sound.

"Don't be silly," she told herself. "There's nothing there."

She turned round. He was standing right behind her.

Best meet the situation head-on and wait for normality to return. Mary swallowed hard.

"My mother always said it's rude to read over people's shoulders."

He grinned. "Mine too, but I'm doing it anyway."

"You could have scared me creeping up like that."

"For the record, I don't creep. I don't need to."

"No," said Mary. "I suppose you don't. Who are you, anyway? Are you.... a ghost?"

"Yes, I suppose that's what you'd call me."

Mary thought for a moment. "Actually, while we're on the subject, what should I call you? What's your name?"

"Mike."

"Hello, Mike, nice to meet you. I'm Mary."

"I know."

"And you're the Office Ghost."

He considered. "I wouldn't call myself that, no."

He walked round and sat on the edge of her desk. Apprehensive, she moved back a little, her heart pounding. What did she think she was doing, talking to this apparition?

Once again, the melancholy child stood before her. Ghosts. Humbug.

"Are you trying to shut me out?" asked Mike.

Mary ignored him.

"Cora sends her love."

Mary started. "How do you know about...."

17

His eyes twinkled.

"Cora was an imaginary friend, nothing more," insisted Mary.

"You know you don't believe that. They made you say it. They made you give her up. She was very hurt, you know. She cried for days."

Mary covered her ears. "Stop it. Go away."

"It wouldn't change anything if I did. You know the truth." He drew up a chair, settled himself comfortably and stared at her over his fingertips.

Mary stared back in consternation.

"You closed your mind and life got easier. Cora understands it was hard having schoolmates shun you and your mother shake her head sadly and give you meaningful looks and hope you'd grow out of it. She forgives you."

"Go away," responded Mary in a hardly audible whisper.

"I won't. Fate put you where I needed a mortal I could talk to. Cora knew you'd react like this and she said not to be stuffy and grown-up and she knows you are because you don't blow bubbles in your milk anymore."

Their eyes met. In spite of herself, Mary smiled. It was exactly the sort of thing Cora would say.

But just in case there was any doubt left in Mary's mind, Mike added: "She also said that lucky charm you lost fell into that old cloth pencil case you've kept all these years."

"I'd have found it by now."

"It went down the lining."

Slowly, Mary took the pencil case from her desk and felt around until she found a lump. She drew out the tiny charm. She studied it, drinking in every detail.

In that moment, Mary knew that Mike really was a ghost and so had Cora been.

"Tell Cora I'm sorry," she whispered. "Tell her I missed her."

"She knows."

Mike waited patiently while Mary composed herself.

"Mike?" Mary ventured. "Why did Cora come to play with me?"

"You'd have to ask Cora but I sense a vacuum in both your childhoods."

Ellen.

Had Cora, too, lost a friend? Or worse, a sister?

"So, why did she go?"

"She didn't want to cause you problems. She's a good kid. Then, as time went by, you grew older but she didn't. For a long time, Cora watched over you from afar…."

Mary looked up, startled. "I wish she'd come and said 'hello.'"

Mary considered. She would still like to see Cora again but they could hardly play together like they used to. What would she say to her if she did come? It would be an odd meeting.

"Thank you for keeping me company after Ellen disappeared," she thought. "That's what I would say."

"You will tell Cora I'm sorry? I know I already said that but you will tell her?" Mary felt tears welling up.

Mike lifted her chin. "She knows."

As Mary sat dabbing at her face with a tissue, Mike's eyes strayed to the still open news channel on her computer.

"You're really concerned about this child, aren't you?"

"Yes," replied Mary.

"Why?"

"He reminds me of something…. of someone. I do hope…."

Mary's voice tailed off; footsteps were approaching.

"Hi, Mary, who are you talking to?" Vicky asked as she walked through the door. She looked around but there was no one there. "First sign of madness, talking to yourself," she joked.

"Ah, but hearing voices is infinitely worse," parried Mary whilst unseen in the shadows, Mike winked at her and disappeared.

The afternoon passed quickly. Gary fretted over his end-of-month report, sufficiently distracted that he took little notice of the others which gave Mary a chance to hunt down a lost invoice without an inquest as how it came to be lost.

"Found it. Finally."

On her way back to her desk, she heard Vicky and Gemma finishing off their inventory of the stationery cupboard. They picked up their bags and clattered down the stairs and Mary heard their voices getting louder and more excited as they discussed their plans for the weekend but today, she was not leaving with them.

'No good deed goes unpunished.' That was another thing Mary's mother used to say. And Mary had proved it so many times but she still kept making the same mistake. Tonight, she was late leaving because she had agreed to finish putting together meeting packs for the contract meeting first thing in the morning. Paul had had to go and pick up his mother from the station – she was earlier than expected – "Mary, *please*? Gary will chop me into little pieces if it isn't done."

Mary was not doing anything special so she had agreed. Eventually, everything was laid out ready for tomorrow and finally, she was going home.

Being winter, the nights were drawing in. It was already damp and dark. Slowly, Mary became aware that someone was walking along the road on the opposite side in the shadows. Odd, she had not noticed anyone get off the bus at her stop. Glancing at him, Mary thought it looked a little like Tom from the floor below but she was not sure because she did not know Tom that well and whoever it was had his woolly hat pulled down over his ears to protect against the cold and a scarf high against his mouth. She looked again but still was not sure. Better not call out "Hi, Tom," it probably wasn't him.

The figure crossed the road and was now walking along behind her on her side. His shadow stretched in front of them and she could see as well as hear that he was gaining on her. Without making it obvious, Mary walked a little faster. So did her pursuer. She was suddenly aware how alone she was in the dark street, houses all with closed curtains glowing dimly from the lights behind.

He drew level. "You looking at me?"

"No.... I...." Her voice tailed off and she stood there helpless, knowing that she could not outrun him and wondering if anyone in the houses would hear her scream.

But as she stared at his face, its expression changed. The menacing look was replaced by curiosity, then alarm. And then he was gone, sprinting down the street as though his life depended on it.

Mary turned to see what had caused this sudden change, and there was Mike. She looked at him questioningly.

He shrugged. "I just drew myself up to my full height – I'm quite tall, you know – and pulled a couple of faces at him. Can't think why he took off like that."

The already familiar mischievous twinkle was dancing in his eyes and Mary thought she could guess exactly why Mike 'drawing himself up to his full height' and 'making faces' might have had the effect it did.

"Will you walk me home?"

"I'd be delighted."

It was not long before they arrived at Mary's flat.

"Come on in," she said. She took off her wet coat and turned on the fire. "That's better." Then a thought crossed her mind. "It's not too hot for you, is it? I mean…. can you feel…. I mean…. sorry."

He sat opposite in her large, soft chair laughing at her. "I'm fine, Mary, thank you."

Mary gazed at the flames of the fire but all the time in the back of her mind she was wondering about ghosts. As a child, she had simply accepted Cora but she was older now.

"May ask you something?"

"Ask away."

"Most people can't see ghosts, can they? My mother for instance. My teachers."

"Correct."

"So, what's special about me?"

"It happens sometimes when a baby is born dead," Mike replied slowly. "A connection is retained."

Mary remembered her mother describing how fear had

engulfed her as the medical team took Mary and tried to resuscitate her, how the minutes passed, how tears washed down her cheeks and soaked her nightie. Then the joy that swept over her as she heard her beautiful daughter cry.

"I haven't seen any ghosts for years, though. Why not?"

"Why should you? There aren't that many of us here and we're picky who we talk to. The fact you are receptive, the fact I *can* talk to you doesn't mean I have to. You avoid Kevin from the office next door. Now, don't you wish you could become invisible when it suited you?"

It certainly would be convenient, agreed Mary.

"So, it's up to the ghosts whether I see them?"

"In your case, we can block you just as you can block us. Or you can try. Failed with me, didn't you?" he finished triumphantly.

"I'm new to this."

"So am I."

"Are there people you can't block?"

Mike nodded. "A few."

"What about people who aren't receptive? Can you make them see you?"

"If we want to. All except the most resistant."

Mary continued staring into the fire. "I'm curious. Given that you are here – and visible – how come you're sitting in my chair?" she asked. "Traditionally, ghosts are supposed to pass through things, aren't they?"

"You mean walking through walls and all that? That's the default position. But I can interact with things – pick up that book, sit in this chair…. It just takes practice."

Mary was looking straight at him as he disappeared then

reappeared on the other side of the room. He walked towards the table – and straight through it. Then he disappeared.

Cora was the same, Mary remembered. She would mess Mary around sometimes for the fun of it.

Something touched Mary's hair. She shivered.

Mike reappeared beside her. He was visible again and behaving like a mortal which was much less disconcerting. But it still left questions unanswered.

Not for long.

"Why are you here? Why have you chosen to let me see you?"

"I have business here but there's only so much a ghost can do. I'm conducting some investigations but there will come a time when I need practical help. You are perfect for the job: you are in the right place at the right time and I can communicate with you.

"For your part, I believe you requested supernatural help…."

"What?" Mary was incredulous. "When?"

Then she remembered. She had said to herself that it was the only way the kidnapping would have a happy ending.

Mike beamed with satisfaction. "I think we will make a great team."

Mary's eyes widened. Team? Her brain froze, not a single thought surfaced. Team? Slowly, she recovered. He envisaged them helping each other but could he really help her find Jared and what did he want her to do for him?

"Mike, I…."

"I think that's enough for one night."

Mike made his excuses and left and Mary found she was glad; suddenly she felt tired. She stumbled to the kitchen and made a cup of tea.

There was no chance of dredging up the motivation to cook, so she called the shop on the corner. The delivery boy placed the warm package in her hands. Her pizza's cardboard prison was thick but it was no match for the smell of oregano rising from it. Mary curled up on the sofa and ate from the box.

She would have an early night but first: Mary turned on the television – in time to hear an appeal for the safe return of the little boy.

First, a journalist outlined the circumstances: It was the third day since Jared had been snatched. His nanny had gone into the newsagent's for a paper and some cigarettes leaving him asleep in his pushchair at the door. She turned to pay and when she turned back, he was gone. Mary's guess had been about right; he was a little over two years old.

And then there they were. The stern man from the bus looking somewhat grey and a younger woman with blonde hair, her face swollen with crying. The policeman accompanying them did most of the talking while the woman wept quietly. They were looking for a man of medium height with light brown hair wearing a bomber jacket. The description fitted Mary's suspect from the bus but then it fitted half the male population of the country. Then, as the news conference drew to a close, Jared's mother looked up at the camera and begged: "Please don't hurt him. We just want him back. Anything, but don't hurt him."

Mary slumped further into the cushion at her back. She felt so powerless. If there was anything Mike could do then she was glad they had met and she would do everything she could to make their alliance work.

WEDNESDAY
DAY 4

Next day, Gary was late. And not just a little bit. As nine-thirty passed and then ten o'clock, Mary, Ben, Gemma and Vicky looked at each other. They had ceased enjoying the more relaxed atmosphere and were feeling more and more on edge. Something was not right.

It was not until nearly eleven that he finally arrived and as he came through the door their fears were confirmed. Gary looked somehow shorter and greyer, shoulders hunched, a broken man. His step uneven and deliberate, he walked to the centre of the room.

"I need to talk to you all."

They gathered round and waited in silence but Gary seemed to be having trouble finding words.

With an effort, he struggled on: "They're closing the office. We're to be absorbed into the London office to reduce costs. There will be room for two people in London but the rest of you – of us – will be made redundant."

They waited, stunned.

"You may record your preferences and hand them to me. If more than two people want to move to London then interviews will be held next week for the posts available."

Automatically, Gary started to walk towards his desk, then he changed direction and made for the door.

"I expect you all want a few minutes time-out. I'll be going down to reception to let Lisa know we'll be vacating the office."

As soon as the door closed behind him, the room exploded into an excited babble of 'Oh my goodness,' 'Can they do that?' and 'Surely these days firms are moving out of London not into it' but once they had told themselves and each other ten times over how surprised they were, the office became quiet.

Of their little group, only Vicky thought London an appealing prospect. Gemma had long been planning her wedding to Max, Mary was actively job-hunting and Ben had never meant to stay at Bramwells long anyway.

Footsteps approached and Gary walked in.

"Mary, if you would spend the rest of today and tomorrow preparing your client accounts for handover. Ben can help you. The rest of you have until the end of the month although you are free to leave sooner if you wish."

* * *

Back at home, Mary stared at the application form in front of her, her mind a blank.

Please give details of your greatest achievement to date and what you consider to be the important lessons you have learned from this.

Tell us about your biggest failure. How did you recover and what did you learn?

Tell us about a time when you had to make a decision without knowledge of the full facts.

By this point Mary was becoming irritated. "Damn silly question. I'm not omnipotent, I don't suppose I ever know the full facts whether I realise it or not."

She was also becoming certain that she was not alone.

"You're looking over my shoulder, aren't you?"

"Only a little bit. What are you doing?"

"Not doing. A job application. But it's one of those stupid competency things, I can never think of anything to put and I don't see the point."

Mike leaned over for a better look.

"What are you applying for, Managing Director?"

"Oh, ha, ha. Just a clerk job."

He picked up the piece of paper, crossed to the middle of the room and holding it in front of him like a stage script, he solemnly read aloud: "Dealing with the unexpected. Give an example of a time when you prevented tragedy using only a goldfish and a flat battery. Include all…."

He was stopped in mid-sentence by Mary springing at him. "Give that here. It doesn't say that, you're making it up…. Idiot."

He grinned. "Made you smile. Come on, you need a break. How about we go to feed the ducks?"

They set off in the direction of the canal.

"All the adverts seem to want the same; a team player who works well on their own initiative. Schizophrenics welcome," complained Mary.

"Ducks," replied Mike.

When they arrived, there were only two ducks but when Mary started throwing them bread, more appeared out of nowhere flapping their wings and skidding over the surface of the water with their feet sticking out in landing position in their hurry not to miss out.

All too soon the bread was gone and Mary stood there apologising and showing the ducks the empty bag and feeling she should have brought more.

"See you again," she told them.

She picked her way back across the grass avoiding the inevitable duck-mess and checked her shoes.

"Now you," she ordered Mike who had been walking beside her. He turned up his feet to reveal shoe-shop clean soles. Did he walk on the ground, she wondered, or kind of hover above it?

Away from the job application, Mary's thoughts turned to the kidnapping, to her last meeting with Mike and to their agreement.

"I'm glad you turned up, Mike. How are your investigations?"

"They're progressing."

"Is there anything you want me to do?"

"No. I haven't reached that stage. I'll let you know."

A small family group passed by and nodded to Mary, unaware of the tall, good-looking man with dark brown hair, warm brown eyes and high cheekbones accompanying her. Where in times gone by they might have thought she was strange talking to herself, now they assumed she was on the phone, an earpiece hidden under her long hair.

Mike and Mary arrived at the flat and Mary let them in,

knowing that if he had wanted to, Mike could have simply walked through the door as if it were not there.

"You know the police haven't found Jared Parker?"

Mike nodded.

"It's too long. The police will assume he's dead and wind the investigation down. If only there was something I could do. Or maybe he is dead."

"He's not," said Mike. "We do have records in the Other Realm just like you have records of births and deaths here. I looked him up before I suggested our little arrangement."

Ellen.

Should she? Mary was desperate to know if Ellen was alive but part of her was afraid to find out. Mary bit off the request. She was not ready to explain how they had been out playing and how 'he' had grabbed them and taken Ellen away and left her, Mary, behind. The pain and the guilt of her own better fortune were buried deep. She did not know Mike well enough; they had only just met.

Once Jared was safe, she would ask. Finding Jared was urgent; it would not change anything for Ellen to wait a few more days.

"But I will find them both."

And she had Mike to help her.

"Do you know where Jared is?" Mary demanded.

"I don't have access to that sort of information. Anyone can look up the register but where mortals are and what they're doing is entirely another matter."

Which meant that Mike could only have told her that Ellen was dead or that she was alive but he did not know where. She had been right not to ask – yet.

"For what it's worth, Jared's traffic light is yellow."

Mary stared at him uncomprehendingly. "What are you talking about? What traffic light?"

"On the register. There's a yellow light."

Mary continued to look mystified.

"If something dreadful had happened to him or was about to happen, it would be red," explained Mike. "When everything is back to normal, it will go green. Meanwhile, he waits. That's what you do at yellow lights."

"Waits for what?"

"For someone to find him and take him home," replied Mike simply.

"He's safe, then? He's not in any danger?"

"The light would be red."

"Well, that's a relief."

Mike watched as Mary's thoughts reflected in her eyes. Yellow was good but not good enough. Only green would satisfy her.

"What if something goes wrong? The light might turn red."

"Why should anything go wrong? As long as harm is not intended – in which case the light would be red – why should Jared be any more likely to meet with some misfortune than anybody else?"

He was right. They sat in the silence then: "Given that he is being looked after, I wonder why he was taken," pondered Mary.

"Ransom? But there has been no demand. Childless couple turned down for adoption?" speculated Mike. "I don't know, there must be loads of possibilities."

Maybe not loads but some. Mary shot him a grateful glance. However, yellow was not green.

"It's been four days already. The police should have got somewhere by now. What if this carries on and they do give up?" she fretted.

"He has you."

"I've no idea where to start looking. What if I can't find him either?"

"You'll find him. I've been around you long enough to know you'll bang your head on a brick wall however much it hurts until that wall comes tumbling down."

"And I will," thought Mary. "Ellen may never have got back home but if I have anything to do with it, Jared will."

Better get started, then. Focus.

"You said we were a team and that we would help each other," said Mary thoughtfully. "There is a possibility we could investigate: it's said that crimes are usually committed by people close to the victim so maybe someone in the Parker family circle took him. You could tail the Parkers and find out more about them."

"I'm sure the police have investigated the Parkers, Mary," Mike replied.

"You can follow people around without being seen so you might find out something the police would never find. You could pay the police a visit, see whether they have any other suspects and who, then follow them."

"I don't know. A couple of the more likely ones, perhaps."

It was not that Mike was against the idea but there are only so many hours in a day, even a ghost's day.

"What about my concerns?" he inquired.

"What concerns?" Mary was genuinely interested. "What *do* you do all day?"

There was a pause, then slowly Mike replied: "Research."

"Research into what?"

"History."

"Are you looking for something in particular?"

"Facts."

"About?"

"The past."

"Can't you ever answer a straight question?" she demanded.

"I just did. Four of them to be exact."

"You're infuriating, do you know that? I'm not trying to pry but you haven't told me why you returned and I think you owe it to me to behave like a team member!"

Mike was surprised by the strength of her reaction but the truth was that it bothered Mary that she had signed up to their alliance without knowing what Mike expected of her.

"You're right. I have been allowed to return to resolve personal issues that cause me disturbance; that is the usual reason why any of us come back. I am here – in this place – because this is where I will find answers. This is where I can find somebody who, if I'm correct, should be behind bars not roaming the world free to cause harm."

"Who?"

"I said 'if I'm correct.' It would be inappropriate to tell you until I'm sure. But you're an intelligent girl, you'll work it out."

Mary sighed.

"Going back to the question of Jared, are you going to help or not?"

"Of course."

"Right, then." Mary became business-like. "First of all, it would be useful if you could establish whether the police have any leads."

"I'll see what I can do," Mike agreed and Mary flashed him that funny little smile of hers.

Mike shook his head and sighed. She had only to look at him like that and she could wind him round her little finger.

"Now, what about the Parkers?"

"Why don't you take that line of inquiry?"

Mary's eyes widened. "How could I get close to them?"

"Leave it to me," said Mike. "I have an idea about that."

THURSDAY
DAY 5

Finally, Mary had found something Ben could not do. He stood looking bemused at the flat-pack box she had given him. Push this bit downwards according to the arrow – but it was too big, it would not fit. Ben turned it over; that was not right either. He turned it back, sucked his teeth. Wait a minute – this way. But Ben's pleasure in his tiny victory was short-lived; the bottom might be in position but the side had bent in half.

"Here, let me help."

"Thanks. Why don't you make them and fill them up since you know what's going to London and what's going to archive and I'll do the heavy work stacking them by the lift ready for the courier."

"Oof," said Mary about an hour later. She wiped her brow with the back of her hand. "Time for a tea break."

Just then, her phone rang. Normally, Mary would have set it to silent mode and ignored the call but this was not a normal day. Gary looked up but merely nodded, his face expressionless, not a hint of criticism.

"Is that Mary?"

"Yes."

"My name is Cameron, I'm calling from Renfrews Rapid Recruitment. Is this a convenient time to talk?"

"Just a minute."

Mary turned to Ben. "Could you put these labels on the boxes?"

She walked to a quiet corner to take the call. "Go ahead, Cameron."

It seemed Cameron had seen Mary's CV online and wondered if she would be interested in a temporary vacancy that had just come up.

"They want someone who can start straight away, ideally Monday morning. It's mostly filing, a bit of typing and so on. Nothing you haven't done before. Would you be happy to work on a construction site?"

"Of course," said Mary.

"Good. I'll send over the details. Eight-thirty sharp."

Mary put down the phone and went back to Ben feeling quietly pleased. She had a job. And she had not even had to attend an interview, competency-based or otherwise.

* * *

Mary was still not sure about having a ghost in her life but he was in her life and she wanted to see him and he did not come.

Then suddenly, there he was. Mike cleared his throat.

"I, er, thought you might enjoy a week-end break before you start your new job," he said.

"Why?" Mary asked.

"Well, I was passing by the Parkers' and I heard Henry Parker arranging for them to go away for a little while. Not far, in case of developments but Mrs Parker – Rachel – is having trouble coping with newspaper people trying to take pictures and she's convinced the neighbours are whispering behind her back. I thought you might enjoy a little break, too – in the same hotel – bump in to them and see what you can find out.

"Oh, and Mary…. watch yourself. It wouldn't be the first time the parents themselves were involved in something like this."

Mike gave her the details of the hotel and Mary booked the last remaining room.

FRIDAY
DAY 6

The next day was frantic, what with it being her last day at Bramwells and having to pack in the evening and look up trains but she made it. As Mary settled into her seat on the train, she was finally able to contemplate the trip with anticipation. The hotel looked pleasant – in the pictures anyway. There was an attractive looking sea-front area and surrounding it all was beautiful countryside with pretty villages steeped in history.

It was only a short journey. The hotel was not far from the station and soon Mary was mentally congratulating the Parkers on their choice. In its own quiet, understated way the place was perfect. Mary arrived in time to fit in a short walk in the evening sunshine before dinner and guided towards the sea by its unique smell, she found her way to the promenade with its fancy black railings and steps down to a sandy beach. She could have stood there for hours listening to the soothing sound of the waves and watching the patterns they drew crossing over each other as they lapped gently on to the shore but Mary knew better than to dip her toes in. It would be cold even in summer and it was not summer yet.

She did not see the Parkers that night and retired to bed realising that it might not be easy to engineer a meeting.

SATURDAY
DAY 7

But luck was on her side. The following morning, Mary went down to the dining room to see what was on offer. A row of tables filled the centre of the room and along the side were silver serving dishes from which a most inviting smell emanated. She peeped into the nearest – bacon – and continued along the row. Eggs. Sausage. Tomatoes. Beans. It was irresistible. One full English coming up. Breakfast safely demolished, she was sitting drinking coffee when who should come in but the Parkers. They collected their breakfast and sat at a nearby table. Mary asked for more coffee and sat listening to their conversation.

It appeared that Mr Parker – Henry – was not feeling well. He had only come down to breakfast to keep his wife company. Mary studied him; he certainly did not look well. He sipped his tea and told his wife not to mind him, he would be fine in a moment and they would go out as planned. But actions speak louder than words and as he hurriedly put down his cup and ran for the bathroom, it was clear he would not be fine. Rachel stared after him in concern.

Couldn't he hurry up? Mary could not justify staying much longer. Finally, he returned, still looking green around the edges.

"I think you may have to go out by yourself," he told Rachel.

She looked appalled. "I can't just leave you. And anyway, you know I hate doing things on my own."

"Yes, but I brought you here for a change of scenery, to get away from it all. It will defeat the object if you sit in the hotel room and watch me being sick."

"They seem genuinely fond of each other and they don't act as though they have anything to hide," thought Mary.

She stood up and began to walk slowly towards the door. As she passed the Parkers' table, Henry added: "I know it's no fun by yourself but I really do think you should go out."

Mary seized her chance. "I hope you don't mind but I couldn't help hearing what you were saying," she remarked. "And....well.... I'm on my own and I was intending to take a trip down to the harbour. Perhaps we could go together. I'd be glad of the company."

Mrs Parker looked doubtful.

"I'm not leaving for about ten minutes," said Mary. "Let me know. Room 214." She went upstairs to collect her bag and before long there was a soft tap at the door. Henry had talked Rachel into it.

Tentatively, Rachel asked: "This might seem a little strange but before we go would you mind taking a look outside to see if there's anybody there?

"Anybody?" queried Mary, playing the innocent.

"A little group of people, perhaps?"

What she meant was reporters. Mary stepped into the bay window and peered about. "No little groups. In fact, not a soul. It's deserted."

Rachel replied: "Oh good. Let's go before…. it gets any later."

The day was bright and still. They walked through the Old Town peering into antiquated shops then headed for the bustling market where Mary bought a table cloth. She was tempted by a pretty necklace made of sea shells and had trouble getting away from a handbag stall where she did not like anything and the seller was reluctant to give up but Rachel was not in a buying mood. Mary did not let on that she knew why.

"I hope you like ruins," she said to Rachel. "There's a castle up there."

They walked towards it. And they walked all round the high stone walls looking for the way in.

"Up there, over the bridge," said Rachel, pointing.

After a steep climb up an adjacent hill, they eventually arrived via the wooden bridge at the entrance to the castle to discover a large open space which had been turned into a pretty garden off which came rooms one of which overlooked the harbour far below.

"Isn't it lovely," said Mary.

"Yes," agreed Rachel.

By now they were getting weary so they headed down to the sea-front. It was lined with cafes offering every type of cuisine both ethnic and traditional but from above they had already chosen a place on the corner right by the water with a wonderful view of the sailing boats in the old harbour. Mary ordered coffee and stared around her.

"Fascinating," she said. "Don't you wonder how they did it?"

"Did what?"

"Well, it said on the notice in the castle that the Romans built those sea walls to break up the waves. The question is: how? They didn't have the technology we have now. Suppose they laid stones on the sea-bed then built on top of them until they had a wall rising out of the water, do you think they dived down with snorkels to lay the first few layers?"

As Mary thought aloud, painting pictures of rows of Roman soldiers with snorkels diving in synchrony on command, even Rachel had to laugh. Her new companion was good company. She wondered whether perhaps they could keep contact since it seemed they lived in the same town and Mary was more than happy to agree.

The logistics of Roman wall-building and their invention of water-proof cement might continue to occupy Mary's mind for a while as they sat in silence but Rachel's concentration wandered. A small boy was running along the promenade and hiding behind the bollards playing peep-bo with his big sister. A sad expression crossed Rachel's face, pain in her eyes.

"Are you all right?" asked Mary.

"Yes, of course," replied Rachel. "Well, actually, no."

She told Mary about Jared and although Mary did not admit to having known all along who Rachel was, her sympathy was genuine enough.

"I can't imagine anything so awful," she said. It had been hard losing her friend Ellen but to lose a child was infinitely worse. "I suppose Henry is a help?"

"I suppose so," agreed Rachel. "Although there's not really anything he can say. And we've gone over it and over it and said it all. He goes away a lot for work, too. Recently, he has been concentrating on local business and staying at home more but the house still seems empty without Jared."

"Isn't there anyone else you can talk to? Don't you have any family?"

"I do. Henry doesn't but I do."

Rachel fished in her bag and produced a photo. "Here we all are," she said. "That's Henry and me and Jared of course…." She drew a breath. "And that's my sister Tess and her husband…. Charles."

Mary looked at her keenly. "You don't like Charles, do you?"

"It's not exactly that. It's just that, well, his business got into trouble and although Henry puts work his way, I feel he resents Henry's success. It creates a bit of a barrier."

"What does he do, this Charles?"

"He's a builder."

Mary resolved to find out more about Charles. But it would have to wait for another day; she must not appear to pry.

SUNDAY
DAY 8

Next day, Henry was better, at least to the point where he and Rachel could resume their original plans. They had hired a car so they could explore further afield and invited Mary to join them but she politely declined, explaining that she needed to leave early.

After a pleasant morning exploring the nearest of the local villages, Mary caught a train home. Back in the flat, she packed a bag with an array of things that might come in handy the following day then turned her attention to what to wear for her new job. Sensible shoes, obviously. Trousers. A cheerful jumper, tidy but not too smart.

Mary rummaged through the wardrobe; she did not have anything matching that description. No matter, there was just enough time to shop. She headed for the department store. Her choice in her hand, she made for the check-out but on the way, right in front of her on a mannequin, was a gorgeous fitted blue dress with long sleeves and a flowing skirt.

She couldn't justify it…. could she? But she had been caught out that way before; she had resisted then along came an occasion and she couldn't find anything she liked. It would not hurt to have something put by…. it certainly wouldn't hurt to try it on. Mary chose her size from the rail and headed for the changing room.

"Mmm…." said a voice, and there was Mike. "Nice dress. It suits you." He viewed from all angles with an approving expression.

"Don't you have any sense of decency?" she hissed.

"Of course," he replied. "Have you ever known me visit you in the bath?"

"I take it that was a deliberately careful choice of words? There's a difference between me not knowing and you not doing it."

"True. You'll have to trust me."

Mary was trying to compose a suitable reply as she headed to the pay desk with Mike alongside when who should they run into but Ben.

"Hey, Mary," he called.

"Hey, Ben. What are you doing here?"

"I came for a present for my grandfather. It's his birthday. How about you?"

"Jumpers. A dress." She pointed. "Like that one over there on the model."

"Oh, wow. I bet you look fantastic in that."

"Thank you," said Mary, feeling slightly embarrassed as she looked around for Mike. But he was nowhere to be seen. She paid for her purchases and turned her full attention to Ben.

"Do you fancy a coffee?" he asked.

"Yes," said Mary gratefully if a little distractedly. "I could do with one."

They went over to the café area and sat by a big picture window looking out on to the street.

"What are you going to buy your grandfather?" asked Mary.

"I thought perhaps a hat. Why don't you help me choose then we could have a meal together if you would like?"

They chose a little Italian restaurant at the end of the High Street and sat in big, comfortable chairs by the window enjoying a glass of wine and waiting for the food to be ready. It would be pleasant not to eat alone for once and even if Ben was annoyingly perfect…. actually, he wasn't, thought Mary, remembering the box. A smile crossed her lips.

"What?" inquired Ben.

Mary thought quickly. "Hats," she replied. "I was thinking about Gary in his Father Christmas hat he wore to hand out the Secret Santa presents at Christmas."

"It's hard to imagine," mused Ben, "but even harder to imagine is Gary at Christmas in days gone by. After all, he must have been a child once."

"In a pin-striped Babygro," contributed Mary.

"And can you imagine Gary with a baby of his own?"

"Nappy exactly symmetrical or do it again."

They laughed.

"Seriously, a baby would be good for him. It's just what he needs," observed Mary.

"That's cruel."

"Perhaps. To the baby."

Ben chuckled thoughtfully, then said: "No, you were right the first time. Babies are instruments of justice. That's what heredity is for. It gives people what they deserve and the grandparents some quiet amusement watching revenge exacted on their behalf!"

"And I suppose meeting the parents and hearing the baby stories is about finding out what you're in for?"

"That is a logical extension of my reasoning. Remind me to keep you away from Mum and Dad."

As Mary met his gaze, she felt suddenly cold and began to shiver. A breeze ruffled her hair. She pulled her coat around her shoulders.

"Are you all right?" asked Ben.

"Fine, thank you," she replied. "It seems draughty all of a sudden, that's all." She turned, looked around and pointed. "Look, those people over there have opened a window."

"We'll go and sit over there in the corner," said Ben, catching the eye of the waiter. "The food's ready now."

Mary hung her shopping bag on the chair and they sat eating.

"Are you looking forward to your new job?" inquired Ben, to which Mary responded with a cautious 'yes'.

"It'll be fine, you'll see," Ben replied.

"Gemma said you're intending to start your own business."

"I was, but events have moved on. Now I'm going into business with a friend of mine," Ben explained. "He needs a partner and it's just the sort of thing I was planning myself. I need challenge.... freedom.... adventure.... there's a world out there...."

His excitement was obvious and a little contagious.

"Wouldn't it be nice," thought Mary. "To be my own boss." But doing what? And where to get the capital to start a business? It was all right for Ben.

They ordered coffee and Ben started to tell Mary more about his plans but the promise of another meal once the business was running smoothly brought another sudden chill to the air. Strange. The restaurant was full now, packed with bodies generating heat, the temperature rising with wine and laughter. Surely it couldn't be Mike? Mary had heard it said that the air goes cold in the presence of a ghost but she had never noticed it before when Mike was around. Then again, the air was still, the slightly open window surely could not have let in enough breeze to ruffle her hair and their cosy little corner was exactly that – cosy.

She looked for Mike but could not see him and turned back to find Ben eyeing her curiously. She shivered once again and the meal over, Ben suggested perhaps she should get an early night. He insisted she wait in the warm while he brought his sports car round and on arrival at her flat, ever the gentleman, he escorted her to her door.

Ben took her hand.

"Goodnight, Mary."

She held him at arm's length.

"Goodnight Ben."

Just think: a second date with the not-perfect-after-all Ben and another in the offing. But was it Mike who kept causing the air to grow chilly or just an open window and too much imagination?

MONDAY
DAY 9

Early on Monday morning, following the directions she had been given, Mary arrived at the construction site. The safe routes for visitors were clearly marked and led straight to a small, grubby Portakabin. The door was open and inside there was a chair and a table with a signing-in book for visitors.

"Ah, Mary," said a man in a hardhat. "I'm Dan. You'll be wanting Pete. Go on over."

Across the way was a larger Portakabin. Mary went over and knocked but it made hardly any sound against the steel door. Dan grinned. He strode up to the door, flung it open and pointed to a grey-haired man at the far end.

"That's Pete."

He let go of the heavy door and it slammed behind her with a loud crash that shook the whole cabin. Mary felt embarrassed that she had not caught it and shut it quietly but no-one else seemed to notice. Pete called her over.

"I'm the Site Manager. That was Dan, the foreman, and over there is Josh – he's Health and Safety. Then over in the far corner are Minty, Bellyache and Ryan. You'll meet the project managers and the engineers and the bean counters and so on later, they're in a meeting. We're glad you're here. We've got a bit behind," he explained gesturing towards a table. "But I'm sure an expert like you will have it all in apple-pie order in no time."

Mary smiled. On the table were rolls of drawings heaped next to a pile of delivery tickets and assorted bits of paper.

"You can sit here. You'll soon get used to things. Any problems, just ask."

Ask what? Mary had no idea where to start; this was very different to anything she had done before. She decided, however, that she had better not let it show and picked up the pile of delivery tickets.

"Dan will show you what to do with those. He's been having to process them while we didn't have anybody," said Pete.

The filing system was inscrutable so Mary chose a piece of paper from the table and hunted through likely-looking files until she came across a similar piece of paper and put it with its twin. As a system it would work until she knew the jargon and what things were and where they went. The important thing was not to lose anything and this way other people would find things – hopefully – even if Mary herself was destined in the short term to end up looking like a startled rabbit if anyone asked if she had seen the greens (Goods Received Notes) or what she had done with the groundworkers RAMS [Risk Assessment – Method Statement] or whatever.

"Cup of tea, Mary?"

"Thanks. I'll come and help." She followed Pete to the kitchen. It was clean and tidy like the main cabin.

"Have you done this sort of thing before?" asked Pete.

"Well…. yes…. but not on a building site."

"You'll be fine. Just don't put up with any nonsense."

They collected the cups of tea and went to hand them round.

As Mary put down a cup on the desk by the window, Minty was saying to Bellyache: "So, I sat in the queue for twenty minutes thinking it was heavy traffic and when I finally made it round the corner, I'd been sitting in a queue for a car park I didn't want to go in and I could have overtaken the whole **** lot of them. Talk about bad traffic design, I don't know which **** brainbox thought that one up…."

His hand flew to his large, muppet-like mouth as he realised Mary was standing beside him. She half turned away to try to hide her smile of amusement. But Pete had noticed. He noticed everything. Mary, he concluded, would indeed be fine. She was sound.

"That's Minty's latest excuse for being late," he explained to her. "We call him that because he's always After Eight."

"Oi," called out Minty. "Not so too. It was only ever once."

"Yeah, yeah," chorused the others.

Mary decided she was going to like it here.

* * *

In the evening, she phoned to tell Ben all about her new job.

"Gosh, that sounds different," he said.

For a moment she was concerned that he thought it was a bad idea but only for a moment.

"Next best thing to the army," he commented. "I had a brilliant time in the army while it lasted and I'm sure you're going to love your new job. Sock it to them, M!"

TUESDAY
DAY 10

The following evening, Mike came strolling in as though it was the most natural thing in the world.

Being more used to him now and less nervous in his presence, Mary went over and deliberately stood near him but she could not feel any discernible drop in temperature.

"I'm glad you're here. I was wondering how your surveillance activities were progressing."

"Like us, the police are looking into the Parker family. They've been looking for witnesses to the abduction but so far without result. And they've been speaking to the neighbours. The sergeant whose shoulder I was looking over wasn't turning up anything hopeful – or not while I was with him anyway – and I saw no point in doubling up on your investigation so I did a tour of the local nursery schools to see whether Jared had been enrolled in any of them. He hasn't."

Mary considered. "That's not surprising. His picture has

been all over the news. I expect the kidnapper is hiding him. It might be something to look into again later, though."

Mike shuddered. "Let's hope it won't be necessary. I've discovered that jingly-jangly nursery music upsets my aura. I don't know why children like it. It goes through my head like hot knives. I feel as if I'm breaking into pieces. At one point, I really thought I might disintegrate."

Mary watched him sympathetically for a few moments before her thoughts drifted back to her own concerns.

It was frustrating. Time was passing and it was turning into Ellen all over again. There had been nothing but silence following Ellen's disappearance; twenty-two years of silence.

"Mike," she ventured. "Is Jared still alive? I know I asked you before but is he still?"

"Yes," he reassured her. "I would tell you if he passed over. Or if his light turned red."

"I do wish there was something I could do."

"I know," he comforted her. "If it's any help, I have a feeling you won't have to wait much longer for something to break. Try to be patient."

Mary's expression said it all. Patience was a virtue she did not possess in abundance.

"Another thing. It's only a little thing but the other day when we met out shopping, you didn't by any chance stay around for a while?"

"I have better things to do than watch you eat."

Mike might have better things to do but had he been doing them, she wondered. He had not actually denied being there. She sighed; she knew it was all the answer she would get.

"I suppose you want to know how I got on with the Parkers?"

Waiting only for his acknowledgement, Mary launched into an account of her trip.

"I really don't think the Parkers had anything to do with it and I only came up with one other possible suspect and I don't know enough about him even to know if he is a suspect," she finished. "Rachel's possibly jealous brother-in-law, Charles Armstrong."

"Charles who?" Mike stiffened. "Where does he live, what does he do for a living this Charles Armstrong of yours?"

"He lives in Bidcome Marsh. He's a builder."

"I might have known. He had better not be mixed up in this. I don't want you anywhere near that man, do you understand?" The vehemence of Mike's reaction startled Mary.

"Do you know him? How? What has he done?"

"Doesn't matter. Promise me." His tone was insistent. Mary promised but Mike still looked disconcerted.

"So, ruining one young life is not enough," he muttered to himself and oscillating violently, he told her he had things to do and disappeared.

* * *

"Patient," Mary said to herself as she headed for bed. "I can be patient."

"Enforced patience doesn't count," said a voice.

"Mike, go and annoy someone else."

Or was it that little voice in her head she could never hide from?

WEDNESDAY
DAY 11

It was only a day or two before Mary was well on top of things. She had made sense of the filing system, one of the design managers had explained what the numbers on the drawings meant and she had stopped calling people by the wrong name and getting teased for it. She was one of the team.

The other main difference compared to her previous job was that it was more active. Instead of sitting at a desk all day, Mary was on her feet sorting out the drawing racks, dealing with deliveries and collaring subcontractors for paperwork as they tried to sneak past the cabin.

She had hardly sunk wearily into a chair at home that evening when there was a knock at the door.

"Hi, Mary. Are you busy?"

It was Ben.

"No. Come in, make yourself at home but I don't think I'll be good company. I'm tired."

"You sounded tired on the phone the other day. I came to cheer you up. There's a good film on the television. Funny. I brought popcorn."

"That's sweet. The thought, not the popcorn. Although that's sweet, too."

Ben smiled.

They sat on the sofa, Ben with his arm around Mary and Mary with her head on Ben's shoulder. The film was, indeed, funny but as it went on, Mary's dipping into the popcorn grew less and her quietness became silence; she was falling asleep. Ben shifted his weight as carefully as possible and reached out to put the popcorn carton on the table. He slid back to his original position, ignoring the ache in his shoulder and sat watching attentively as the film ran to the end so he could tell Mary what happened. She was bound to ask.

The jarring music of the news programme roused her. Mary got up and turned off the television.

"That kidnapping case they've been on about. I saw the boy and his father on the bus the other week," said Mary and fell silent, thinking.

"I expect a lot of people did," said Ben.

"I expect so," agreed Mary shaking herself out of her reverie. "Coffee?"

"No, I'll be going. I have work to do. You get some sleep."

Mary yawned. "I'm sorry. I shouldn't be this tired."

He gave her a peck on the cheek.

"Don't worry, you'll soon get used to the job."

THURSDAY
DAY 12

The last thing Mary wanted to do when she arrived home from work was clearing out but she had received a call to say that the new flat she wanted was available for her to move in from Saturday. It was smaller than her present one but it had a definite charm in its compact little way.

First, however, she needed to pack up the old flat and move out, not taking with her rubbish she did not need. She was revolving in the middle of the living room deciding where to begin when Mike appeared.

"I thought I'd call by," he explained.

"Any particular reason?"

"I was passing by the police station and I saw a lady handing in a cuddly toy she had found in the park. She thought it looked like the one Jared was holding in the picture they showed on the television and in the papers. I thought you might like to know."

"Is there any reason to think it might be Jared's? Cuddly toys aren't exactly unique, after all."

"This one had a chewed ear. So did Jared's. They're taking it to Rachel for identification."

"Do you know if it was freshly lost?"

"It wasn't dirty or wet so it can't have been there long."

Another visit from the police would add to Rachel's stress, thought Mary, but it would give her hope that Jared was still alive or how could he drop his toy? Poor Rachel. This roller coaster of emotions must be as hard to take as the silence that had characterised Jared's disappearance so far.

There was a short pause then: "I don't wish to seem unwelcoming but I have things to do," said Mary.

"Didn't look busy when I arrived," commented Mike.

"That's because I hadn't started yet."

"Ahh," said Mike knowingly. Mary's eyes narrowed. Quickly he added: "Anything I can help with?"

"Why not?" She relaxed. "All offers gratefully accepted. We will start by – drumroll, please – clearing out the hall cupboard."

Mike groaned. He had walked straight into that one.

Mary knew she was indecisive when it came to clearing out. She knew how frustrating it must be for Mike as patiently he reminded her yet again: "You need to decide whether you actually want that or whether you want the space more."

They were doing well when Mary suddenly yelled: "Spider! It's a spider!" and recoiled from the cupboard.

Mike looked from her to the arachnid and back again: she was white as a sheet and shaking. The spider, meanwhile, was acting deaf as they generally do and remained precisely where it was. Viewed through Mike's eyes, it was pretty inoffensive: it was not particularly large or knobbly; it did not appear to have friends; in fact, its only crime was that it was there. Mary's attitude seemed like an over-reaction but no matter, phobias are irrational. Mike picked it up and put it out of the window.

"Thanks. If it's not too much of an imposition perhaps you could stay while I put the saucepans in a box. The living room and the bedroom should be all right, it's just the kitchen."

It did not take long to pack the kitchen items because there were no decisions to be made; everything was needed and into boxes it went. Mary could exist on sandwiches and take-aways for a day or two.

"Can you manage now?"

"Yes. Thank you, you've been a great help."

"You're welcome."

The reminder of the shed, however, was not, neither for itself nor for reminding her of the growing parallels between Jared's disappearance and Ellen's.

FRIDAY
DAY 13

Slowly, Mary became aware of a smell. It grew stronger, and her attempts to think of the right words to end the email she was writing were rudely interrupted by Ryan issuing through the door, the foul odour wrapped around him, an aura of evil. The door slammed behind him with its usual loud crash, sealing them all in the metal cabin.

"Hi, Mary," he called cheerfully. She held her nose.

"Hi, Ryan."

"Got some pictures for you for the site file."

It took a moment for Mary to realise she was looking at the records of his camera investigation of the drains. Charming.

"Wow," commented Bellyache, looking over her shoulder. "That's a good 'un. Bet someone felt better for that."

"And we know who," replied Ryan triumphantly. "That picture is from that short pipe run up by the Lea and the only person whose house is on that run…"

"Is Grumpy-guts Holden. No wonder he always looks constipated."

Their shrieks of mirth attracted the others, who examined the pictures critically.

"I think I can see a crack," said Dan.

"Unlikely. We were very discreet where we aimed the camera."

When their howls of laughter finally died down, Dan said: "You'll have to jet it, though, to be sure."

"The drain," he added before Ryan could say what he was obviously thinking. "It's a good job Mary finds all this funny."

And Mary did find it funny. Very funny. It was much better than working in an office.

As she headed for the bookcase to file the photographs, Mary thought she heard a faint chuckle. "Mike?" she whispered.

"Just going," replied a disembodied voice. "It was only a flying visit."

* * *

"I don't know about Rachel, I'm finding this stressful," thought Mary as she watched another television appeal that evening. Jared might be alive but would he ever be found? Ellen had not been.

But Ellen was dead. Almost certainly. However, there was a chance…. In her mind, Mary pictured a happy reunion, years of questions finding answers as she pounced on her friend with a loud 'Where have you been?'

But this was not the time to brood about Ellen, it was the time to concentrate on Jared. Mary forced her thoughts back to the present and to the broadcast.

There was to be a re-enactment of the crime. Those often resulted in witnesses coming forward, so Mary had heard.

SATURDAY
DAY 14

Mary looked around, still hardly able to believe her luck in securing the flat. A gorgeous ginger cat called by to inspect the new tenant but most of the human neighbours seemed to be out.

She gave the place a thorough clean even though it was not dirty, it was just part of making it her own. Then she unpacked her clothes and books and kitchenware. As a final touch, she had bought some pot-plants; carefully, she peeled the wrapping from a chrysanthemum with large red flowers, placed it on the kitchen windowsill and stood back to admire the effect. Then a cheerful yellow one for the living room. She was going to like it here.

"Oh yes," approved Mike, appearing from the hall as though he had just walked in like a regular person. "This feels more like it's a home, not just passing through."

"I know," agreed Mary. "I think it's partly having your own front door and letterbox rather than picking up the post from the hall table and that sort of thing. I'm glad you've turned up; it gives me a chance to show the place off."

"At your service," replied Mike, bowing slightly.

Mary smiled, then wistfully observed: "You're not, though, are you? I can't phone you if I want you."

"You've never tried calling me, have you?"

Mary's eyes opened a little wider. "You mean I can? How?"

"Just think me. But you'll have to mean it."

Mary sat down and started to tell Mike about the cat and how nice it was to have a lawn and be able to sit out in the summer but apparently, she had to mow it and she wasn't sure where her bit stopped and the neighbour's started and she didn't have a mower…. and before long she was fast asleep in the chair, exhausted from the day's exertions.

SUNDAY
DAY 15

It had rained all night and it was still raining. Gemma was out with Max and a call to Ben rapidly established that he was busy on the computer, something about his new business venture and would remain bogged down in whatever it was for some time.

"Sorry I couldn't help you move in. Did it go all right?" he asked.

"Yes, thanks. I even managed to read the meters at the third attempt with a bit of help from the chap next door."

Ben laughed. "And you like it? You don't miss the old place? You'd been there a while."

"I'm loving it already."

"Good. How's the job going?"

"Fine, fine."

"See, I told you you'd be brilliant, didn't I?"

Mary needed some milk but she did not want to go out. No help for it though, it was not going to get itself. According to the internet there was a supermarket not far away; a bigger, newer one than where Mary had been living before. She put on her coat, collected her umbrella and headed out. The rain was coming down as though under pressure and she was soaked. She squelched up the aisle past the bread – and then she saw him.

It was the little boy from the bus. And with him was – the man who had sat opposite her that night she had first seen him, the man who had turned so white.

It had to be him who had kidnapped the child. She had better try to find out where they were going in order to have something to tell the police other than 'You remember I told you I saw a man on the bus watching Jared Parker? Well, I saw him again and they were together.'

Shopping finished and back outside, they did not notice Mary discreetly following them because the little boy was jumping in every puddle they passed and shrieking with excitement and his companion was completely absorbed with avoiding getting splashed.

"That's enough," he pleaded.

"Mummy lets me," returned the child. His voice was husky and the words indistinct. The man sighed with exasperation but did not say any more.

Finally, the rain began to ease and safely back on the main road, the pavements were in a better state of repair and the puddles fewer and shallower. The man paused to point out the rainbows in the oil on top of the puddles by the kerb to the little boy and Mary became worried they would spot her.

'Think me' Mike had said so she tried to imagine him, concentrated on the image and tried to beam her thoughts skywards. Nothing.

"Come on. I need you."

And there he was.

"Thank goodness. I need you to follow that man and that boy." Mike looked at her quizzically. "We can discuss it later. Please. Meet you at home," she said impatiently and ducked down the nearest side-road.

Mary had been back at the flat long enough to get changed and have a nice hot cup of tea before Mike appeared.

"Well?" she demanded.

"They went home," said Mike simply.

"But there must be something," insisted Mary.

"Nothing obvious," said Mike. "When I left, the little boy was eating jam sandwiches and drinking juice and watching the television. His father hung their clothes up to dry then sat down at his computer with a cup of tea."

"It's not his father," said Mary. "That was the man who was on the bus that night, the one I told you about."

"Ah. I suppose that is a bit odd," Mike conceded. He continued thoughtfully, "Kid behaved as though he was at home, though, and the chap acted like he was his father."

"Well, I don't know. Maybe they're used to each other; it is two weeks since the kidnapping."

"I'll keep an eye on them," Mike promised. "Don't you go getting into mischief."

The subject of the boy in the supermarket being exhausted: "Your new place of work is an improvement on Bramwells," said Mike.

"I know. It's interesting seeing all the plans and watching them prepare the site. I can't wait to see the building go up. And they're a great bunch of people." Mary thought for a moment. "I haven't seen you there above once," she said.

"Would you have noticed?" he countered. "You've been pretty focussed."

"I should have done this before," said Mary. "It's much more fun than the old job."

"I prefer it, too," replied Mike. "I always did like something going on."

But in spite of half-promising Mike not to get involved, Mary could not get Jared out of her head. The minute he left, she fished out her phone and dialled a number she knew by heart, a number that was indelibly imprinted on her brain.

"You have reached the phone of Andrew Beresford. I am not available at the moment. Please leave a message after the tone."

Mary hung up.

Andrew had been a young inspector on the case when Ellen was snatched and he and Mary had kept in contact over the years. She still remembered how kind he had been. She had seen the man who took Ellen; she was the only person who had and she could not describe him. She had looked at pictures but nothing brought an image of his face back to her mind. It would have made a difference, *the* difference, she was sure it would have and she still blamed herself for the blank that sat above a checked shirt where his face should have been. She may only have been five years old but she could remember every detail of Ellen's face so why not his?

Mary called back and left a message. She would prefer to talk to Andrew but if he did not call by morning, she would go to the police station.

MONDAY
DAY 16

Andrew called back first thing.

"How did you know I had been asked to take over the case?" he asked.

"I didn't but I'm glad. I need to talk to you. You see, I know where Jared is."

"I understand you live in Borrowdale Road now? As it happens, I'm not far from there. I'll come over. Five minutes."

Mary had spoken to Andrew now and then but she had not actually seen him for many years and she was surprised how little he had changed. He took out a notebook and prompted gently.

"You say you followed them."

"It's all right, I didn't let them see me."

"That's not exactly the point. It could have been dangerous. And you have the address?"

"Sort of." Mary thought she had better not tempt too many questions. "I didn't want to get too close but they went into a block of flats on Queen Street."

Still pretending she had personally tailed them all the way home, Mary continued: "A light came on straight after on the first floor, far end on the right."

"And you're sure it was the same boy?"

"Yes. Completely sure."

"All right. We'll look into it."

"And will you let me know what happens?"

"Yes, Mary, I promise."

TUESDAY
DAY 17

Mary was sitting with her feet up reading her book. It had been a busy day at work and she was tired.

"Hello, Mary."

Mary shut the book. "Hello, Mike."

"I'm not disturbing you, am I?"

"No, no. Come in – oh, you are in."

"Very funny. I drop by to do you a good turn and…. I'll just go then, shall I?"

They both knew he was teasing. Mike sat down.

"First of all, Rachel confirmed the toy that was found in the park was Jared's. She put it in his room and she goes up there and picks it up and has a little cry now and then."

"Did you really need to tell me that?"

"Sorry."

"Anyway, I guessed she had identified it from the fact there was another television appeal at the weekend. I hope that implies the police think Jared is alive."

"We know he is."

"But they didn't and I'd hate to think they were winding the investigation down. I don't suppose you know whether it resulted in any more witnesses coming forward?"

"Nothing useful. A couple of dead ends."

Mary could not hide her disappointment.

"I'll give Rachel a call. She must have been hoping – I know I was."

There was a pause then Mary continued: "You said 'first of all.' How about second of all?"

"Henry broke up with his mistress."

"He had a mistress?"

"He did, and she was so keen to see him after the Parkers' trip to the seaside that when he didn't call her, she went to his office, pretended to be a lawyer on urgent business and tricked his secretary, who had never seen her before, into saying he was at his country retreat and had left orders he was not to be disturbed. She knew that meant he was at the apartment where he used to take her – nice place, by the way, a rather exclusive conversion in the country – so she went over to see him. The secretary was still upset about it when I went to the office which is how I got to know all the details. She was talking to her friend who was comforting her saying it was not her fault and she should stop dwelling on it.

"Anyway, the apartment and the office use the same cleaning firm and conversations, especially loud ones, are prone to be overheard – and repeated – and it seems that the mistress thought that now she and Henry would be able to be together and threw herself into his arms. But before Henry could answer, another girl came out of the bedroom and demanded to know what was going on. Then," he finished triumphantly, "they all started shouting at each other."

"So, Henry told his mistress that he would leave Rachel for her." Mary thought for a while. "He probably never meant it. From what I saw, he loves Rachel."

"Whatever the reason he gave for delaying, the mistress thought it wasn't relevant anymore."

"Which I suppose means he said he couldn't leave until Jared was older. With Jared gone…."

"You needn't to worry, the mistress has gone now. And Henry dumped the other girl," said Mike.

"Good," said Mary.

WEDNESDAY
DAY 18

It was two days since Mary had seen Andrew. Then, late in the evening, he knocked on the door and asked to come in.

"I just called to give you an update like I promised," he said. "We went round to the flat and interviewed them." He paused. "The thing is, Mary, I can see why you thought it was the same child; he is very like but, well, there were photographs on the wall of Darren – that's the lad's name by the way, Darren Danesford – growing up, you know, baby pictures and then a bit bigger and on his first birthday and with his Mum and how could that be if the bloke had only just kidnapped him?"

"Perhaps he stole them," said Mary. "Off Facebook or something."

"I don't think so. Mrs Parker and Mrs Danesford seem to have very different ideas about what small boys should wear. Plus, the Danesfords aren't so well off and the kid seems to get a lot of hand-me-downs whereas it's strictly designer in the Parker household. And then there are photos of all three of them, Darren and his parents, at a holiday camp at the seaside. The Parkers would never be seen in a place like that.

"I tried speaking to the kid himself and he responded equally to 'Darren' and to 'Jared'. So, I asked him his name and he said 'Darra'. Which doesn't help at all. He's too young to say the 'j' sound so he could have been trying to say Jared just as easily as he could have been saying Darren. Besides which, he doesn't speak clearly even for a two-year old."

"Could he point to himself in the photos on the wall?"

"We tried that and he pointed and said 'me' then hid his face and went all shy. And that was that; he wouldn't cooperate any further."

Mary knew Andrew of old. He liked the i's dotted and the t's crossed. He would not have left it there. She waited.

"I sent a couple of WPC's round yesterday – in plain clothes of course – and they sat and played with him until he was at ease then they introduced a new game identifying picture cards. You know: horse, sheep, man, lady, car. He's very clever, apparently, and a lovely kid. Then they slipped in photos of his parents."

"And…."

"Well, he said 'Mum' to the photo of Mrs Parker…."

Before Mary could interrupt, Andrew carried on: "But when he was shown a photo of Mrs Danesford, he also pointed and chuckled and said 'Mum'. The two of them do look similar, unfortunately."

"What about photos of his father?"

"He slid off the chair and went to sit on the floor with his toys."

"He doesn't like his father, he's strict. And he doesn't know this Danesford." Mary defended her position. Nor was she giving up yet. "How about the nanny? He spends time with her."

"Actually, he doesn't spend much time with her. She's a student who lives nearby and helps out on occasion to earn some money. Anyway, Mrs Parker didn't have a photograph of her and she was off on a field trip so we couldn't take one." He held up his hand to silence her. "We will get a photo and try again but it won't do any good."

"Why not?"

"Her name is Ramona or Nona for short. He calls her 'No'. So even if we show him a picture and he says 'No' it does not get us far."

Mary imagined the conversation over the photograph. 'Who's this? Do you know her?' A solemn nod accompanied by the word 'No.' 'Is that her name?' 'Yes. No.' Andrew had a point.

"What about the neighbours?"

"None of them know the Danesfords. They only recently moved in and the neighbours know nothing of their habits. They didn't even know Mrs Danesford was away in hospital."

Mary contemplated. She was not ready to give up yet. She had been so sure.

"Could you get a DNA sample? That would settle it one way or the other."

"As things stand, Mr Danesford would be within his rights to refuse."

Mary had one final try.

"Could you arrange for Mrs Parker to see the child? See if the boy runs to her?"

"We have to tread carefully. Mrs Parker is in a fragile state and Mr Danesford has already been muttering about harassment after we showed the kid the pictures and he started to cry and say 'I want my Mummy' so no, I don't think so, not without more in the way of evidence. In any case, I honestly don't think the child you saw with Danesford is Jared. We have no reason to think so."

"Look, I'm sorry if I've wasted your time." Mary was disappointed and in spite of everything she was still convinced she was right. She had seen what she had seen. Why would Mr Danesford react like that on the bus? There was some connection, she was sure of it.

"It's never a waste of time. We'd rather chase a hundred dead ends than miss an important lead. Especially in a case like this."

Mary jumped on the opportunity to try to find out what progress they had made without actually asking. "You're not getting anywhere, then?"

"We're doing everything we can." There was a short pause then Andrew sighed and said: "Sorry. That sounded like an official non-answer, didn't it? Truth is, it's gone on too long for my liking. I can do without history repeating itself."

In the pause that followed they were both thinking of Ellen.

Andrew sighed again and continued: "Often with these crimes there's something connecting the victim and the perpetrator but not always. There doesn't seem to be anything in this case. It doesn't give us much to go on. The family aren't aware of having been followed around and the description of the suspect could fit anybody."

Mary's thoughts flew to her own inability to provide a description of Ellen's abductor. No, that was different. She had been young and scared out of her wits, not that that was any excuse. Someone might remember something yet.

"Is it too much to ask for an independent witness?" muttered Andrew more to himself than to Mary. "Somebody picking up some shopping or walking the dog or out for a stroll…."

"I'm sure you'll get a breakthrough soon," Mary said comfortingly.

"I hope so, although I can't see where it will come from. We've questioned people living in the flats over the shops and stopped people in the street and shown them photographs hoping to jog someone's memory. Nothing. He has vanished into thin air. And yet somebody must know something; perhaps a child 'coming to stay' next door around the right time or strange noises through the party wall…."

"Unless he's in a lonely farmhouse somewhere," said Mary then immediately realised that was about the least comforting thing she could have said. "Sorry." She stood up and headed for the kitchen. "I'll make some more coffee."

"No thanks Mary, I'd better be going."

She showed him out. "Goodbye Andrew. Thank you for coming."

"Goodbye Mary. Let me know if you think of anything else."

THURSDAY
DAY 19

Mary could not help brooding upon Andrew's visit. She had been sure it was Jared she had seen in the supermarket. She sighed. It was a good thing work was more interesting than it used to be. She immersed herself in making sure the drawing files were up to date and joining in the banter as she dished out cups of tea.

"You make a lovely cuppa," complimented Josh, the safety manager.

"You're just saying that to make sure they keep coming," replied Mary.

"No, really." He pulled a packet of chocolate biscuits from his desk. "Want one?"

"No, thanks."

She returned to her desk, picked up a pile of skip tickets and went over to the printer. It took a while to scan them onto the system and fill out the Waste Register but it was one of the things the environmental people were hot on so Mary liked to ensure it was in good order. Then she put the tickets in an envelope to go to Head Office where Accounts would check them against the invoices and went to wash her hands. It was best not to inquire what was on some of the dirty bits of paper she was given.

On the way home that night, Mary walked through the park as she often did since moving to her new flat, especially since Mike had told her about Jared's teddy being found near the playground area. It was a little out of her way but a pleasant walk. Of course, it had nothing to do with hoping the Danesford family might be there which they never were.

Until today. There on the merry-go-round sat the little boy, dressed in an old anorak and jeans. She could have spotted him a mile off. Casually, Mary drew nearer, sat on the grass and producing a book from her bag, she pretended to read.

"Jared…." she called softly. No reply; he did not even look up. Mary tried again: "Darren…." No reaction. He was totally engrossed in enjoying the sensation, laughing with joy as the merry-go-round spun and the breeze stroked his face.

She edged a little nearer. "Jared…."

Still the child did not respond but she had attracted the attention of Mr Danesford who had been crouching behind the merry-go-round out of sight making sure it did not go too fast. He came storming over.

"I don't know who you are or what you think you're doing but you can leave my son alone."

"Sorry. I'm sorry, I thought he was someone else." Her protestations were irrelevant because Mr Danesford had already gathered up the child and was heading away across the grass.

* * *

Back at home, Mary kicked off her shoes. It was disheartening but for the moment, there was nothing more she could do.

She had not heard from anyone for a while so she decided to phone them and catch up.

Vicky was delighted to hear Mary's voice and settled down for a good gossip. In the end, she had not stayed with Bramwells, she had gone to work for an advertising company and enjoyed the energy and bustle and the fake histrionics produced by a flamboyant young man named Calvin in response to some of the assignments. Mary could hardly get a word in edgeways.

"It's such a contrast to Bramwells," she said excitedly and Mary knew exactly what she meant. As to her own job, she could hear Vicky pulling faces at the other end of the phone but she did not care.

"Speaking of Bramwells, do you know what happened to Gary?" asked Mary.

"No idea," replied Vicky.

But Gemma knew. He was running a care home called Silverwood Hall.

"What?" Mary was stunned.

"We never really knew him," pointed out Gemma, "but it seems that all the time we worked with him he was carer to his mother and knows a lot about the needs of the elderly. But the time had come when he couldn't manage any more. He didn't want to put his mother in a home and anyway he couldn't find one he would have been prepared to put her in. So, when he lost his job, the answer was obvious. Combine the management skills with the caring. Apparently, the Home is seeing quite an improvement in its reputation even though he only took over two weeks ago."

"And how about you?" inquired Mary. "What are you up to?"

"You'll see," said Gemma. "I can't tell you because we haven't told Max's parents yet."

"You're not pregnant?" exclaimed Mary in surprise.

"No, nothing like that. But it is something that involves you so keep your diary free. By the way…" she continued in mock-casual tone: "How's Ben?"

"Well…."

"You like him. I told you so," crowed Gemma and hung up.

"Something involving me," wondered Mary. Something about Gemma and Max. There was only the wedding but that was not for another year.

And now for the final call. Mary took a deep breath and dialled Ben.

"Ah, Mary…. I'm a bit busy. Can I call you tomorrow? Better still, the day after? I have a few arrangements to make and then…. I'll call you, all right? In the afternoon."

FRIDAY
DAY 20

Just as Mary got off the bus the following evening, the heavens opened. Carefully, she stuck her hand in her bag and felt around for her umbrella; it would not do to open it wide and let the rain in.

No umbrella. It must be here. Then Mary remembered: she had hung it above the radiator at work to dry days ago and forgotten to pick it up again. Drat.

The beep of a horn attracted her attention. A car door opened right beside her. "Hop in, I'll take you home. You'll get drenched in this."

"Thanks Andrew." Gratefully, Mary climbed into the passenger seat. It was not far from the bus stop to the flat but Andrew was right, she would have been soaked to the skin.

"Good job I was passing," he remarked.

"Now you're here, would you like to come in for a coffee?"

Andrew dithered. "Why not."

As they walked up the path and into the apartment block, it was obvious to Mary from Andrew's demeanour that he had not had a good day.

"I don't know about bad day, it's been a dreadful week and yesterday took the biscuit," he admitted glumly.

The second television appeal and re-enactment of the crime had been a disappointment in terms of witnesses coming forward. Mary did not let on that she knew that. Andrew continued: a ransom demand had been received.

"We were to hand over the money yesterday in exchange for Jared but whoever sent the note outwitted us and made off with the cash.

"It was an open-air rendezvous, not a vast space, we had all the exits sealed off, we had checked the place over thoroughly for old tunnels because there used to be mine workings there, we had searched sheds and undergrowth for a hidden motorbike and so on and so on.

"So: handover. He picks up the money which was left in a holdall by the wall as instructed while we kept our distance watching. Then suddenly, this nearby crane starts up – we had checked it, there wasn't a driver in it – then the bloke hitches the jib to a harness he was wearing under his coat and sails up and away before we could grab him. On to a bridge. He must have had a car waiting down the road. Turns out the crane was rigged for remote control. No sign of the kid, though; he wasn't at the rendezvous and he hasn't been returned since."

"Whose was the crane?"

"Hired. In a false name."

"Didn't you have a tracker on the money?"

"They found it and got rid of it. All we know is that we are looking for somebody who could access or create a false identity and knows about electronics."

The description did not fit Mr Danesford.

"Why wait so long before demanding a ransom?" pondered Mary.

"I don't know." Andrew's exasperation was clear from his tone. "If it's money he – or she – is after, I would have expected the exchange within days. Having to mind a kid is nothing but a nuisance under those circumstances."

He did not need to say it for Mary to know what was concerning him: he was afraid Jared had been killed and if not, that he would be killed now the money had been handed over.

Andrew finished his coffee. "Thanks for putting up with me, Mary. It has helped just having someone listen."

Sympathy shone back at him as he stood a moment then turned and left.

Within seconds of his weary departure, Mary was calling Mike.

"Is Jared still all right?" she asked breathlessly, the moment he appeared.

"I told you I would tell you if anything changed. Now what's all this about?"

Mike listened gravely as Mary recounted Andrew's news.

"Whoever has him didn't kill him straight away and I promise you they haven't killed him since the ransom was paid. And his light is still yellow. Doesn't that suggest that there's some other reason for all this rather than extortion and murder or worse? I know it's hard but try to put it out of your mind and await developments. There's nothing else you can do."

What other reason? Did Mike know something? No, he would tell her – or would he? Mike, the secretive team member who knew something about Charles and told her only to keep away from him.

Mary sighed. There was nothing she could do but await developments, he was right about that.

SATURDAY
DAY 21

Put it out of her mind. Easy for Mike to say. Normally, Mary looked forward to a Saturday morning lie-in but today she felt a need for activity. She jumped out of bed.

She was half way across the room when the phone rang. Mary made a dive for it.

"Hi, Mary."

Of course: Ben had said he would phone.

"Sorry about the other day," he continued. "You caught me at a bad moment. How are things?"

"Okay."

Determinedly, she tore her thoughts from the kidnapping and started to tell him about work and phoning Vicky and Gemma but Ben cut her short.

"Before you carry on, how would you like to tell me in person tonight? I thought we might go out."

"That would be lovely," Mary replied and she meant it. Not only would it stop her dwelling on why Jared had not been released now that the money was paid but she had been counting the days since she had last seen Ben and wondering when his pre-occupation with his business would die down a little.

"Is six o'clock too early?" There was a brief pause. "I don't want to spoil the surprise but dress up a bit, we're going posh."

Having no idea where they were going except that it obviously was not the local McDonald's did not give Mary much idea about what to wear. The new blue dress? No, that might be too much. She would save it for another day. After a little thought, she chose a midi length burgundy dress with balloon sleeves and elegant but sensible shoes. It was a reliable favourite that suited her and somehow managed to blend in and look more or less smart depending on what other people were wearing. Mary called it her camouflage dress.

"Perfect," approved Ben who arrived looking debonair in trousers, jacket and open-necked shirt.

He offered her his arm and escorted her down the path.

"I'll put up the top on the car. It's dropping chilly."

They drove towards town. "Are you hungry?"

"Average."

"Good. I'm glad you didn't say 'famished,' we have a little way to go."

He turned onto a country road. Mary looked around. It seemed to be going nowhere.

"Ben?"

"Hmm?" He turned down a track and they found themselves on an old airfield.

"I think you went the wrong way."

Ben just smiled. He drove up to one of the hangars, stopped the car and helped Mary out. A man in overalls paused, wiped his oily hands on a cloth and waived. They went over and Ben greeted the man with a playful shoulder punch. He turned to Mary.

"Ready, M?" he asked. "Good." And before Mary could collect her thoughts, they were climbing into a helicopter.

"That's Jack," Ben told Mary gesturing towards the pilot who greeted her with a cheery smile. The ever-considerate Ben handed Mary a scarf to put over her hair and the next half hour was occupied looking out of the window at a patchwork of fields, at tiny houses and even tinier cars and at trains that looked like clockwork toys in an old-fashioned toy-shop window.

"Look, sheep." Mary pointed delightedly.

Soon, however, the fields gave way to a large urban sprawl. As they flew over, Mary began to recognise famous landmarks.

"We're in London!" she exclaimed. "Well, above it, anyway."

"Quite right," agreed Ben.

"Where on earth are we going?"

"Not *going*. We're here. See there…. Look straight down." He pointed at the heliport. Jack circled talking to the control tower then landed the helicopter like the expert he was. Ben helped Mary out.

"See you later," he told Jack who nodded acknowledgement; he knew the arrangements and set off to kill a few hours until they were ready for the flight home.

Ben shepherded Mary to a waiting car. "Relax," he reassured her. "It's only dinner."

Ben was right, it was dinner but to Mary's way of thinking there was not much 'only' about it. They arrived at an exclusive hotel. The mosaic floor and marble columns of the entrance hall gave way to a sweeping staircase as wide as the ocean leading to a balcony which wrapped around the whole atrium. Mary stopped to look over, unable to tear herself away from the swirling patterns in the marble, gazing at the sheer opulent grandeur.

Ben steered her to the dining room. In the context of the vast space, the furniture seemed tiny and Mary felt as though she had stumbled into some strange dolls house as she was seated at a table with a crisp linen cloth and a beautiful floral centrepiece. Her practical mind could not help wondering how they got up there to change the bulbs in the chandeliers but only for a moment; the splendour of it all suspended such thoughts even in Mary. She stared around at the ornate arches and smiled at the way the light flooding through the tall windows cast rainbows from their glasses.

Ben watched her fondly.

"If you can tear yourself away…. they do actually serve food here," he chided.

"Good," said Mary, suddenly realising she was hungry.

The waiter appeared, a little white cloth over his arm, to fill their wine glasses then kept re-appearing to top them up whenever they were empty as though he had nothing at all to do but watch over her and Ben. Mary found it a little disconcerting but Ben did not seem perturbed by him at all. Mary tried to ignore the man and concentrate on the food; it was presented as though every plate was a work of art and delicate sauces brought out the flavour.

Ben reached for her hand and squeezed it gently.

"Enjoying yourself? You're very quiet," he observed.

Mary looked up from her now empty plate and as she did so, she felt a wave of happiness spread through her from her head to her toes. Her smile enveloped Ben in a shower of stars.

"Wonderful," she answered. "There's just so much to take in."

"We'll go to a theatre next time we come," he said. "Then we can come here or try somewhere else as you like."

"But how can you afford all this? I don't mean to pry but you can afford it can't you? You aren't over-stretching yourself?"

"Wise investments. I saved like mad when I was working in insurance, then I made a killing on the stock market – twice – now I'm in the air freight business with Jack. Once we're properly up and running there'll be plenty more where that came from. This is just the beginning."

That, thought Mary, explained the easy access to the helicopter. She remembered Ben saying that he might go into business with a friend rather than wait through the start-up phase of setting up on his own. An enterprise like this would instantly provide the excitement and challenge he craved so she could see why he had jumped at the chance. And that Jack should need a partner to put in a bit of capital just at that time….

"Real stroke of luck, that," Ben observed. "Of course, it doesn't hurt to make your own luck and, in this case, I confess to maximising mine. Jack needed help but he didn't realise how much until he saw my business plan. He didn't take much talking into it once I showed him, though."

The curtains ruffled and Mary noticed that the night air leaking through the old window had gone surprisingly cold. She fished a little shawl from her bag.

Ben beckoned to the waiter and pressed a tip into his hand. Mary noticed how pleased the man looked and guessed that for most of the diners he did not even register on their radar. She threw Ben an adoring look. He met her eyes and in his own she saw an irresistible seductiveness. That mop of hair above them, the perfectly shaped nose.... he was without doubt the most attractive man she had ever met.

Tonight, they would kiss.

They walked towards the entrance but before they reached it, Ben pushed Mary gently towards a big oak door. Faintly, she could hear music.

"Shall we finish with a dance?" he inquired, opening the door.

To Mary's surprise, the music coming from behind it was actually fairly loud because at the top of the room on a little platform there was a live band. It was early yet so there were not many couples on the dance floor and as Ben, who turned out to be an expert dancer, took her in his arms and swept her round, Mary felt as if she was floating on a cloud of happiness. The perfect end to a perfect date.

Back at the heliport, Jack helped Mary into the helicopter. He nudged Ben in the ribs.

"You look pleased with yourself. Impressed, was she?"

"Yep."

Ben stood for a moment lost in thought. Not only had Mary been impressed by the lavish style of the date, she had been concerned about him and whether he could afford it. She had cared about the waiter.

He nudged Jack back. "I think it's time for a little charity work."

Jack looked mystified.

On the journey home, Mary snuggled sleepily against Ben's shoulder. Before long, she was roused by the night air and clambered out of the helicopter and into Ben's sports car. It was late when they finally arrived at her door.

"Thank you for a lovely evening," she said.

"I'm glad you enjoyed it," replied Ben.

They stood a foot or so apart gazing into each other's eyes. Mary could feel that Ben was about to pull her closer but at that moment, the family next-door-but-one clattered into the corridor. Seeing Mary, the little girl ran to insert herself between them, standing on Ben's feet in the process.

"Mary, Mary," she began excitedly. Mary bent down.

"Yes, darling?"

But the girl stood there suddenly tongue-tied. Ben could see this was going to take a while. As the kindness that seemed to come so naturally to Mary flowed from her to the child, Ben shot Mary an adoring look.

"I'll see you later. Don't mind me, it's fine, honestly," he said.

The little girl told Mary they had been to the circus and now that the unfamiliar Ben had gone, she was settling down for a long and breathless description of all that they had seen but her mother called her away.

"Tell Mary tomorrow. It's time for bed."

No kiss after all.

Mary went to the door of the block and watched Ben drive down the road. When, finally, she entered the flat and turned on the light, it was to find Mike was waiting.

"Nice time?" It was only two words and yet Mary thought she detected an edge to the question, a hostility.

"Amazing," replied Mary without thinking. "We went to London."

"I know."

Silence. Then: "Have you been spying on me?"

Silence.

"Ben is going into the air freight business," explained Mary.

"What's he going to carry?" asked Mike.

Mary ignored his tone. "Whatever anyone commissions them to transport. So far, mostly express parcels and flowers."

"Drugs, people…." continued Mike sourly.

There was a short silence. Then he said: "It's late, we're both tired, I'll pop in tomorrow," and disappeared.

SUNDAY
DAY 22

Come Sunday, Mike appeared bright and early. Mary had only just finished getting dressed and could not help wondering if he had been there, invisible, waiting for her to be decent.

"If only I could put a bell round his neck," she thought irritably.

Patiently, Mike waited while she had a cup of coffee then dragged her into the garden.

"Come and see what I got you."

There stood a smart electric mower.

"It's time you took your duties as a tenant and neighbour seriously," he joked.

Surely Mike wasn't trying to compete with Ben? More to the point, where would a ghost lay his hands on a mower?

"How did you get it?"

"Good old-fashioned bartering. Occasionally, it suits me to find a psychic and trade although I keep away from the professional ones. I would do the grass for you but the neighbours can't see me so they would find the spectacle rather odd."

"How do you know none of the neighbours are psychic? Then they would see you, well some of them would and you could wait until the others went out and give me a hand."

"I can sense whether they are," Mike replied.

Back in the house, the conversation turned to the kidnapping.

"Andrew followed up on my sighting of the little boy in the supermarket," offered Mary. "But he doesn't think it's the same child."

"Ah," said Mike.

"It is him, though, I know it is."

"No, you don't, it's just a pet theory you have because you saw them on the bus and you thought Danesford was behaving strangely and you hate being wrong."

It was a somewhat cruel analysis but it struck home. Mary did hate being wrong but he was not being fair; her interest in the case went far beyond saying 'I told you so'.

"I do think you should consider the possibility that Andrew might be right."

"I am. I mean, I have. But I still think we should investigate further just to make sure."

"We?"

"All right, you."

"I will pay the Danesfords a few visits," agreed Mike.

Mary flashed him a smile. He smiled back.

He was in a good mood. Relaxed. This could be a good moment to probe for information.

"Mike, what's your other name?"

He considered, then: "It's Mallory-Quinn."

An unusual name, and one that Mary felt she had heard before but could not think where. Her face, however, was a picture of innocent acceptance.

"Do you have any family, Mike? Do you keep in touch?"

"Of course, I have family," he replied light-heartedly. "I didn't just appear out of thin air aged thirty-four, silly. And as to keeping in touch: not really."

Not *really*. He'd done it again: avoided the question. What did not *really* mean? That he didn't visit them? Or just that he didn't let them know when he was around? Mary sighed.

"At least tell me something. What did you do for a job before…. you know?"

"I was a pilot. And no, I didn't crash my plane…. I lived life in the fast lane and died of influenza. Ironic, isn't it?"

"I need a cup of tea," Mary announced. "Would you like…." Her voice tailed off. He probably couldn't drink tea.

"Do you have any ice cream?"

"Ice cream?" she questioned in surprise.

"Yes, ice cream. Brilliant stuff. Smooth and cold. I do have to get energy from somewhere, you know. All this maintaining visibility and substance, all this bartering has worn me out. And ice cream is much nicer than plugging myself into those nifty little electric car charging points. Harder to come by though."

It would be.

"There's a shop on the corner. I'll go and get a couple of tubs of caramel."

She soon returned, then watching him, Mary could not help asking: "Were you by any chance fond of caramel ice cream as a child?"

"How did you know," asked Mike rhetorically, an expression of pure contentment on his face as he licked the spoon.

"What happens if you run out of energy?"

"I fade. But I can feel it coming on so I don't let it happen."

He seemed to be at peace with the world. Mary decided to risk another question, a question of a completely different sort which had been taking shape in the back of her mind for a while and rising towards the top of her consciousness as the television appeals and her own sighting of Mr Danesford and 'Jared' in the supermarket had failed to produce the hoped-for breakthrough. Perhaps the answer lay elsewhere – with Jared's Uncle Charles or the mysterious mistress?

"Mike, do you remember when I was telling you about my tailing of the Parkers? What did you mean when you said Charles Armstrong ruined a young life? Is your private business connected to the Parkers?"

Mike's face darkened. The brooding Mike was back.

"When there's something you should know, I'll tell you."

He left soon afterwards.

So, she was supposed to continue 'awaiting developments' was that it? But if Mike would not take her into his confidence, he must expect she would be curious. Background research was out of the question because she had no idea whose life Charles had ruined or when or in what way. Perhaps if she went to Bidcome Marsh? Unfortunately, as Mary soon established, Bidcome Marsh, although not far, was not the easiest of places to get to on the bus. She needed a car….

MONDAY
DAY 23

Mary did not know whether work was a relief from what was becoming an increasingly complicated private life – it was all so simple when she just went to Bramwells and had no boyfriend, no resident ghost and no kidnapping investigation – or whether it was an unwelcome but necessary distraction from what was really important. Whatever it was, Monday was here and duty called.

The radio Minty had carelessly left on Mary's desk crackled into life. "Dan to Ryan. I thought you said you'd put in that new pipe by the Rectory end?"

"I did."

Static drowned Dan's reply but his tone was unmistakeable.

"Quick, Mary, turn it up, Dan and Ryan are having a domestic." The speaker was Josh. Mary obeyed.

"Didn't catch that," came Ryan's cheery voice.

"I said: I'm standing looking into the ****ing hole and there's no ****ing pipe."

"Get your ****ing eyes tested…. Hang on, I'm coming over."

"No swearing on the radio," intoned Pete's voice.

Mary giggled.

"I think I'll take a little walk over there too," decided Josh. "In my capacity as Health and Safety manager, of course."

"I'll join you, you nosey bastard." The voice was Pete's.

Mary watched them go, envious that she was missing all the fun. She knew she would never hear what happened because they seemed to live entirely in the present. By the time they came back, it would all be forgotten and they would have moved on to something else.

* * *

That evening, Andrew knocked on the door.

"It's all right," he reassured her. "Nothing has happened. I was passing and I did promise to keep in touch, that's all."

Mary made him welcome and tried to think of conversation. The only thing she knew about Andrew was that he liked vintage cars and was restoring an old Morgan so she told him of her ambition to buy a car herself and asked him for advice on what sort of car she should purchase.

"Depends on what you want," he replied. "Something stylish? Something cheap to run?"

"Something small, I'm useless at parking," replied Mary.

"It will come with practise," Andrew assured her. But his attempts to establish what might suit her were doomed to failure because mentioning any type of car brought no picture to her mind. The only car Mary could reliably recognise was a Fiesta because she had learned on one.

"Perhaps I should look for one of those," she speculated.

"You'd be in good company, a lot of people buy the car they learned on as a first car," replied Andrew.

Sitting there, relaxed, his thoughts gravitated to work. She was in good company being unable to recognise cars, too.

"We found Jared's pushchair dumped by the side of the road. No prints, unfortunately. A local resident fed up with fly-tipping ran after the culprit but couldn't catch him. She didn't know what sort of car it was but we dispatched a police constable to show her photographs of cars and she picked out a Mondeo as being the right sort of shape. We checked on Mondeos and discovered Mr Danesford hired a Mondeo last week. When we asked him about it, he said he had some holiday due and had decided to take a trip to Wales with his son. The constable checked with the hire company to see how many miles he had travelled and concluded that he was lying; he had covered only about half the distance to Wales and back."

"So, I was right," said Mary.

"I wouldn't go that far," replied Andrew. "And please don't repeat what I just said."

"Of course not," Mary assured him. "But it's a bit coincidental that the pushchair is dumped the first time he has access to a car, don't you think? Makes one wonder if he hired it to get rid of the evidence because the new television appeal and coverage of the ransom demand have got him rattled. Are you going to pick him up?"

"For what?" asked Andrew. "Not being straight with us about where he went for a day out? There's still no proof he had anything to do with the kidnapping and until there is, his private life is his own business."

Back to Danesford but still no evidence.

TUESDAY
DAY 24

Four days had passed since Gemma had been so mysterious on the phone. Mary had left Gemma a number of messages but there had been no reply. She was composing another message in her head as she got ready to go to work when a white envelope made of paper so thick it was practically cardboard arrived in the post. Inside was an invitation edged in swirling gold requesting the pleasure of the company of Mary and Ben at the wedding of Gemma and Max. Mary stood staring at it. Then, as her mind started to work again, the date struck her: the wedding was less than a month away. Thoughts whirled through her head: what about my dress; why the hurry; I had better call Ben; I had better call Gemma! But before she could do anything, a voice behind her said: "Hi," and there was Mike.

Talk about bad timing. Startled, Mary turned towards him hiding the invitation behind her back, her face red.

"Are you all right?" he asked. She nodded. His eyes gravitated to her arm. "What's that you're holding?"

Slowly, she drew it out and placed it on the mantelpiece. 'Mr and Mrs Winter request the pleasure of the company of Mary Chadwick and Ben MacKay at the wedding of their daughter Gemma to Max Townsend….'

"Ah," he said.

There was a pause.

"You remember Gemma from when we were all at Bramwells."

"I remember Gemma," Mike agreed staring at the invitation, transfixed. Quickly, Mary pushed him into the kitchen.

"I have to make my sandwiches," she said. "Why are you here, anyway?"

"I stopped by to apologise for Sunday. I was ungracious."

"That's all right. It was my fault. Your private business is exactly that – private. Unless and until you choose to tell me."

By now, Mary was running late. She tried to phone Gemma as she walked to the bus stop but Gemma's phone was still engaged. Finally, sitting on the bus, she got through. Gemma was excited and breathless.

"Sorry," she said. "The phone is busy all the time. The phone is busy, I'm busy, we're all busy, there's so much to do. Can you call round tomorrow?"

Waiting only for Mary to agree, she rushed off to answer the doorbell.

"Don't wear yourself out before the wedding," warned Mary as the call clicked off.

Mary peeped out of the window. There should be enough time to call Ben before she arrived at work. She dialled his number.

"Hi, Ben."

"Hi, Mary, this a nice surprise. What's with the wake-up call, you don't usually phone so early."

"I just wanted to say Gemma is getting married and we're invited."

"Congratulations. Tell her congratulations for me. When's the wedding?"

Mary told him.

The surprise was obvious in Ben's voice. "Gosh. Why the tearing hurry?"

"I don't know. Ben, please don't tell me you can't come."

There was a faint rustling of paper at the other end as Ben checked his commitments then he replied: "Of course I can come. I wouldn't miss it for the world."

The bus bumped over a pothole and Mary realised they were nearly at her stop.

"I've got to go, talk to you later," she said and hung up.

WEDNESDAY
DAY 25

Mary called at Gemma's the next evening. She was about to ask why the hurry but there was no need; words came tumbling out of Gemma at speed on every aspect of the big day.

She had wanted the event at a beautiful country house hotel but it had been all booked up for the next two years nearly. She had left her contact details and looked around for somewhere else but in her disappointed state, nothing seemed as good. Then all of a sudden, the hotel called to say there had been a last-minute cancellation.

Gemma had called Max immediately and he had agreed they should go ahead with their dream wedding as originally envisaged even if it did mean a bit of rushing around.

Quite a lot of rushing around, in fact. The house was in chaos and the telephone kept ringing. Gemma's mother, however, seemed to have it all under control, indeed she seemed to be in her element. This gave Gemma time to catch her breath and talk to Mary.

"You are free that day? You will still be my Maid of Honour?"

Of course, Mary would. Gemma showed her a photograph of the dress she had in mind for Mary to wear and the moment Mary agreed that she liked it, Gemma rushed over to her mother and added calling the bridal shop to arrange a fitting to her mother's already long list of things to do.

* * *

It was late when Mary got back to her flat and her thoughts were centred entirely on food. The smell of soggy chips and vinegar emanated from the bag in her hand. She peeled back the paper. Steam warmed and dampened her face. It was naughty but she would forgive herself; she did not do it often.

Mary was picking up her first chip when Mike appeared.

"Carry on. Don't mind me," he told her.

"Hungry," replied Mary, her mouth full. "Sit down. Keep me company. I didn't expect to see you so soon."

Mike sat at the table opposite her. "I had a reason for calling."

"You've been spying on Danesford like you promised after you told me I didn't know it was him all along I just wanted to be right but I should listen to Andrew," guessed Mary. "And you found something out. Well, so did Andrew; Danesford hired a car and coincidentally, Jared's pushchair was dumped."

"It's not about that. Goodness Mary, it's only three days since I said I'd pay him a few visits. What do you expect him to do in that length of time?"

"I don't know," conceded Mary. "Carry on with what you were saying."

"I happened to be passing the police station and Andrew was holding a piece of paper and looking fed up. Mind you, he looks like that a lot these days. So, anyway, I had a little peep over his shoulder and it was another ransom note."

Mary swallowed her latest chip. "Was there any proof Jared was still alive? A photo holding a newspaper or something?"

"No. You're thinking of Rachel, aren't you?"

Mary nodded. Mike pulled a face.

"Nothing to comfort Rachel. Worse. This second note came with a threat. 'You betrayed me and now you will pay.'"

Mary shuddered. "Any idea who sent it?" she asked.

"The police are looking into personal contacts of Henry Parker's and also business associates who might have a grudge. A successful man like that makes enemies when contracts go bad and expectations aren't fulfilled."

"Does that mean they've eliminated family members?" Mary asked, thinking of Charles.

"No. That line of inquiry is still ongoing."

Mary wanted to ask if Mike himself had eliminated Charles but decided she had better not risk causing him to go into one of his moods and leave. The important thing now was the new note and whether it might lead to the arrest of the kidnapper and the recovery of Jared.

"The first hand-over was a failure. Whoever-it-was got clean away...."

"I know what you're going to say," interrupted Mike. "You want me to attend the next handover, then if all goes to plan – Andrew's plan – well and good and if it doesn't, at least we'll know who is behind this. I'm making it a priority to find out where and when it is. Although where they think the Parkers will get another half million from, I can't imagine."

Mary smiled her gratitude.

Mike patted her shoulder. "Enjoy the rest of your chips."

THURSDAY
DAY 26

The door of the cabin closed quietly and immediately Mary's attention was caught. It took real effort to make it do that. She looked up.

"Ryan?"

He looked round the cabin and seeing no-one, approached her desk, holding out a flimsy white box. "Could you hide this somewhere?"

Mary took the box and peeped inside. "Whose birthday is it?"

"Pete's. And if I had known earlier what I know now, I'd have bought a bigger cake. We're going to need it."

"Before you go…." called Mary as he hurried to the door: "Where is everyone? Has something happened?"

"The ground floor is under two inches of water. New recruit put the prong of the forklift through the rising main."

Ryan had hardly left when Dan issued through the door. "Call the hire company, Mary. Order some pumps and tell them now not tomorrow." He was only in the cabin for a moment and then he was gone.

The familiar crash of the steel door heralded Pete's arrival. "Mary, we need some pumps…."

"Already on the way," Mary assured him.

"Good girl."

Alone again: "I should have known something was up the minute I arrived," thought Mary. "Even Minty and Bellyache aren't here."

"It's like a comedy film out there. Shame you're missing it," said a voice.

"Whilst you are not. Hello, Mike. You might give me some warning when you're going to creep up behind me."

"I've told you before, I don't creep. I noticed you were on your own so rather than wait until tonight I thought I'd pop in and tell you the second handover is scheduled for Sunday, at the picnic spot by the canal at two o'clock. And now," he said with a grin, "I'm going back to watch the entertainment."

He was annoying. There was no need to rub it in that she was missing the excitement. Mary sat down and checked her emails. She looked at her watch; lunch time was long past. She stood up and looked out of the window. Figures in orange coats were spilling out of the building and scattering. The fuss must be over. She had better order some pizza to go with that cake.

FRIDAY
DAY 27

Thank goodness it was Friday. Mary found it hard to settle at work knowing the second handover was coming up but she went through her list of jobs, one at a time, slow and steady, bitesize chunks, until the list was finished and the day was over.

On the way home, Mary called at the supermarket. She had only just arrived at home when the doorbell rang.

"Hello, M."

"Hi, Ben. Come on in. You don't mind if I finish putting the shopping away?"

As Ben made himself comfortable, Mary looked around uneasily. They seemed to be alone. Good.

"Thank you again for that wonderful trip to London."

Ben looked smug. "I'm glad you enjoyed it."

"Are you hungry? The dinner will stretch to two."

"Anything I can do to help?"

He came up behind her and put his arms around her, nuzzling her neck.

"Not helping. Later." Laughing, she pushed him away. "Don't let it get cold."

They ate in the kitchen area sitting on wooden stools then moved to the living room. Ben gravitated naturally to his new business venture and his eyes lit up with enthusiasm as he talked. Mary listened wide-eyed. He was casually knowledgeable and he made even the technical bits sound gripping. He plucked anecdotes from the air to illustrate his narrative. Mary could not help wondering how he had ever thought he needed to go to Bramwells. Never mind; fortunately for her, he had.

She tucked her feet up underneath her on the chair; it was growing chilly. She supposed that the problem was Mike bitching invisibly about Ben's success again.

"Ben, do you mind turning up the heater next to you?"

Pausing for breath, Ben remembered to ask how Mary was getting on in her new job.

"It's much more fun than Bramwells," she assured him.

"Good. I'm glad." Mary could see that he meant it even if the inquiry had been an afterthought. "I told you it was the next best thing to the army, didn't I, M?"

They arranged to meet at the weekend and Ben stood up to leave. Mary followed him to the door. He put his arms around her, their lips were close and Mary's eyes were beginning automatically to close. Then suddenly, they were wide open and she was screaming.

"Spider. A spider!" She stared transfixed as the unusually large specimen abseiled down from the ceiling and landed on Ben's shoulder. He brushed it away and put his arms around her shaking body.

"It's all right, it's gone. Mary?"

It was true, the spider was gone but so was the moment.

"Would you like me to stay?"

"No, I'm fine. Really."

She would phone Ben later to say goodnight.

And she would give Mike a piece of her mind when she saw him. To begin with, she had told herself it was all in her mind – the feeling that he was watching, bouts of coldness in the air as if in judgement whenever Ben got too close or talked of the future – their future – but as time went by, she had become more and more convinced it was not mere imagination. As for today, he had been there, invisible, doing it again – definitely.

Mary did not get the opportunity to take him to task that night, though. The air remained warm and Mike did not appear so Mary deduced he was busy somewhere.

SATURDAY
DAY 28

Mary headed for the bridal shop to try on the dress Gemma had chosen. It was mauve silk, elegant and sleek and complemented perfectly Gemma's stunning white gown. Both had chiffon sleeves and a plain, round neckline.

"Oh, it's beautiful!" Mary exclaimed, feeling the material between fingers and thumb.

"The colour suits you, I thought it would," approved Gemma.

Mary looked in the mirror. The dress looked a little odd with her tousled hair above it but no matter; Gemma had arranged for a hairdresser and make-up artist to be present in the hotel on the morning of the wedding.

Carefully, she hugged her friend.

"You look pretty good yourself."

Both turned to look at their reflections in the mirror. Gemma spoke first.

"We need an excuse to do this more often. Now, I wonder who else could get married?"

* * *

Come evening, Mike appeared.

"I found time to pay the Danesfords a few more visits," he explained: "And they didn't do anything unusual. Again. They behaved like a perfectly normal family – except, of course, that Mrs Danesford isn't there."

Was that a thinly disguised 'I told you so'?

"Andrew said she was in hospital if you remember. If she really is in hospital – still – why doesn't he visit her? Perhaps she's left him," mused Mary. "But surely, she would take Darren. Perhaps he killed her."

"Now that's letting your imagination run a bit wild! Just because you suspect him of kidnap on no real evidence when it may be that all he's guilty of is having a child who looks like Jared…."

"Why doesn't he visit his wife, then?" she demanded.

"Maybe he does visit her. I haven't been keeping a twenty-four-hour watch on them, you know."

"Perhaps you should," returned Mary. She had not intended it to come out rudely but it had, a little. An uncomfortable silence followed. It was time for a change of subject.

But as she looked at Mike, the subject that came to Mary's mind was not exactly calculated to improve the atmosphere. She had adjusted to having a ghost in her life but a possessive ghost was a step too far. She needed to tell him straight out that their alliance did not give him the right to choose her friends and now was as good a time as any.

"Mike, I don't want to cause an argument, really I don't, but I know you don't like Ben and you must understand that your views on the matter are irrelevant. I'm not going to give him up. I know what you're up to, you're trying to break us up and it's not going to work."

Mike looked straight back at her but all he said was: "Noted."

"Wonderful," thought Mary as she climbed into bed that night. No promise to respect her space, just 'noted.' And now there was an atmosphere between them, which upset her although she could not think of a good reason why it should.

SUNDAY
DAY 29

The day the second ransom was to be paid. Mary had decided to attend the second handover herself and had gone to bed late the night before to prevent her from waking too early so it was with some irritation that she read the time: seven o'clock. The handover was not until two (although she would be there long before that) which left hours to kill.

She threw herself into doing the chores. She made herself some toast. She mowed the lawn. And all the while, the clock sat ticking and tocking very slowly, laughing all over its poker face.

One-fifteen. Finally.

Mary set out for the picnic spot. She found a vantage point from where she could clearly see the heavy-duty paper bag with string handles – the sort of bag take-away food comes in – which had been left by the litter bin on the canal bank as directed and from where she also had an overview of the whole picnic area. Not wanting to tip off the blackmailer, the police had not closed it so there were quite a lot of people around. They all seemed unremarkable although Mary guessed that some of them were plain clothes officers.

As two o'clock approached, a woman went to the bin. She had been sharing sandwiches with another couple who had now left. The woman looked closely at the paper bag. Mary's fingernails dug into her palms. Would she pick it up? She seemed to be wondering. Then she dropped her empty juice carton into the bin and walked away.

Noticing she had left the bag, a park attendant went over to clear it up but his eye was caught by a man in dark trousers and a beige jacket. One of the policemen, concluded Mary.

She scanned the area. A girl was walking along talking on the phone and pushing a bicycle at the same time. She was a good candidate; the bicycle for a fast getaway, a basket on the front for the bag of money. The girl went towards the bin…. yes…. yes…. no. She veered away.

Apart from that, there was a nervous moment when a dog showed interest but sniffed the bag and decided there was no food in there and that was it. Two o'clock had come and gone.

Mary stood wondering how long she should wait. Then she noticed the girl again. She was still on the phone, pushing the bicycle and not looking where she was going. The bicycle hit a stone and knocked her off balance and she fell. People went over to help but she waved them away and just sat there next to the bicycle, talking on the phone without even pausing for breath.

Stay or go? Mary looked at her watch again. The kidnapper should have picked up the money by now. And there was no sign of Jared nor had there been. She would go. She would follow the girl.

Fortunately for Mary, the limping girl was unable to ride her bicycle so it was an easy matter to trail her home to one of the big houses overlooking the park not far from where Mary lived.

Having sent the note, why not pick up the money? Why no Jared? Mary sat alone over her Sunday dinner, bitterly disappointed.

MONDAY
DAY 30

Mary was pinning photos to the wall showing the progress of the building when the door was flung open and Ryan bounced in, soaked from head to foot, his orange waterproof trousers squeaking with every step. It shut behind him with its usual crash. He sat down, little puddles of water collecting around his feet.

"Make me a cuppa, Mary," he pleaded.

"Only if you stop dripping on my floor."

"No can do," Ryan replied cheerfully. He untied his boots and slipped them off, adding mud to the equation. Then he started pulling at the bottoms of the trousers. The elastic round the ankles was tight, as was the elastic at the waist.

"Cut you in half, don't they?" remarked Bellyache from the far end of the room.

"And keep the farts in. Yeesh!" re-joined Ryan.

"Ryan!" Returning with the tea, Mary failed to sound properly outraged, mainly because she was trying not to laugh. "Here's your tea. You can sit there and enjoy the smell on your own, don't bring it over here."

"Fact is," interjected Minty, "fact is, you should be subject to air pollution controls. You have no idea what we have to put up with, Mary. With exhaust emissions like that he'd have been scrapped years ago if he were a car."

Ryan went over to his desk and produced a towel. "That's better. And now for lunch. It's your lucky day, Minty, I'm going to the kitchen to make some toast. I would have gone over to the van and got baked potato and beans but it's too wet."

* * *

Mary stood washing salad and thinking about yesterday's handover. Perhaps the money had been picked up after she left. She picked up her phone and put it down again; she could not ask Andrew because how did she know about the handover and anyway, he should not tell her.

"I hate lettuce."

"Why buy it then?" and there was Mike.

"Some of us have to eat something other than ice cream," Mary retorted.

"But not lettuce, it's not food."

"Is. Anyway, I like it."

Mike shook his head. He was not even going to try to make sense of this conversation.

"You enjoy it, then. Did someone mention ice cream?"

"Dinner is served." Mary placed a plate of grated cheese and salad on the table. Mike pulled a face. "Don't panic." She added a dish of ice cream. "Now, what brings you here?"

"I felt your waves of negativity."

"I'm entitled. The so-called handover was a waste of time."

"From Andrew's point of view. The police waited two hours past the appointment time then Andrew gave the order to retrieve the money and withdraw. Mr Danesford bottled."

"You're saying it *was* him!" Mary exclaimed.

"I don't know…. I mean yes, but it doesn't make sense."

"I didn't see him," observed Mary. "Perhaps I should have stayed longer."

"It wouldn't have made any difference. He didn't go to the rendezvous."

"Hang on. If he didn't go, what makes you think it was Mr Danesford that was due to make the collection?" asked Mary.

"I was flitting backwards and forwards between the canal bank and our favourite suspects and I heard him on the phone. He was talking to a woman. Even if the police were tailing him, they would think he was just taking the long way back from work. But I heard him say 'I can't go through with it' then the person at the other end said something and he replied 'Yes, but there are police everywhere. I'm not going to do it. Leave me alone. Look, I know about you and him, don't pretend it doesn't suit you the way things are.'"

"That's odd," said Mary. "It's as though Danesford was being blackmailed himself into blackmailing the Parkers."

"Yes. That's the impression I had."

"Which suggests he took Jared and she knows he did," ventured Mary, "Except that apparently, he didn't. Do you think the 'I know about you and him' referred to this woman and Jared, that she took him and has him hidden somewhere? And it 'suiting her the way things are' means she intends to keep him?"

"In that case, Danesford would be blackmailing her, not the other way round."

"True. Well, how about this? Danesford only just found out she had Jared. Then she calls to threaten him not knowing that he has found out and he tells her to get lost. Of course, there's another interpretation of 'you and him,'" said Mary thoughtfully. "Danesford was talking to Henry Parker's mistress. But who is she and how would she know Danesford let alone his darkest secrets?"

"I'll see what I can find out although I haven't much to go on," offered Mike.

"Thank you." Mary rewarded him with a warm smile.

"So, do we think Danesford was talking to Jared's kidnapper or Henry's mistress?"

"Don't know. Maybe it's one and the same person."

"Doesn't matter either way. I'll keep my eyes and ears open, try to find something out."

"Danesford was talking to a woman," reflected Mary. "I saw a girl with a bicycle at the picnic area. And she was on the phone. Suppose she was talking to Danesford.... but if he refused to pick up the money, why didn't she pick it up?"

"Because like Danesford before her, she realised she'd be caught? Because she went there to see he did the job but never meant to risk having any part in it herself?"

It made sense.

"I don't think Jared is with the girl I saw," said Mary thoughtfully. "There were no signs of life in the house when she returned home – but could you call by and make sure? The note said 'you will pay.' If that was a threat to harm Jared…."

"Yellow light," Mike reminded her.

"Or it could have referred to the money. But the money wasn't handed over."

"Which worries you. Understandably. Although: yellow light." Then, catching Mary's expression: "But I'll still check the house. Of course. Won't be long."

Ten minutes later, he was back. "I searched the entire house and the garden shed. He's not there. And your biking friend is called Hazel, by the way."

"Where on earth can he be? Oh, this is getting us nowhere," muttered Mary in exasperation. She sat reflecting. "Do you think I should tell Andrew about Mr Danesford?"

"No," said Mike. "How could you possibly explain knowing Danesford was the one who was supposed to keep the appointment let alone what he said on the phone? If we want to know who is blackmailing him and with what, I will have to keep an eye on Danesford myself."

"Thank you." He could only do what he could do. "Do you think they'll be another note?"

Mike considered. "Not from those behind this debacle; Danesford doesn't have the courage for the job and the woman he was talking to clearly isn't prepared to collect the money herself. I think it's more a question of whether or not she exposes his secret whatever it is to pay him out for failing to deliver."

"If she does that, he might expose hers."

"All in all, they're probably out of the picture. And I don't think there'll be another note from whoever organised the first handover either. I don't think Danesford and this woman were the architects of that, it was so much more professional, properly organised and efficiently carried out. That was done by someone hard-headed and scheming who would probably have the sense not to push his – or her – luck. Whether anyone new will join in, who knows?"

Mary sighed. "You said you were tailing Danesford and 'our favourite suspects.' Who else were you tailing?"

"Charles…. Henry…. Ben."

"Why Ben?" Mary was shocked.

"I was curious about the source of his money. There was a previous ransom paid, remember," said Mike evasively.

"Ben has always been rich. Well, all the time I've known him. Why Henry?"

"As I said before, it wouldn't be the first time the parents were involved."

Mary drew a deep breath. "And Charles?"

"Nasty piece of work."

This time, his avoidance of the real question was not deliberate, thought Mary. He had simply said what he felt. And done nothing to alleviate her curiosity.

TUESDAY
DAY 31

"I may not be able to afford a car but I could get a bicycle," decided Mary. "At least then I could follow Hazel and find out where she fits in."

She turned on the computer. How could there be so many? It's got *how* many gears?

She turned to Ryan. "Do you know anything about bicycles?"

"No," he replied cheerfully.

"My wife has one she doesn't want. I'll phone her," called out Pete. "Ryan can pick it up; he's going past on the way to the builder's merchant."

"I should have thought this through," thought Mary, as she wobbled away from site that afternoon. She had not been on a bike in years. This was going to take some living down.

It was useful of Hazel to live opposite the park; Mary could sit on a bench eating her hot dog and watching the house until she came out. Except that she did not. She sat at the table in the window all evening and if Mary had stayed to observe, she would have known that she sat there into the night.

"She's an illustrator," Mike informed her. "Children's books."

Wearily, Mary put her feet up and took a gulp of tea. "What are you doing here? You might at least have stopped by the park and told me I was wasting my time."

"Sorry. I was busy. As to what I'm doing here – I observed Andrew holding another letter. I didn't think he could look more fed up than he did the other day but apparently, he can."

"Another ransom demand? Who from – one of the original blackmailers or someone new?"

"Who said anything about a ransom demand? I said Andrew had had a letter. This one was addressed to him not the Parkers. 'You messed that up, didn't you? The instructions were no police. You've put the kid in danger. You think you know best but you don't.'"

"Poor Andrew. I'm sure he feels bad enough without that. Did you find out anything else?"

"No-one has called Danesford and Hazel has done nothing but sit and draw if that's what you mean."

Mary sighed. "I'm going to bed."

"Sweet dreams." Mike blew her a kiss and left.

WEDNESDAY
DAY 32

A light was blinking on the answerphone when Mary returned home the following day.

"That's unusual," she thought. "Most likely it's only a junk call."

Curiosity piqued, she went straight over to the machine before even taking off her coat and found a message from Rachel. Would she like to come round for coffee on Saturday morning?

Mary called Rachel straight back.

"I got your message. I'd love to come."

Rachel sounded pleased.

Mary put down the phone with a feeling of satisfaction; she had been intending to ring Rachel with the same suggestion in the hope of finding out more about Charles. But that aside, she liked Rachel.

Charles…. Henry…. Hazel - who might or might not be one and the same person as the mysterious mistress. And Danesford, of course. Mary counted her suspects.

Danesford: the sort of spying needed there was not her department. Charles: she might discover more about Charles on Saturday and Henry too.... The mistress: if it was not Hazel, then Mary had no clue who she was. Hazel: Mary would go to the park and watch her house again tonight.

Hardly had she reached the park bench and opened her box of chicken nuggets than Hazel came out of her front door. Hastily, Mary put away her meal and jumped on her bicycle.

She caught up with Hazel at the traffic lights. One behind the other they rode along wide urban streets and down little side roads until Hazel stopped outside an unprepossessing semi in a street of identical houses. She knocked on the door.

Mary rode on; it would look suspicious if she stopped. From round the corner, she saw a young man come out. He, too, had a bicycle. They kissed by way of greeting and set off at pace.

Mary intended to stay close enough to see where they went without them becoming aware of her but it soon became apparent to her as she struggled to keep up that cycling was not so much a hobby for these two as an obsession, also that their bikes were better than hers.

"It's good for me," she muttered to herself as she panted up what she hoped would be the final hill. It was: but only because Hazel and her boyfriend had disappeared. Mary looked all around; they must have sped down the other side and turned off. They could be anywhere.

There was nothing for it but to go home.

THURSDAY
DAY 33

"Bellyache," bawled Pete. "Get yourself over here and explain what the electrician is sulking about."

"All I did was point out that he'd installed a sensor in the washroom area but not the one the plans show over the cubicles. So, you're in there, obeying an urgent call of nature and you take a bit too long and all the lights go out. He didn't have to be such a drama queen about it."

"It seems to be the day for upsetting people," grumbled Pete. "I thought you'd have more sense, Mary. What was that pile-up at the turnstile all about?"

"All I did was expire the welders' fingerprints so they couldn't get through to site without coming to see me. Their hot works permit was missing the signature."

"If I hear the phrase 'all I did' one more time," exploded Pete.

Bellyache nudged Minty. "What's eating him?"

Minty shrugged.

"Meeting in the conference room, ten minutes," announced Pete. "All of you."

Engineers, site staff, quantity surveyors, design managers filed in to the conference room in silence and sat down. Pete looked around the table.

"There has been an audit of the server. You all know you are to back up the documents on this list," he waved a piece of paper. "You have all assured me you were on it – 'work in progress' I believe is the phrase – which is curious. Would anyone like to tell me what was backed up in the folder for this site?"

Eyes dropped: fingernails were studied.

"Nothing. Not one of you has uploaded a single document."

They filed out like naughty children.

"He got a roasting but he'll get over it. Better upload a few documents, though," Ryan advised Mary. "I've got things to do on site. I don't suppose you'd like…."

"No," replied Mary. "I've got plenty of my own. Not that I'm behind, you understand."

"Of course not. Like we told Pete, we're on it."

* * *

The evening was half over by the time Mary arrived home but at least she had broken the back of uploading the documents that were her responsibility.

On balance, she considered it unlikely that Hazel had been Henry's mistress but it was still possible she had an involvement in the kidnapping. After all, she had been on the phone at the right time and did not hang up even when she fell over and hurt herself. However, it was getting late and Mike could more easily check out the boyfriend's house and make sure that Jared was not there. Mary called him.

"I suppose so," he agreed.

"I would have gone myself, honestly."

"It's fine, Mary." Gently, he took hold of her hand. "You have a rest."

It was nearly ten o'clock when he returned.

"You've been a long time," observed Mary.

"When I got to his house, he was on his way out shopping," replied Mike. "He bought – amongst other things – smarties, refreshers, chocolate fudge and jelly fruits."

"What about actual food?"

"I doubt Jared likes rump steak. Anyway, he only bought one. Naturally, I accompanied him back to the house – no Jared by the way – but he didn't go out again. He did, however, have a wooden toy train on his window sill new in its box."

"Interesting."

Just then, Mary's phone rang. Ben's voice spilled out. Mike glared at it, marched across the room and straight through the wall.

"Hi, Ben."

"You sound stressed, M. Preoccupied."

Determinedly, Mary put smarties and wooden trains out of her mind. "It's nothing. I had a bad day."

Ben listened sympathetically. "Never mind. You've uploaded most of it now."

"Cheer me up. Tell me something nice."

Nice. His shares had gone up. They had a new client. He had been approached to join the golf club.

"What sort of something?" Ben inquired.

"Something. Anything."

"You're beautiful. I love you." Ben thought for a moment. "Is your computer turned on?"

"It can be."

A beep alerted Mary to the receipt of an email. She clicked it open to find a photograph of a bunch of flowers accompanied by a jolly tune.

"How's that?"

Mary smiled down the phone. "Brilliant."

"Good. Send them to yourself at work to buck you up when required."

"I might do that. Thanks, Ben."

FRIDAY
DAY 34

No need for virtual flowers today, though. Work went smoothly and by four o'clock they were tumbling out of site to start the weekend. Pete stood preparing to lock up.

"I don't know why I bother holding fire drills," he remarked to the air in general. "I know they can evacuate the building in minutes. Every Friday, as soon as the word is given." But his tone belied his words; Pete bore no ill feeling.

Dan came up behind him. "They're all out, I'm the last."

Mary accepted Dan's offer of a lift to the bus stop and before long, she was back at her flat, kicking off her shoes and setting up her computer in the middle of the table. The flowers might not be real but they could pretend.

A shiver in the air sent Mary diving for the computer to close the email, nearly upsetting her coffee in the process. She did not need another sulk from Mike.

"Steady on." He waited while she collected herself.

"I was in the area, on the way back from Hazel's boyfriend in fact, so I thought I'd give you an update.

"He's a financial advisor of some sort. He paid a wealthy client a visit this morning and stopped off at home for lunch. Tuna and salad." Mike paused. "Our cycling enthusiast seems to be a fully paid-up fitness fanatic. I had a look in his kitchen cupboard: protein shakes, nuts, brown rice. I looked in his refrigerator, too: eggs, steak, yoghurt…."

Mary's hands clenched in frustration. "Get to the interesting part."

"After lunch, you mean? He pored over a magazine about mountain biking for nearly twenty minutes…."

"You're doing this on purpose, aren't you?"

Mike exhaled slowly. "All right, all right, keep your hair on. He took some birthday paper from the cupboard and wrapped the train and the sweets then he wrote a card – one of those with a badge and a big '2' on it and put it on top and tied a ribbon round it all. Next stop on the way to the office – his sister's house. It's his nephew's birthday."

"Oh." Deflated, Mary asked: "I suppose there was only the nephew at the sister's? Jared wasn't with her?"

"No. And so you know, Hazel is off to her wealthy parents for the weekend. One thing she isn't is short of is a bob or two. She doesn't need to get involved in a kidnapping."

"And she is obviously attached to her boyfriend which makes it unlikely she was Henry's mistress."

That seemed to close that line of inquiry.

There was always Charles and Henry tomorrow. She would see what tomorrow brought but Mary could not help feeling despondent.

* * *

That night Mary fell asleep thinking about seeing Jared on the bus. He was bored, he was kicking the seat, he was…. kidnapped…. kidnapped…. Just like Ellen. Where was Ellen? Mary was alone in the musty shed. Night was falling. The door would not budge. There were spiders everywhere, in her hair, on her face – and she was screaming, screaming. Don't scream, close your mouth, a spider might go in…. she shut it quickly. Sit up, brush them away – and Mary was awake, flailing her arms and gasping for breath. She sat very still, sipped her water and told herself to get a grip.

SATURDAY
DAY 35

Mary looked all around for signs of Mike. She knew he did not want her getting too close to the Parkers after his reaction to finding out that Charles Armstrong was a member of the family.

Quietly, she let herself out of the flat and walked softly down the street to the bus stop. Sitting on the bus, she reflected on the ludicrousness of it all; it did not matter whether she was quiet or not but she still she felt compelled to behave that way.

Rachel welcomed her like a long-lost friend.

"Are you all right?" Mary asked, seeing how pale she looked but Rachel assured her she was fine.

However, it was obvious the strain was taking its toll.

"I miss Jared so much," Rachel burst out. "I go to his room and I sit there remembering his voice and how he would turn his head to one side and look at me and say 'Mama.' How we'd drive his toy cars across the carpet to the 'garage' under his bed or put his little jigsaw together and he'd tip it straight over and demand to do it again…." She lapsed into silence. Then: "We're thinking of offering a reward for information leading to his safe return. Do you think it's a good idea?"

"Yes, I do," encouraged Mary. "Something might come of it and if it doesn't, you'll know you did everything you could."

"That's what I think but I think Henry is afraid it will get my hopes up again then time will go by and I'll make myself ill waiting for news. I think if he could do it without me knowing, he would. But this is one occasion when discreet inquiries through the old boy network won't work, isn't it?"

"The more publicity, the better. I say do it but on one condition: you must eat and sleep. Promise? I'll come and check," Mary threatened.

"I promise." Purpose took hold in Rachel's eyes. It was obvious she would contact Andrew as soon as Mary departed.

They reminisced about the holiday and Mary asked what Rachel and Henry had done after she left. Rachel showed her a portrait a street artist had drawn of her and photographs of wonderful chalk pavement pictures.

"Sad to think that they're all washed away," commented Mary.

For her part, Mary told Rachel all about what she had been doing which was mostly going to work. Rachel enjoyed Mary's stories of site and from there it was easy for Mary to turn the conversation to matters construction and Charles.

"You said Charles was a builder. What does he build?" she asked.

"Oh, gosh, nothing like you're involved in. He just does little jobs for people, house extensions, that sort of thing.

Well, actually," she continued: "He has been involved in one or two larger projects. Do you remember that derelict house over in the Old Town – Lower Meadow Hall – that burned down? Charles was doing the refurbishment when it caught fire. Terrible business." Rachel shuddered.

"It's a small world, construction," commented Mary. "I suppose you and Henry met through Charles, did you?"

Rachel looked baffled but Mary explained: "I remember you saying Henry put business Charles' way."

"Oh, Henry's not in construction," said Rachel. "He's an investment banker. We met at a dinner party; I think the host sat us together because we were both boring and he didn't think anyone else present deserved to be landed with either of us."

Before Mary could say she was sure that was not true, Rachel continued: "It worked out well, though, don't you think?"

"So how does he put business Charles' way?" Mary was sorry to push but she would not get another chance like this one.

"He dabbles in property. With our money, not the company's. He's quite successful, too."

"Sounds interesting," said Mary. "I'd like to take on a renovation project."

"Yes," agreed Rachel. "I used to get involved before we had Jared. I discovered I have a flair for interior design. Tess and Charles and I used to get on well before the business ran into trouble…. but it seems to be picking up now so you never know, we might become closer again. Tess and I were close as children."

"You don't see much of her now, then?"

"No." Rachel paused. Almost inaudibly, she added: "I don't see much of anyone."

Her thoughts turned inwards and almost in a trance she continued: "I never found it easy to make friends then when Jared was born, I gradually lost contact with the few friends I did have. We just drifted apart. I had a new life. We joined a toddler group so Jared would have playmates his own age but after what happened, the parents of his little friends seem to be avoiding me."

"They probably don't know what to say. Or whether to say anything at all."

"No. And to be fair, I don't want to see people. I mean, I do but I don't."

Mary knew only too well from her experience with Ellen how unwelcome concerned interest could be but that acting as though Ellen, or in this case Jared, had never existed was equally painful.

Rachel looked at her and there was understanding in both their eyes.

"Sorry. I get a bit maudlin. Where were we?"

"You were saying you used to get involved in renovation projects with Charles and Tess."

"We worked well together, too – not that I got involved in many projects and only Henry's – because we have different interests so we didn't stand on each other's toes. I did the interiors and Tess has always done the accounts. Tess still does the accounts for their company but she has just started working a few hours in the evening doing the books up at the care home as well."

"You mean Silverwood Hall?"

"Yes. Have you heard of it?"

"Only that it's under new management and the manager has really made something of it." Mary made a mental note to visit Gary.

"Interiors sounds interesting," she continued.

"Yes. Especially when you're trying to create a period look for a historic house or something like that. I had a lot of fun sourcing furnishings for an Art Deco place one time."

Mary would have liked to continue the discussion but she was determined to try to get a little more information about the Parkers' family life so she turned the conversation back to the reasons why Rachel had given up.

"But you found it didn't mix with Jared?"

"No. He was very active, not the sort of boy to give you any peace to do anything. If he was awake (which he seemed to be day and night) then he wanted attention and action. Not that I minded; he was my world."

She looked sad.

"He'll be back, I'm certain of it," said Mary. She wished she could tell Rachel that she knew he was safe and well.

She waited a while then remarked in a casual tone: "I wonder how on earth does Tess manage what with working in the evenings and everything."

"Oh, they have no children," replied Rachel. "That became something of a wedge, too, to be honest. They were jealous of us and Jared. Perhaps I should have told them the trouble we had having him but it's no-one else's business, is it?"

Mary agreed. So, Tess and Charles were jealous of not only the Parkers' money but also of the fact they had Jared? Had everything, apparently.

Mary helped herself to another cake. "These are wonderful. You must give me the recipe."

"They're Henry's favourite," said Rachel reaching for a piece of paper and a pen. "Not that I do much cooking now. Not that I do anything now. I can't be bothered. It's all so pointless."

Mary leaned over and squeezed her hand.

They parted soon after with an arrangement to meet next time at Mary's, date to be confirmed.

SUNDAY
DAY 36

Mary felt a little excited on Sunday morning as she put on some tidy jeans and a pretty shirt for the trip to meet Ben's parents. Ben had stressed that it was to be an informal event, he probably would not even warn them that he would not be alone but she wanted to make a good impression.

Mike, however, had other ideas. In spite of their little chat, he had left a large bouquet of flowers in a vase on her mantelpiece where Ben could not possibly miss them. Mary moved them to the bedroom. While she made her toast, the flowers moved back.

"I know when I'm beaten."

When Ben rang the bell, Mary opened the door just a crack and squeezed out.

It was only a short journey to where Ben's parents lived. They drew up outside a pleasant suburban house with an immaculately groomed garden. Ben rang the bell even though he had a key and greeted his mother, Flora, with a hug.

"This is Mary," he said and Flora accepted the statement at face value. Either she already knew all about Mary or she was a remarkably incurious individual.

They were shown to a large room with little furniture other than three enormous sofas from where they had a clear view of the garden and Ben's mother produced tea and freshly made scones. Mary felt slightly on edge but there was no sign of Mike so she began to relax. Perhaps he couldn't be here so he had left the flowers in an attempt to cause trouble between her and Ben since he could not do it personally.

"Your father will be along soon," Flora said. "I can't think where he has got to."

Ben's father, Gordon, appeared shortly afterwards from the direction of the shed. His curly hair stood on end and boasted the odd cobweb and there were fibres of pink insulation on his trousers.

"Have you been in the loft messing with that aerial again?" inquired Ben.

Gordon gestured to Mary. "Listen to Sherlock Mackay."

"Well, it's not difficult," replied Ben. "I've got something for you in the car. Come on."

Together they collected a large box which turned out to contain a satellite dish.

"It's time you came into the modern world," explained Ben. The pair of them disappeared to fetch a ladder and put up the dish on the side of the house. Gusts of wind disrupted their efforts – something which made Mary highly suspicious – but they managed to hang on to the dish and eventually it was secured in place. Then up, down, up, down plugging in wires and making adjustments until finally it was declared to be in the correct position and Ben called his mother for the grand demonstration which took place amid expressions of delight from both Gordon and Flora.

"He's such a good boy," said Flora to Mary and (silently) Mary had to agree he was a son to be proud of. "And good with electronics and computers, too. I'm always pressing the wrong button and losing everything. I don't know what we'd do without him."

Ben retrieved the ladder and took it back to the shed.

When he returned, Mary was looking at photographs on the mantelpiece while Flora proudly elaborated with indiscrete stories.

"You joined the army cadets after school, then?" questioned Mary, holding a picture of Ben and a small group of other young men on a rock-climbing expedition.

Ben looked wistful. "Good times. Joe there joined up but I failed the medical because of a rugby injury."

"They were like brothers," commented Flora. "Let's see…. that's Harry in the background and Robert and Alistair and Malcolm."

In an aside to Mary, she whispered: "Never did like Alistair," before continuing: "Joe is out of the army now and he and Ben still go climbing and anything else dangerous…."

"Exciting, fun," substituted Ben.

"That they can think of," finished Flora.

Ben winked at Mary.

"When we get the time, which isn't so often these days."

Mary was reaching for a little clay model that was right in the centre when suddenly it moved on its own. It was only Mary's quick reactions that prevented it from smashing on the floor – which would have been embarrassing since it would have appeared to be her fault. Carefully she replaced it, glaring at where she imagined Mike must be standing. Fortunately, Ben and Flora were still bickering in a playful way about the photographs and did not seem to have noticed although they certainly would have if Mary had not caught it.

There was a short silence then Flora suggested: "Why don't you show Mary the garden? Your father is going to enter the dahlias in the show next week."

Ben and Mary went outside but were not so far out of earshot that Mary did not hear Flora say to Gordon 'She seems like a nice girl. Better than his usual' as suppressing a smile she followed Ben to the greenhouse. But the air seemed heavy as though a sudden storm was brewing; in fact, it was positively claustrophobic and in the house, she heard Flora start to cough.

"Mike?" whispered Mary crossly but there was no reply.

"We'd better be going," said Ben. "Anyway, it's time I was somewhere else. That little diversion with the television took longer than I thought it would. You wouldn't mind if I dropped you at the bus stop, would you?"

"Of course not."

A wave of relief swept over her; now she would not have to find an excuse not to invite him in, would not have to excuse those flowers on the mantelpiece.

"I hope you've enjoyed the visit," he said as he opened the car door to let her out.

Mary assured him that she had. "And the baby photos on the sideboard and that little hippo you made when you were seven were great," she teased.

"It was a cat," he retorted. "Talk to you later. 'Bye."

MONDAY
DAY 37

With the weekend over, Mary had time to collect her thoughts. She must visit Silverwood Hall but on what pretext? A sudden concern for Gary? They had never been close. She could not simply turn up; he was so prickly. Mary sighed.

It had been good to see Rachel, though. And meeting Ben's parents had gone well. "In spite of Mike's best efforts," thought Mary.

Mike. Aside from personal gripes, talking to Rachel had started her wondering once again where Charles' and Mike's paths could have crossed. And whose life Charles had ruined and whether it was deliberate. If it was…. Rachel had intimated Uncle Charles resented Jared's existence.

Enough to hurt him? The light would be red. But carelessness might suffice and resentment was unlikely to breed concern and consideration.

"I need to find Jared. For his own sake and for Rachel's. I'm not five years old any more, there must be more I can do. Poor Jared…. and Ellen, poor Ellen…. she would be twenty-seven now, she would have a job, perhaps she would be married….''

Mary was staring unseeingly at her computer screen when her reverie was interrupted by Ryan.

"We're all going down the pub on Friday, would you like to come?"

"No-o…. thanks," said Mary. "It's nice of you, though. But I've got things to do."

"Again?"

"Yes, again."

"Aye, aye. Secret boyfriend?"

Mary blushed. "Of course not," she said.

She might as well have saved her breath because Ryan turned and called out: "Hey, everybody, Mary's got a boyfriend."

From half-way down the room Pete called back: "Leave the poor girl alone."

He advanced towards them. "Take no notice," he said to Mary, who had almost returned to a normal colour. "Now then, I was on my way to see you. There's a little job I need you to do."

She waited.

"About this time of year, we hold a Spring Fete," he continued. "Helps connect with the local community, raises money for charity, you know the sort of thing."

Mary's eyes may have widened a little but that was all; she made sure her expression did not alter. Inside, however, she felt horrified; she could guess what was coming. She couldn't organise a fete, she had never done anything like that in her life.

"It's all right," Pete reassured her. "You don't have to do it all by yourself. As a company we do these things regularly so Christine in the office is well on top of it. Give her a call."

He sauntered off in the direction of his desk.

Mary stared at the telephone. She did not know Christine; she did not know what to say. Her eyes followed Pete across the room. There was no way out of it so she had better get on with it. She took a deep breath and picked up the receiver.

"Hi, Mary, I thought you might call." The voice at the other end was friendly and warm. "I expect Pete explained part of my job is to organise events across the region. I just need you to sort out the local stuff," she said. "Pete has already found a venue – he'll explain all about that – and the other thing is: choose a theme."

"Theme?" questioned Mary.

"Yes, we find it helps to arouse interest. For instance, you can have a theme-related fancy dress competition and theme-related music – such as jazz if it's an American theme – and you can get the local school-kids involved in designing posters or doing a write-up for the school magazine and things like that. I can send you some little paperweights that look like hard hats and ballpoint pens and so on we usually give them for entering and then there'll be book tokens for the winners."

Together they chose Victorian Days and by the time Mary came off the telephone having discussed the various stalls they might have, she felt much more confidant and quite excited. It would be fun to dress up as an elegant Victorian lady.

* * *

"Rachel didn't hang around. I didn't think she would." Mary sat watching the appeal for information on Jared's whereabouts. One thousand pounds. That should motivate people to come forward. "I do hope Rachel is all right. Henry had a point about it being stressful."

Mary poured herself a glass of wine and put a DVD of her favourite musical in the player.

TUESDAY
DAY 38

"I told you before I won't give him up whatever your opinion," exploded Mary the moment Mike walked through the door the following evening.

"Don't you have something better to think about than that arrogant big-head," he responded.

"That's not the point. You didn't listen to a word I said."

"I listened to every word."

"And took not the blindest bit of notice."

"Meaning?"

"Don't act the innocent."

Mary outlined her complaints.

"All this is about a few temperature fluctuations and the fact you nearly dropped an ornament?"

"I may not be able to prove it was you but that makes no difference. We both know you don't like Ben and you just admitted it when you called him an arrogant big-head."

"All right, so I don't like him."

Mary glared at him.

"And you can keep your opinions – however expressed – to yourself."

She sat down plonk in the chair. This was where he was supposed to see the error of his ways. Just because they had an alliance, he did not own her. He had to back off Ben.

"You like him, I don't. Why don't you take it slowly and see how it works out?"

It was the sort of thing her mother would say. Or a big brother. In fact, come to think of it, he fitted the profile perfectly: solid, reliable, never complained about being taken for granted….

My big brother I always wanted. The thought made Mary smile and as she did so, Mike's expression softened in return. Perhaps his behaviour was understandable. Unacceptable but understandable.

It suited them both to change the subject.

"I visited Rachel Parker and Charles' business seems to be doing better," offered Mary.

"I will do some more checks on Henry Parker's finances."

"Henry's? Surely you mean Charles'?"

"I meant Henry's. Just to make sure there wouldn't be any point in staging a kidnapping himself in order to access funds he wouldn't normally be able to touch. Everything was in order when I last looked but you do hear of these things."

"When you last looked?"

"As I was saying, you hear of these things – you know, investment banker gets into trouble gambling or dodgy deals on the stock-market or whatever and has to come up a lot of money fast…. and yes, I am checking on Charles' finances as well," he added.

Mary had the distinct feeling there was something he was not telling her about his investigation of both the Parkers and the Armstrongs.

In spite of his reaction the last time she had mentioned the subject, Mary could not help herself. "Mike, what is your interest in Charles? Is it to do with why you came back? Is Henry part of it? Is Jared?"

"Now look, Mary. I thought you wanted me to help you investigate Charles and the Parkers. If our interests coincide, is that a problem?"

"No, of course not. Do they?"

Mike sighed. "No. We just have some of the same players in common."

"Have you found out yet whether you were right about that person you said should be behind bars?"

His lips pursed. "I was right. Wistfully, he continued: "If I could simply lift the documents that incriminate him and leave them on Andrew's desk…. but I can't. Interfering in the lives of mortals is not permitted."

"Surely that's what you've been doing ever since I met you?"

"When you think about it, all I have done is observe," Mike replied haughtily.

Mary thought about it. "And reporting your observations to me?"

"Is different to direct interference. It could influence events, then again, it might not. For instance, when you wanted to book a room in the same hotel as the Parkers, there might not have been one available. When you decided to attend the handover, you might have had some mishap on the way and never got there."

He was sailing close to the wind, thought Mary.

"Come on," he wheedled, "the practice of spirits giving mortals messages or warnings has been going on for centuries."

"Well, I hope you know what you're doing."

Mike grinned. "So do I."

"What about our alliance? My part of the bargain was to furnish practical help when the time came. So, why don't I collect this evidence you were talking about for you and take it to Andrew?"

"Point one: Not very subtle. Unless you're up for a little breaking and entering, I would have to give the documents to you. Close to direct interference, don't you think? Point two: I'm not ready. I would like to make further inquiries into the exact circumstances of…." He grimaced "…. a certain event…. and try to establish what his accomplices knew or didn't know. Point three: Events have moved on. The way things are, it would be wrong to ask you."

"Does that mean our arrangement is over?" asked Mary, panic in her voice.

"No. I will help you look for Jared as I promised and it may be that circumstances will change and you will help me yet, who knows?"

Mary desperately wanted to ask what the event was that Mike seemed so upset about but knew she should not.

Mike's thoughts turned inwards and Mary watched strong emotion register on his face.

He looked sad and broken, not at all the Mike she knew.

WEDNESDAY
DAY 39

Mary was in the shower when the phone rang. Quickly, she rinsed the shampoo off her hair, turned off the water and opened the door to grab her towel. Silence. The phone had stopped. Mary finished showering at her usual leisurely pace then crossed the room to the blinking phone to play the message.

"Hi, Mary. It's working. There have been two sightings." There was a clattering and a soft thud. "Sorry, dropped you. I'm so nervous. Look, don't call me back, it takes years off my life every time the phone rings. I just thought I'd tell you but I've done that now so…. well…. 'Bye." Rachel rang off.

"I was about to tell you the same thing," said Mike, materialising in the corner. "The sightings are both in the same area, around one hundred and fifty miles from here."

No chance of taking the long way home after work in the hope of seeing for herself, then.

"I thought I might pop over if I have a few minutes," observed Mike.

All day, Mary kept glancing at the clock. Had Mike been yet? Were either of these children Jared? The day dragged and the bus home seemed to be grinding along particularly slowly and waiting longer than usual at every bus stop. Even the walk to her flat seemed to have grown longer. Back at home, the minutes ticked by until finally, Mike appeared.

"I went to see the 'Jareds,'" he said. He seemed amused about something.

"Go on then, spill," Mary prompted impatiently.

"I arrived at the first house at the same time as a constable from the local station so I hung back and watched. He knocked on the door and explained they had received a report of a little boy matching Jared's description living at that address and asked if he could see her son. The woman gave him a withering stare and replied 'You'll have a job. My 'son' is a girl.' You should have seen the constable's face.

"He was obviously intending to proceed to the next address so instead of going on my own, I decided to accompany him. It was another girl," he said in delighted tones. "Although to be fair, there was a strong resemblance to Jared in both cases."

"This is no laughing matter," Mary scolded him.

"I know. I'm sorry. It was amusing, though. The expression on his face...." Mike smiled at the memory but Mary's expression remained serious.

"We're back to square one."

"Don't give up. It's only two days since the media campaign began. It's a sizable reward; people will be looking out for Jared in a way that maybe they weren't before. Or someone might struggle with themselves then report suspicions that they've been squashing. Go on, make yourself some coffee and let's talk about something else. I want to see that smile of yours before I leave."

THURSDAY
DAY 40

At work, the theme of the day was phone calls: Mary made a lot but to no purpose. How could it prove so difficult to source a burger van?

"Problem?" inquired Bellyache.

"Just that the regular bloke says all the burger vans are out the day of the fete and I can't find anyone else."

"Hmm…. typical." He stood there a few moments but came up with no suggestions.

"Not to worry," said Mary. She carried on phoning round and by the end of the afternoon she was able to report to Christine.

"Hi, Christine. I'm doing quite well – maybe – that is to say I've found a local band and some people who will do us a hog roast and someone to sell hot potatoes but I would like to run an idea past you: one of the dumper truck drivers reckons he knows a fortune teller who is very good. Do you think having something like that will offend anyone?"

Christine thought. "No, that sort of thing goes down well. Most people regard it as a bit of fun. I know what you mean, there are those who take it seriously and say you shouldn't meddle with the occult but I don't think you will offend anyone." She paused then continued: "Did you ask Pete about the venue?"

"No, not yet, I simply haven't got round to it."

Mary was fairly sure Pete was out on site but she went to check just in case and found that he had sneaked back in when she was not looking and was in the kitchen.

"Hi, Pete," she said.

"Ah, Mary, what's up?"

Mary explained that she needed to give the various vendors a proper address for the venue, not just that it would be local to site.

"That's all right, Mary. There were details to be worked out which is why I didn't confirm before but it's all sorted now and we'll be able to hold it in the grounds of Lower Meadow Hall. We've bought it as a development site, you know. The area where the original Hall stood requires clearing before we can build but it's all fenced off and there's plenty of room in the grounds for the fete. It'll be much better than the second-choice option, Moorca Reach, the ground is very rough there."

"What are we going to build?" asked Mary.

"A college and accommodation and a shopping complex," Pete replied. "It should keep us occupied for a couple of years and be a good project to work on and quite profitable. I reckon the owners of the Hall did well out of it, too – I gather there was a big insurance pay-out and we gave them a good price for the land."

"Who were the owners?" inquired Mary.

"I don't know, some company called 'HP Property Development.'"

Mary thanked him and left. Lower Meadow Hall again. The place Charles was refurbishing when it burnt down. She must Google it. And look up HP Property Development in Companies House to see who the directors were.

For now, however, she fished out the contact details the dumper truck driver had given her and completed her day of phone calls with a call to Mme Delphine, who sounded perfectly ordinary on the telephone and why wouldn't she? Having established that Mme Delphine would be delighted to attend and needed no facilities other than a place to pitch her tent, Mary packed her bag and left; it had been a tiring day.

FRIDAY
DAY 41

Mary sat watching the rain bouncing in the puddles. In came Ryan leaving a trail of mud behind him. In came Pete, water dripping from his hat and the end of his nose.

"Wrap up whatever you're doing, Mary. We'll finish early today."

Mary looked at him questioningly.

"Kind of now-ish," he elaborated. "We're ahead of schedule so why not?"

Mary closed down the computer, put on her coat and headed out of the door. Ugh! That bus had better not be late.

She hung her wet clothes in the hall and went to the kitchen. It was a good day for a nice hot curry. Mary stood frying the curry powder and inhaling deeply. Mmm.

The doorbell rang and Mary pulled the pan off the heat.

"Andrew."

"Something smells good."

"You can stay and have some if you like."

Andrew looked longingly from Mary to the kitchen and back to Mary but: "I'd better not," he replied. "I was passing on my way home and I saw the lights were on and thought I'd call. I didn't mean to intrude."

"You're not." Mary settled him in a chair with a mug of tea.

"Did you get any useful information from the media appeal? Is anyone in line for the reward?" asked Mary disingenuously.

"Waste of time," replied Andrew, shaking his head. "A few sightings reported of Darren Danesford and three of other children."

Three? Mary waited.

"You're never going to believe this but two of the three were girls. We double-checked, of course. Dressed in trousers, but girls."

"It is the more practical playwear," Mary replied. "How about the third?"

"That one only came in today. The child was a boy but I always thought it was a long shot. The photo we were given along with the information wasn't exactly confidence inspiring as you might say. But we checked it out – we had to. The poor constable fared as badly as his fellow officer who responded to the sightings of the girls. To say we got short shrift from the mother is an understatement. She glared at him and said 'Is this a joke? My lad doesn't look remotely like that missing child. You should have something better to do – you *do* have something better to do. You could start by catching the **** who burgled my house. It's been twenty-six days now. You lot couldn't detect dog mess if you stepped in it.'

"To summarise: a waste of time, like I said." He stared dejectedly into his coffee. "To make matters worse, I've had another note. I had one before; this is the second. 'You're no good at this, are you? You offer a reward, you get the public staring at their friends and neighbours and you still can't find me.'"

"You will, I know you will."

Her confidence in him meant a lot to Andrew. He had let her down over Ellen and although generally regarded now as 'successful' and 'a safe pair of hands,' Andrew himself had never quite moved on.

SATURDAY
DAY 42

Ben dropped by at the weekend.

"You seem jumpy," he told Mary, who assured him she was not but continued looking tense. His visits seemed to have that effect, he thought, even though she clearly liked him.

"Let's go outside, it's a beautiful sunny day," suggested Mary.

"Actually, I was going to suggest a car ride. I have to go over to the children's hospice. It won't take long, then we can go for lunch somewhere."

"No-one is ill, I hope?" Immediately, Mary was concerned.

"Well yes, of course they are but not like you mean. That is to say, no relatives or anything. Although I have got to know a couple of the children a little on previous visits. I'm only going over to take a cheque but I'll call by the ward while I'm there. I've been doing well and one must give back, don't you think?"

"I do. And I would love to come with you. Give me a minute to get ready and we'll go."

Mary rushed to change her shoes and not keep Ben, or more importantly the children, waiting.

It was not far to the hospice and they were soon there but as it turned out, it was quite long enough. The bright sun made Mary squint. Her eyes began to water and she started to sneeze.

"I hope you're not sickening for something, M," remarked Ben.

"It's only hay fever," she assured him.

He looked at her doubtfully.

"Perhaps you had better not come in just in case."

It was a pity but Mary could see his point.

Ben walked smartly up to the door. Mary had not noticed anyone else around then suddenly, she heard a voice shout: "Turn around, hold it there."

A photographer aimed a camera and startled, Ben bashfully put up his hand to shield his face. Too late.

"Thanks. That's a good one. Any comment on your generous donation, Mr MacKay?"

"Just trying to help these incredible people who are doing an incredible job. I wish them all the best."

A series of flashbulbs went off as Ben waved and ducked inside the hospice. He was not long but by the time he came out, Mary's face was swollen and her eyes were streaming. She was overcome with a desire to hug him but had to resist the urge.

Lunch being cancelled, Ben dropped her off back at her flat. In spite of her repeated assurances that it was only hay fever, he kept his distance and left soon afterwards. He had an important meeting with the bank coming up that he simply could not miss.

"You do understand, don't you, M?"

Mary did. Ben had put a lot of effort into putting together plans for the future development of the company; it was only natural he should be keen to avoid delay.

* * *

Ben had not been gone long when Mike materialised in her armchair.

"I wish you wouldn't do that, you made me jump."

"Sorry. Just checking up on my favourite girl. I came by this morning but you were out," he said.

"I went to the children's hospice with Ben," she replied, suspecting that he knew that already. "I didn't dare go in because I was sneezing but it's just as well because there was a photographer and I would hate to be in the paper."

Mike snorted.

"This photographer being there, an accident, was it? Good publicity for Ben and the re-launch of his company."

"You're doing it again. You can't bear the idea that Ben is generous, public-spirited, decent and honourable, can you?"

In the face of the obvious stars in Mary's eyes, Mike bit his tongue.

He settled himself in her armchair.

"How's work?"

"I'm extra busy what with the fete and all the usual stuff – drawings and Health & Safety files and so on."

"Fete?" questioned Mike.

"Oh gosh, thanks for reminding me. How did you know about the fete?" Mary was getting flustered. "I need to go and hire a costume. But I don't even know where to go for anything like that."

"Calm down. There's a costume hire place by the Corn Market. I'll come with you; a walk will do us good. Better get a move on, though, they shut soon."

Mary allowed Mike to hurry her out. The Corn Market was not far but he was right, they did shut soon. They also turned out to have a vast choice in Victoriana; apparently, it was very popular. Mary was pleased, not just because it made her own task easier but because it should be easier for other attendees to get costumes too.

Mission accomplished and back in the present, Mary soon realised she also needed to buy dinner.

"Order a pizza and tell me all about this fete," suggested Mike.

Mary obliged.

"Let me get this straight. Hot potatoes, pig roast but no ice cream," he observed.

"Don't you think it's a bit cold for ice cream? Anyway, not everyone is like you."

"Spring is here and anyway, it's never too cold for ice cream," replied Mike. "Honestly, call up some vendors and I bet you'll find they'll be more than happy to come."

"Before you go," she said, "will you be coming to the fete with me? The arrangements are coming along well, it looks like it'll be good fun. And I'm told the venue is quite scenic, too; we're having it in the grounds of Lower Meadow Hall."

Was it her imagination or did he look startled? No, not startled.... horrified. But only for a moment; instantly, he regained his composure.

"No, thanks, Mary. I'll give this one a miss if you don't mind."

SUNDAY
DAY 43

Another sighting. Please let it be Jared. Mike had stayed just long enough to give Mary the details and knowing she would not see Andrew again for a while: "I will check it out myself," she decided. It was not as though she had anything better to do today and she could not simply sit and wait for news.

After a hurried breakfast, Mary set off. It was not far but it was an awkward journey and Mary had to change bus three times. "Roll on getting that car," she thought.

The scenery slid by, lush and green. "At least it's a day out," she told herself, not that it was much comfort. Time was passing. Memories of Ellen intruded.

Mary had not thought what she would do when she arrived at the address Mike had given her but now the question stared her in the face. The door was closed, the windows were closed and there was no child playing in the garden.

"They're out," called a neighbour.

"Do you know when they'll be back?"

"No."

"I'll come back later." Mary walked off down the street.

The town centre was compact and mostly closed because it was Sunday but Mary found a garden centre where a falconer was giving a talk and demonstration. A little boy in jeans and a bottle green top pointed excitedly at a large tawny owl.

"Don't poke your fingers too near, Paul," warned his mother. The owl spun its head round. "Hooo, hu hu hu hooo."

Paul toddled forward but his mother grabbed him. "Let's get that pretty flower for Grandma then we'll come back here before we go home."

"Gamm-ma," repeated Paul, holding out his arms to be picked up.

Mary stayed watching the falconer then headed to the café.

"I can't stay here much longer. It's a tedious journey and the Sunday bus service finishes early."

Mary returned to the house where 'Jared' had been seen. All was still quiet, closed windows, no lights. Obviously, the family had not returned. A cloud of depression settled over her. She dithered briefly then began to walk away.

At that moment, Paul and his mother came walking down the street. He looked worn out.

"But that was probably the idea," thought Mary.

They opened the gate and walked up the path to the 'Jared' house. Surely not: Paul didn't look anything like Jared. Well, maybe a bit. The odd expression from the right angle with a desire to see it….

"Aided by the obscuring effect of pound signs in the eyes."

Mary caught the bus – or rather buses – home.

She sighed. "I should have persuaded Mike to go instead of going myself."

"So, it's better I waste my time than you waste yours?" inquired a disembodied voice but Mike's tone was playful rather than cross.

He appeared on the sofa beside her. Mary jumped visibly.

"That's not what I meant."

"Difficult to see what else you could have meant."

Mary was not about to crown a wasted day by losing a battle of wits with Mike.

"Merely that it was wrong of me to deprive you of potential amusement – it might have been another girl – and of a chance to further your new career in preventative crime. You know, hanging around watching people and then catching them red-handed doing whatever it is they shouldn't be doing before they get the chance to do it so to speak. And, of course, facing serious hazards like jingly-jangly nursery music…."

She dodged the flying cushion aimed at her head, catching it in mid-air and lobbing it straight back.

"Good shot," Mary congratulated herself, grinning widely, but already it was on its way to her again. She caught it just in time. Mike sprang over, Mary was ready for him and straight away she was beating him with it; a blow round the ear, a body blow right to left, another on the way left to right was intercepted and the cushion yanked from her grasp. After that, it was an easy matter for Mike to grab her wrists and pin her to the sofa.

"Truce," she begged as they collapsed in a heap, laughing.

"Oof." Mary sat up and caught her breath. Their eyes met…. and Mike's were full of longing.

Mary moved along the sofa to put a distance between them. They had an alliance, that was all. It helped that they got along – had become friends, even – but he was a ghost. He could not be in love with her. And she was not falling in love with him, definitely not. There was affection: he was her honorary big brother so of course there was. But that was all. She was in love with Ben.

Mike straightened his clothes, his face impassive. Mary brushed her hair off her face.

"I had so hoped this reward idea would lead somewhere."

"I know you had. Something will come along, you see."

Did he know something or was he just naturally optimistic? Mary shook her head and sighed.

MONDAY
DAY 44

At least the arrangements for the fete were progressing. To Mary's surprise, Mike had turned out to be correct: ice cream vendors were keen to come and ply their wares. She looked at her watch; Mr Mario should be arriving soon with his hygiene certificate. Which he did, bang on time. Mary put it on her desk and went to show him out but as they walked towards the gate who should be coming the other way but his arch-rival, Tubs.

Mr Mario (or to be exact, Rob) turned purple.

"What are you doing here?"

Tubs grinned. "I happened to be in the area so I thought I'd call by. I heard I was needed – that is to say, I heard a top-quality ice cream seller was needed – you know: proper, decent…"

He got no further.

"You? Decent?"

They squared up to each other.

"I thought I told you if I saw your van on my turf again, I'd tow it to the lake and push it in."

"*Your* turf is it? And I'd like to see you try."

"What was it they said on the conflict management course?" wondered Mary. Something about keeping calm and taking charge. She took a deep breath and was about to step forward when Pete's voice boomed across the yard.

"Knock it off you two." He strode over.

"Take these gentlemen to the meeting room, I'll be with you in a minute," he said to Mary.

Neither spoke as Mary escorted them to the meeting room. Politely, she offered them tea and biscuits – Mary was a firm believer that chocolate made everything better – but they declined. Then Pete appeared. Mary was about to show one to an adjacent room but Pete interjected.

"It's all right, Mary, I'll see them both together."

Turning to them, he laid down the law. "Now look you two, there's room enough for both of you, one each end of the field and no funny business. Identical terms of business and the rest is up to you."

They trooped out.

"Do you know them?" asked Mary.

"Yeah," replied Pete. "We used to be in the same football team. Sometimes I think they're no older than the kids they sell to." He rubbed his hands. "Don't look so worried. It's going to be a good fete."

TUESDAY
DAY 45

Ben and Mary spoke frequently but it was unusual for Ben to phone her at work.

"You weren't feeling well when I saw you on Saturday and you haven't called since," he explained.

"Nor has he," heckled Mike, who Mary had not realised was there.

"I'm fine, Ben, really. It was hay fever, I told you."

"As long as that's all."

It was fortunate Ben could not hear Mike, thought Mary as: "Was that concern for your health or a veiled dig? Feeling neglected, is he?"

"I've been busy," she informed Ben. No need to tell him she had been wasting her time chasing imaginary 'Jareds'.

"Which is fine – when it's him that's busy," contributed Mike.

"Shut up," Mary mouthed at him. She turned her attention to Ben. "Are you looking forward to Saturday?"

"You bet. I love weddings. I like parties of any sort."
He paused. "What about your hay fever? Do you have any
medication? I assume you'll be holding flowers."

"All under control," Mary assured him.

Now to chase Mike away without attracting attention.
She looked round the cabin. No Mike. She looked in the
kitchen. No Mike. He had gone.

"Good," thought Mary. Explaining Mike to Pete and
Ryan – of all people – was an idea she did not relish.

* * *

Mary arrived home to find Andrew on the doorstep looking
harassed.

"I hope you don't mind me turning up again so soon," he
said. "You shouldn't be such a good listener."

"Come in, Andrew. I'll put the kettle on."

"It's these notes," explained Andrew. "I've had another
one."

He took his phone from his pocket and held it out to
Mary. On the screen was a photo of the note. 'I'm getting
bored. Another sighting, another failure. You've no idea
where Jared is, have you?' read Mary.

"He's not wrong, either. I shouldn't take it personally but
I can't help it. And it piles on the pressure."

Mary took a mouthful of tea.

"It feels personal," Andrew repeated.

"Perhaps it is."

"It can't be, I don't know the Parkers or I wouldn't be on
the case," was Andrew's first reaction but as he sat slowly

drinking his tea: "Mary, you've done it. It *is* personal! Why didn't I see it?"

Mary looked mystified.

"I'll explain another time," said Andrew. "For now, this is the best cup of tea I've had in a long while." He drained his cup and stood up to leave. A pained expression crossed his face. "Sadly, ending these notes won't bring us nearer to finding Jared but the less red herrings, the better."

WEDNESDAY
DAY 46

No more ransom notes, no more sightings and soon, apparently, no more challenge notes. Mary sat on the bus brooding. Danesford.... Henry.... the mistress.... Charles.... Lost in her own thoughts, Mary walked slowly towards site but her pace quickened along with her heartbeat at the sight of a police car parked at the entrance. It couldn't be about Jared – could it?

Andrew would phone her; he wouldn't turn up here. Mary stifled the rising feelings of panic and hurried to the cabin.

A uniformed policeman was talking to Pete. They showed no interest in her as she hung up her coat, walked to her desk and sat down; obviously, it wasn't about Jared. Slowly, Mary calmed down. She went to the kitchen to make them some tea.

"What's going on?" she asked Ryan, who came in shortly afterwards.

"We were burgled last night. They took the total station."

"You mean that tripod with the prism on top that the surveyors use?"

"Yep. Expensive things. It won't hold up work, though. We'll hire one."

Mary arranged some biscuits on a plate, took Pete and the constable their tea and quietly got on with her work. The others, however, were not so lucky. In spite of Ryan's optimism, the hire company were unable to supply a replacement total station due to a shortage caused by a spate of thefts in the area whilst the disruption caused by the incident meant that Pete had to delay a meeting from early to late afternoon.

"Will it be all right for you to stay late, Mary? I need this meeting minuted for legal reasons."

Mary assured him that it would be no problem. Secretly, with the hunt for Jared having stalled, she was pleased to have a chunk of her evening taken up by work.

THURSDAY
DAY 47

By the following day, site was back to normal. Mary typed up the minutes, Pete congratulated her on a thorough job, tea was drunk, banter was traded and everyone left in a good mood.

Following Hazel and looking into the 'Jared' sighting having concentrated the mind wonderfully, Mary called at a car dealership on the way home to get an idea of prices. On the up side, they were not as high as she had feared but on the down side, there was nothing there that she liked. Never mind; there were other places.

Back at the flat, Mary picked up her book but it was not long before her evening was disturbed by the arrival of Andrew.

"After your help the other day, I thought I'd tell you what was going on," he said. "Once I realised it really was personal, it all fell into place. 'You messed up,' 'You think you know best,' 'You're no good at this' – I thought it was the kidnapper taunting me and making it personal to get under my skin. But it wasn't.

"When I was promoted, there was another candidate who thought he should have got the job. Recently, he was transferred here to work under me.

"The first note said: 'You were told no police.' We brought people in from outside the area to infiltrate the second handover in order to be as sure as possible they wouldn't be recognised if the kidnapper was local. Experienced people. I'm not saying there was no chance they would be spotted but I thought they did a good job.

"And the last note: 'Another sighting, another failure.' We hadn't made that public. The note writer had to be someone who was well-informed about what we were doing."

"And you've caught him."

"Not yet. I've laid some misinformation. A neighbour overhearing a woman shouting at a child she addressed as 'Jared' for going to the window where he might be seen. I've organised a 'raid' on the house and I've assigned my quarry to another task so he won't be involved in it or around when it – supposedly – takes place. The others in the team have been sworn to secrecy.

"'They will return from their supposed raid and report signs of recent habitation and hurried departure making sure he is there to hear. I'm expecting another note soon afterwards and when I get it, I've got him.'"

FRIDAY
DAY 48

"Have you seen this?" Bellyache's loud and scandalised tones were the first thing Mary heard on entering the cabin.

"What?" Minty clearly had not.

Ryan took no notice of either of them. He collected a pile of paper from the whirring printer, put it on his desk and plugged in the laminator.

"This!" Bellyache beckoned Minty round to read the email on his computer screen. Emblazoned across the top in the usual, coloured strip were the words: 'Health and Safety.' Then, on the next line: 'Walking Speed Initiative.' Minty read on.

'There have been a number of recent incidents involving personnel running on site. This dangerous practice is to cease forthwith. Furthermore, it must be understood that dawdling is equally unacceptable, causing – as it does – build-ups of personnel in a single area and rising levels of frustration which lead to the aforesaid running.'

"And that's not all. Guess who has been chosen to set up and man check-points at the main entrance to the building and at the welfare facility? We are to 'monitor the problem and encourage improved behaviours.' Then we report to Josh who will recommend appropriate next steps and expansion of the scheme."

Minty opened his mouth and shut it again.

Ryan bounced over. In one hand, he held a pile of laminated paper showing a red circle containing a silhouette of a running man which had been crossed through with a red line: No Running on Site. In the other hand, a sad-looking silhouette stood, head bent, feet together, immobile. He, too, had been crossed out.

"You're to put these up all round site."

Bellyache groaned. However, there was no help for it, so muttering under their breath, Minty and Bellyache collected a staple gun, tape and a sharp knife and went outside. Mary watched them from the window then crossed the room to her desk. As she turned, she caught sight of Ryan: she could have sworn there was a flicker of a smile playing around his lips but it was instantly suppressed. Mary frowned.

"Ryan?"

"Yes, Mary. Can I help you?" He was the picture of innocence.

"Nothing."

For the next two hours, Mary processed hire tickets and work sheets.

"Haven't you had enough of that? I'll tell you what, put on some hi-vis and come out with me," Ryan invited her.

She kitted herself up and followed him outside.

"This way."

By a circuitous route, they came up behind Minty. He was sitting at a small table recording names and times and calling them through to Bellyache on the radio. Ryan raised his finger to his lips, spun Mary round and led her back the way they had come.

"Let's go and see how it's going at the other end."

A large man in an orange jacket was standing over Bellyache threateningly. "Yes, mate, I did get here a bit quick. If you must know, I've got a bit of a runny tummy and I need the facilities urgently."

Bellyache looked confused. "Says here 'Pedestrian speed limit: three miles per hour. No running, no exceptions.'"

"I wasn't running. Look, I haven't got time to argue about this and I don't care what it says there, all right? It's ridiculous."

"It's company policy."

"It's ridiculous."

"It's for your own good."

The man stormed past him and into the welfare cabin. Ryan pulled Mary out of sight behind the corner of the building, leant against the wall and let out the bellow of laughter he had clearly been trying to contain for some while.

"Priceless," he gasped, hardly able to speak. "Absolutely priceless."

"Ryan, you didn't?"

"I did." Tears of laughter rolled down his cheeks. "That's the best one yet."

Come lunchtime, Minty and Bellyache returned to the cabin. Ryan, who had seen them coming, was nowhere to be found.

"I'll kill him. I will, I'll kill him." Bellyache rounded on Pete. "Were you in on this?" he asked accusingly.

Pete did not answer.

"Bellyache will get over it," he quietly informed Mary, "But it could take a while which is why it is a good idea to play jokes like this on Fridays."

* * *

After all the set-backs in the hunt for Jared, Ryan's little prank had been perfectly timed to cheer Mary up before the wedding tomorrow. She smiled to herself and settled down to a quiet evening and early bed.

SATURDAY
DAY 49

Ben collected Mary in his sports car 'so we can arrive in style.'

Ben and Mary drove up the sweeping driveway to the hotel and as it came in to view, Mary could easily understand why Gemma had been so taken with it. It was an attractive stone building with creeper growing across part of the façade and in front there was a tiered fountain in the centre of a large round pool, all surrounded by vast, perfectly manicured green lawns.

At the rear, lawns swept down to a lake.

They entered over a polished, dark wood floor and set off to find the rooms that had been set aside for changing. Gemma welcomed Mary and introduced her two nieces who were to be flower girls.

Obediently, Mary sat while the hairdresser put up her hair and wove white flowers into it. Mary hardly recognised herself when finally, dress on and make-up complete, she looked in the mirror. The little girls had their hair in ringlets and wore white dresses with mauve sashes and looked so sweet it was not true but even so there was no danger of upstaging Gemma. Hers was the only dress with sparkles and she looked amazing.

They walked up the aisle of the chapel past bunches of white flowers adorning the end of every pew and arrived at the altar where Max was waiting. The service was simple and the smiles broad as, holding hands with the flower girls, Mary and the best man followed Mr and Mrs Townsend back down the aisle past the assembled family and friends.

A photographer took a few pictures before moving them outside to take pictures by the lake. Mary and Ben found themselves called over by a second photographer who was taking portrait pictures of each couple whilst the first completed his studies of the bride and groom. "Smile, please."

There was one more thing to do before they ate; throw the bouquet. Gemma turned her back, closed her eyes and threw it over her head, no cheating. It arced through the air and began its descent; Mary was nowhere near and in spite of his best flying tackle, Ben failed to catch it. He went to look for their names on the little cards on the table to see where they were sitting for the reception and Gemma came over to Mary.

"Hold out your hands," she said and dropping a single white carnation directly above them from a height of about five inches so Mary could not possibly miss: "Catch," she instructed. "I took it from the bouquet before I threw it."

Ben called to her from the dining room and Mary went to join him taking her flower. She put it beside her plate; Ben already had a flower in his button hole.

"Lovely wedding," they agreed.

"And lovely food," said Mary who by now was hungry.

They were sitting near Vicky who had brought Calvin but could not see anyone else they knew. Vicky talked excitedly about work until she realised Calvin was conducting a mime behind her which explained the smiles of her neighbours but it broke the ice and theirs was the liveliest table there.

"Can't take you anywhere," Vicky admonished, giving Calvin a playful shove.

"Nope. Go on, admit you love me just the way I am."

Vicky wrinkled her nose and raised her eyes to heaven.

With the once immaculate tables a wreck of screwed up napkins lying amongst side-plates and wine glasses it was time for the speeches. Then the tapping of a microphone and a loud burst of disco music called them next door.

First onto the floor to open the dance were Max and Gemma. They were closely followed by Calvin who had no inhibitions whatever and threw himself about in such a way as to make it clear that this was so much fun that it was impossible not to join him.

Ben caught Calvin's eye and mouthed 'Well done!' He would have been there beside him in an instant but Mary preferred to wait until the dance floor was filling up a little.

The music was too loud to allow talking but she and Ben smiled into each other's eyes, bodies gyrating as they moved from foot to foot. With her hands above her head, Mary turned a half circle – and who should be behind her but Mike. As he mouthed 'Surprise!' she noticed her white carnation in his button hole. Her arms dropped but she recovered instantly and turned back to Ben. Then it was back to Mike to execute a few steps before half turning to Ben.

She laughed aloud as she rose to the challenge of dancing with them both without Ben realising. And as they caught Gemma's eye, Gemma was merely pleased to see Mary enjoying herself and noticed nothing amiss. Ben went to get some drinks, which was one thing Mike could not do, and Mary bagged some chairs so that they could rest.

"What on earth are you doing here?" she hissed at Mike.

"Partying," he replied.

Ben returned and suitably rested, Mary kicked off her shoes and began to dance again, this time moving around the floor to say 'hello' to Gemma's parents. Then it was back to get her shoes.

"Excuse me a moment," she said to Ben and obliquely also to Mike as she headed for the ladies room.

On the way she bumped into Max.

"Hi, Max," she said. He gave her a patient stare, nodded curtly and walked away.

"How odd," thought Mary staring after him. "And how rude."

But by the time she had adjusted her hair and was on her way back to look for Ben (keeping an eye out for Mike as well, of course) it was forgiven and forgotten. Max was under a lot of pressure.

But Ben was nowhere to be seen.

"Are you all right, Mary? You look a little lost." The speaker was Max.

Hardly pausing to wonder how he had got there: "Have you seen Ben anywhere?" she asked.

"Over there," he pointed. "Are you having a good time?" He seemed genuinely concerned that she should be.

"Great time," she assured him. "Lovely wedding."

"Yes, it has gone off well," he agreed.

Mary went to find Ben.

"Let's go in the garden," he suggested.

The air was cool which made a refreshing contrast to the ambience indoors. A few of the other guests had strayed outside also but no one they recognised – until Max appeared on a collision course. Again, he nodded curtly to Mary. Surely, he would greet Ben who he had been friends with since before Bramwells? But no. His eyes swept across Ben and dismissed him. He headed for the lake.

"What on earth is wrong with Max? I've never known him behave like that before," Mary said to Ben, but Ben, too, was at a loss.

At that point Mary spied a familiar figure walking along beside the orangery and hurried over.

"Gary?" she asked incredulously. She had not realised he was here. Trust generous Gemma to include him along with all the rest of the old crowd. He looked different, younger and definitely chirpier.

"Mary. Lovely to see you." They bumped cheeks. "And Ben: Hello."

They compared notes on what they had been doing since the demise of Bramwells and all agreed it had been a blessing in disguise. Gary was obviously proud of Silverwood Hall and eager to show Mary around.

"Come any time," he told her.

"I would like that very much," Mary replied and she meant it.

Together, the three of them strolled back towards the

hotel but before they could reach it, who should appear but Gemma and Max, arm in arm. Mary looked a little doubtful as they approached.

"Beautiful, isn't it," she said making harmless conversation and gestured around the garden. But as she looked across the lake she saw – no, it couldn't be – Max was here. Then she realised.

"You didn't mention Max had a twin," she said to Gemma.

"He doesn't. That's Oliver. They're brothers – there's a two-year age difference – but lots of people make that mistake. They're like peas in a pod, aren't they? And they're both the image of their father."

"That explains a lot," thought Mary. Max was not acting oddly; Oliver was fed up with being accosted by people who thought he was the bridegroom and having to explain that he was not.

Mary and Ben took their leave and headed back to the dance floor. The time of night had arrived when the DJ was putting on smoochy tunes and winding down. Gemma might be running on adrenaline and have boundless energy but Mary was a little out of condition (although she would not have admitted it) and so was pleased that the pace was slowing. There was a problem, however; she should have been totally wrapped up in Ben but Mary was conscious of Mike's presence coming between them. Ignoring him, she hooked her arms around Ben's neck and put her cheek against his. Mike's disapproval was icy. Ben noticed her draw back and looked at her questioningly but she said nothing.

The best thing to do now was to retire to bed. They had booked rooms at the hotel rather than drive back that night (no chance of sharing, Gemma's parents were very old-fashioned) so they made their way upstairs. Thankfully, Mike was nowhere to be seen.

Mary's room was first. Ben stood looking at her as they prepared to part.

"Did I tell you how beautiful you look tonight?"

He had, but Mary did not mind him telling her again. The party was still in full swing downstairs and for once there was no-one around to interrupt them as he drew her close and they kissed.

Wow.

Mary fondled Ben's ear, reluctant to part. He could smell her hair, he kissed her shoulder, her eyes…. she threw her arms around him and they kissed again.

"Goodnight, Mary."

"Goodnight, Ben."

Mary went inside and leaned her back against the door. There was something special about that kiss, a tingle, an intensity she had never felt before. For the first time, she understood the point of kissing. She stood there re-living the moment, feeling that tingle all over again all the way to her toes.

Slowly, she came back down to earth. She looked nervously around to see if Mike was there.

No.

Good.

Mary crept into bed. Only one thing was left: Mike came in and kissed her goodnight.

Mike's kiss was not at all like Ben's: it was cautious and questioning rather than passionate and yet there was something about it…. a warmth, a depth. Mary felt as though she became a part of him just for that instant…. no, for longer than that.

Because later on, it was Mike not Ben who appeared in her dream and kissed her again.

Dreams. They mixed people up and put them in places where they did not belong. It should have been Ben she was kissing. Mmm. What a kiss. Mary snuggled down into the pillow and slept like a log for the rest of the night.

DAY 50

In the morning, Mary went down to the dining room where she had arranged to meet Ben for breakfast. They were chatting quietly when Vicky and Calvin joined them. Mary had never seen the sophisticated Vicky in jeans before, only office wear and party clothes.

"Gosh, you look different!"

"Doesn't she." Calvin gazed adoringly at Vicky. It was obvious he was smitten whatever she wore.

Mary dug Ben in the ribs and made a slight nod towards them to ensure he noticed.

"Did you enjoy the wedding?" she asked conversationally, knowing quite well what the answer was.

"Oh yes," replied Calvin enthusiastically. "And we made lots of new friends."

He would, thought Mary. He was so outgoing: the perfect complement to Vicky's reserved, slightly formal ways.

"Speaking of new friends and thinking of old ones, have you seen Gary this morning?"

"He left last night."

"I should have known that," thought Mary. No matter.

"We're going walking in the country this afternoon," offered Vicky. "Calvin reckons it'll be the perfect way to clear our heads after yesterday."

"Not a bad idea," seconded Ben. "We might borrow it. M?"

"Sounds good to me although I don't know where we could go around where we live."

"I do," responded Ben.

Over toast and marmalade, Calvin entertained them with a guide to the true meaning of various enticing sounding advertising terms then, promising to stay in touch, they went to their rooms to pack.

"First stop, my flat," Mary informed Ben. "I need to change my shoes."

The air was fresh as they strolled along a footpath at the edge of a field. Clambering over a stile, Mary caught her foot and fell straight into Ben's waiting arms. He kissed her passionately.

"Good job I was there to catch you."

They walked on, stopping every now and then for another kiss.

"We should go for country walks more often," remarked Mary. "This was a good idea of Calvin's. Speaking of whom, did you see the way he looked at Vicky? Gemma and I were speculating whose would be the next wedding. I think we know."

"Don't bet on it," replied Ben.

Mary smiled up at him – and looked round nervously for Mike.

MONDAY
DAY 51

Monday morning arrived like a bucket of cold water. Mary checked her emails, found there was nothing urgent and faced up to the idea of sorting out the bookcase; people had an annoying habit if a file was full of cramming in a bit extra, after which the thing did not open and close properly and you could not turn the pages, so every now and then Mary labelled up a selection of empty files and distributed them through the filing system ready and waiting. Or maybe she would do that this afternoon and start by updating the architectural drawing files. No, best get going.

A commotion by the door interrupted her indecisiveness. Ryan had two visitors in tow. He crossed the room and whispered to Mary: "It's the drug and alcohol testing people. Is Pete about?"

Pete was in a meeting but Mary knocked softly and went in, walked quietly round the large table to where Pete was sitting and gave him the message. A short coffee break ensued while Pete went to get the day's attendance list and help the D&A men select some random victims for their tests.

"Your fault, Mary," joked Ryan. "They seem to be able to sense when anybody has been out partying. They turned up the day after we had our Christmas do. Speaking of which, are you coming to the summer one? You could bring that pain-in-the-arse boyfriend of yours, the one you don't have but can't go out with us because you're always with him. Or not. Lots of us go on our own, it's a good laugh."

Mary had heard tales of previous years' exploits and wondered how they had not been arrested. She would give it a miss, pain-in-the-arse boyfriend notwithstanding.

"Don't you ever let your hair down?"

Mary showed him a photo on her phone Ben had taken of her dancing at the wedding, pointedly ignoring his opportunistic inquiry as to the identity of the photographer. He continued: "Actually your hair looks good up, you should do it like that every day."

"No chance."

"It's not a very good photo, though," he concluded. "See, there's a massive shadow on it."

He was right, but that was another thing Mary was not about to discuss. She knew what (or rather who) had made the shadow.

"Skedaddle," she said. "I've got things to do."

And places to go. Brooding about the kidnapping and with the wedding fresh in her mind, she decided to strike while the iron was hot and call Gary.

"Come on over after work, I'm always here," he said.

The first thing that struck Mary as she walked up the path was how bright the place looked. It was in a good state of repair, the fresh paint gleamed in the sun and the gardens were neat and full of colour. The path itself was lined by borders of bright bedding plants and hanging baskets framed the door. Silverwood Hall positively beckoned visitors inside.

The heavy wooden outer door stood ajar and Mary passed through a small lobby into the hallway where on an ornate dark-wood table there was a visitors' book, a vase of flowers and a bell. She noted that although the place was spotlessly clean there was no institutional disinfectant smell. As soon as Mary rang the bell, an efficient-looking girl in an immaculate white uniform appeared and showed her to Gary's office.

Gary welcomed her enthusiastically. He obviously could not wait to show her round so they set off immediately to tour the building.

"The residents all have their own rooms most of which are en-suite," Gary explained. "And when they have finished the upgrading, all the rooms will have their own bathrooms."

There was a television room, an activities room, a quiet room and even a gym/ physiotherapy room. Back in the office, Gary showed her pictures of the building as it was when he had taken over and he certainly had a right to be proud of what he had achieved. Furthermore, his exacting standards were exactly what was needed in the day-to-day running of a place like that.

He looked at his watch.

"I hope you don't mind but I have to go and have tea with my mother. It's a sort of ritual. You're welcome to come along."

Gary lived in a ground floor flat in the south wing overlooking the garden. His mother, Violet, had a suite of rooms between Gary's flat and the main part of the Home that was accessible to the nursing staff from one side and to Gary's flat from the other. She was sitting in a chair next to a coffee table on which was arranged a beautiful china tea set.

"I'll pour," she said. Mary was a little nervous that the cup of tea extended towards her by shaking hands would be mainly in the saucer by the time it arrived and leaned forward to take it. Miraculously, it arrived safely.

"Biscuit?" inquired Violet.

She was a sweet old lady who had obviously been used to taking care of other people but it was clear that she herself needed taking care of now. Looking straight at Mary, she asked: "Where's your lad? I thought I saw him playing outside a moment ago."

Mary looked confused. "I don't have…. a child," she said hesitantly.

Violet thought. "He must have gone for sweets. He'll ruin his tea." Creakily, she rose from the chair and went to the window to call after him. "Now, wherever has he got to?"

"She regresses into the past, Mary," said Gary by way of explanation. "When she looks outside, she sees children playing in the garden. She sees me out there. I was an only child but it was always open house to all the children in the street. She loved children. The time when I was little was a happy time for her when her life had real purpose the way it doesn't now."

He went to the window and looked out. "Come on, Mum, let's sit you down again. There's no-one there."

"Sorry about that," he said to Mary, taking care that his mother did not hear.

"Not at all," Mary replied. "She's lovely."

A nurse came to collect the tea things and Gary took Mary back to his office. They arrived to find a dark-haired woman sitting at a computer in a side-room.

"This is Tess, my accountant," explained Gary.

"Pleased to meet you," said Mary.

Tess was older than in the photograph Rachel had shown Mary but still easily recognisable. She turned and smiled but seemed disinclined to chat.

"Just leaving, won't be long," was all she said.

Mary, too, left soon afterwards. The evening was still young so she decided to walk back through the park. There were a few people around, mostly middle-aged and walking dogs. Mary paused to watch a drunk, knees bent, body bent to the shape of a lightning flash, walking along carefully balancing an imaginary tray of drinks in his hand so as not to spill a drop. She walked on, then in the distance she saw what looked like Tess. Her clothes were not in any way distinctive; indeed, she was not herself distinctive in the sense of being particularly tall or having an unusual hair style but having only just seen her at the nursing home, Mary was sure it was her.

She would have liked to go over and engage her in conversation but she could not think what to say. She moved nearer; it was Tess. But Mary still could not think of anything to say so she hung back, watching.

Tess sat down on a bench and now Mary's attention was fully caught. Tess was not resting, she looked tense and straight. She looked all around her then pulled out a mirror and pretended to fix her make-up but in fact she was checking behind her to see who was there.

Tess continued to sit there and after a while, a woman jogged up to the bench and sat down for a rest. She pulled a drink from a tiny rucksack she was carrying then surreptitiously took out an envelope. She put it beside her on the bench next to Tess's bag and rested her head on her hands, elbows on her knees. The envelope was directly in Mary's line of sight. Tess moved her bag to reveal a package, fumbled and dropped something, leaned to pick it up and the envelope was gone. The jogger stretched her legs, first one and then the other, swept the package into her rucksack and got up to continue her exercise. Nice manoeuvre, thought Mary, but what was going on?

The dilemma was: which should she follow? If she followed Tess, she might find out what was in the envelope but only if Tess opened it where Mary could see. That, Mary considered, was unlikely. She would be better to follow the jogger in the hope of finding out who she was.

The jogger set off down the path in Mary's direction which meant that Mary had a head start, which was fortunate since she would not be able to jog after her without risking attracting attention; she was not dressed for exercise. She walked briskly until the jogger was safely past then speeded up further until she was walking so fast it was nearly a run. The gap between them widened but the road at the edge of the park was wide and busy and the jogger had to wait for the lights to change before she could cross. Even so, Mary could not get there in time to cross with her but by now she had caught up enough to see where she went next: into the grounds of the hospital.

It was too much to hope that Mary would find the mystery woman when a break in the traffic finally allowed her across and she was right; the hospital was a maze of buildings and the woman had disappeared. She could have gone into any one of them or she could have simply carried on through the grounds and out the other side.

Mary walked purposefully back to the park just in case Tess was still there but she was not, so Mary continued home lost in thought. What was in the package? It was thick and oblong; it could have been money. Yes, money. But what was in the envelope? Something thin, square.... what could it be? .... And what should she do now? Should she ask Mike to follow Tess.... true, he had told her to keep away from Charles but was it her fault she had accidently bumped into Tess at the Home then seen her in the park? Perhaps another visit to Gary.... Gary.... what if his mother really had seen a child in the garden? Surely Gary couldn't be involved?

TUESDAY
DAY 52

Mary arrived at work the next day in time to hear Pete sending Minty and Bellyache over to Lower Meadow Hall.

"Could I tag along? I'd like to have a look at the site."

"Fifteen minutes. We have to load up the truck and we'll be going."

It was a squash fitting them all in but the journey was short. They stopped by the gateway where a huge puddle had collected in a dip in the ground following the recent rain. Minty and Bellyache began unloading old railway sleepers from the truck to bridge it in order to ensure that the fete-goers first experience of the event would not be wet feet while Mary set off to check for any more hazards – or in reality, to explore the grounds. There was nothing aside from the odd piece of wire which she cleared away so she went over to peer at the remains of the old Hall.

It was not long before Minty and Bellyache meandered over. "What's up?"

"We ran out of sleepers. We thought we might scrounge something from here."

They made a hole in the fence around the ruins, then Mary sat on a flat stone which had been part of the front wall and watched as they shifted some charred but still substantial beams and tugged them clear to cut to length and drag to the gateway. Alone again, something caught her eye as it glinted in the sunlight. There was a bare patch of earth where Minty and Bellyache had moved the beams and something was lying there. Mary stretched out her hand and picked it up; it was a pretty bracelet made of individual links each comprising a polished stone in a gold setting.

Mary looked back at the ground where she had found it and noticed a piece of wood not far away. It was thin and flat and painted in shades of cream and gold. It, too, was unusual and strangely out of place. Mary picked that up too.

"Time to go," the others called. They wound the wire of the fence back together.

Mary wrapped her finds in some napkins from the coffee shop which were still sculling around in her bag, put them safely in a zip pocket inside and then it was back to site.

After dinner that evening, she emptied them onto the coffee table and looked at them carefully. What did the rather odd piece of wood belong to? Not a painting, the finish was not right. Nothing structural, not even a kitchen cupboard or a painted wardrobe, the wood was too thin.

She turned her attention to the bracelet: it was muddy and the mud seemed to be baked on, presumably because of the fire. Mary put it in a glass of soapy water to soak and went to fill the washing machine.

Nearly bedtime. Mary peered into the glass and gave it a swirl. The soapy water seemed to be working. She fished out the now much cleaner bracelet then as she was drying it, Mike suddenly appeared. Mary dropped it on the table and turned to him.

"Hello, Mike. Did you want something?"

"Not especially, I was just lonely."

There was a short silence then Mary began casually: "I went to Lower Meadow Hall yesterday. It's a big site. And I found something – look – do you know what this is?"

She handed him the wooden shard and he examined it critically but "Hmm…." was all he said.

The bracelet lay on the coffee table partly obscured by a tissue and as she took back the piece of wood, Mary's sleeve caught it and it fell. Automatically, Mike reached out to catch it. As he drew back his hand, the bracelet dangling from his fingers, glinting in the light, he saw what it was. He sat staring at it with an anguished expression.

"Mike? What is it?" but he would not, could not, answer.

"Mike, are you all right?"

"Of course, …. Mary, you must promise to look after it for me. Promise?"

"Promise."

He relaxed a little but still seemed upset as he sat in silence.

"Promise?"

"Yes, Mike, I promise. Why is it important?"

"Oh…. well…. It should be returned to its owner, don't you think? When the time is right."

He was being evasive again was what Mary thought but there was no point in saying so. Hastily, she wrapped the bracelet in an old embroidered handkerchief and put it in the drawer out of sight.

"Come on, let's see what's on the television," she suggested. Anything for a distraction and in the end, it worked although it took a long time. Preparing to leave, he reached for her hand and his touch was cold.

"Are you sure you're all right?" Mary asked solicitously.

"Of course," he replied. "Why wouldn't I be? I have had a pleasant evening with my girl."

"He wasn't all right, though," thought Mary as she lay in bed that night. "He was cold."

She thought also of what he had said. 'I have had a pleasant evening with my girl.' Ever since their cushion fight, she had had concerns about exactly how he felt about her but she had pushed them from her mind. That look in his eyes…. was nothing. She had been mistaken.

Unasked, unwanted, a feeling surged through her to be instantly dismissed. It was the feeling of his kiss after the wedding.

Weddings. Champagne. They made people act in a way they would not normally. It had not happened again.

There was nothing between them. He was the self-appointed big brother she never had.

WEDNESDAY
DAY 53

On the way home the following day, Mary spied Andrew coming out of one of the houses near the bus stop.

"What brings you here?" she asked.

"Police business," he replied then seeing the expression on Mary's face: "Nothing to do with Jared."

They walked together along the road. .

"I'll tell you what, though. I was right about my colleague writing those notes. He confessed."

"I suppose there haven't been any more sightings?"

"No. I should imagine anyone who was going to come forward would have done so by now."

They had almost reached the place where Andrew's car was parked. Not wanting to let the opportunity to fish for more information pass, Mary inquired: "Have you discovered anything you're allowed to tell me about the family?"

"Rachel's sister doesn't have much to say for herself and brother-in-law Charles is a surly individual. Sadly, I can't arrest him for that."

"Mike doesn't like him, Andrew doesn't like him," thought Mary. She still wondered whose life he had ruined and Mike clearly was not going to tell her so: "Does he have a record?"

Probably, he would not tell her but: "No," replied Andrew. There was no harm in her knowing that he did not.

So, what had he done? If it was not criminal but he had ruined a young life…. Perhaps he had got a girl pregnant. Whatever it was, Charles was a good suspect, especially after she had seen Tess and the jogger in the park. No doubt about it, he was top of her list but he was not the only person on it.

Mary hesitated.

"Go on, what's on your mind?"

"I was wondering if Henry upset any business associates."

"He's old-fashioned, strait-laced. He gets up noses but commands respect. The consensus was that his reputation is such as to intimidate colleagues and rivals alike so no-one has ever been brave enough to make an enemy of him."

By now they had reached Andrew's car.

"Can I drop you at the flat?"

"Don't be silly, we're almost there. But thanks, anyway."

* * *

Sitting quietly in her big, soft chair, Mary's thoughts reverted to the intriguing subject of what was in the package Tess had bought and who had she bought it from. She had only two possible sources of information: Rachel and Gary. After a little thought she decided to pay Gary another visit; that way, she could not only try to find out what Charles and Tess were up to but also whether Gary was involved.

It was a bit soon to call at Silverwood again but she would think of some excuse.

THURSDAY
DAY 54

When she arrived, Gary was having tea with his mother. Recognising Mary from before, the receptionist directed her to his office and Mary sat down to wait. Tess was in the anteroom. Tess typed away in silence, periodically consulting a calculator and made no effort to make conversation then after a short while, she got up and left the room. Her bag lay on the table beside the computer and on the spur of the moment, Mary decided to seize the opportunity to look inside. Her heart was pounding as she went over to pick up the bag; she had never done anything like this before. Quickly, she unzipped it and peeped in: her luck was in; the envelope was still there. Fingers trembling, she fumbled it open to find two passports. Mary looked over her shoulder, listening hard for approaching footsteps: nothing. She leafed through to see who the passports were made out to: a David James and a Vera Tomlinson.

But someone was coming. Mary's heart was beating so violently she felt it would break through her chest. Her eyes darted in all directions. There was no time to return to the chair because already a shadow was falling across the semi-opaque internal window to the corridor. Any minute the door would open…. Mary shoved the passports up her jumper: at least she would not be caught with them. She would have to work out how to put them back later. She stood trying to look innocent as she gazed out of the window.

"Tess?" The nurse had need of a signature.

"She just popped out."

"I'll leave the papers here."

As soon as her back was turned, Mary hurriedly pushed the passports back into the envelope, zipped up the bag and went back to her seat. She was glad she did not do things like this often; she was sure it had taken years off her life.

It was a few moments before Tess returned and Mary used her time well. She searched through the ringtones on her phone so that all she had to do was press select and the tune would begin. Surreptitiously she did so as Tess sat down then pretended to answer the ringing mobile. The 'call' over, Mary turned to Tess.

"I have to go," she said. "I'll catch Gary another time."

That was a turn up for the books. Why were Tess and Charles buying passports? And what to do next? Mary thought hard.

"I could hang around and follow Tess home or I could go home myself and find out Charles' and Tess's address from the electoral roll."

Mary opted for the second alternative.

"Then I will need to tail Tess and Charles to see where they go and what they do. For that I will need a car. I mean,

I need one anyway but I can't stand outside their house for hours on end waiting for them to come out then run after them."

Mary went home and inspected her bank account; she might just have enough.

FRIDAY
DAY 55

It was only two days to the fete. If Mike would not go with her, perhaps Ben would. In fact, that might be better if Mike's absence was guaranteed and his reaction to finding out where the fete was to be held suggested it would be. Ben could give her a lift – her costume would be awkward on the bus – and they could have a day out together.

Mary finished work early on a Friday so she decided to go over to the airfield and pay Ben a visit but as she tramped across the airfield towards the hangars, Mary began to wonder whether this had been a good idea. The landscape was flat and desolate and even though she had walked a long way she did not seem to be getting any closer. Nor could she even be sure Ben would be there; he was not answering his phone and she could not see anyone moving in the vicinity of the hangars.

Finally, however, she arrived at the rear corner of the largest hangar. She leaned against the metal wall to rest her aching feet. At that moment, Ben came out of the open door at the other end dressed in grey overalls, his hair standing on end. Mary felt too weary to call out and simply stood there, head resting on her arm against the wall, facing towards it, shoulders hunched, eyes on the ground.

Mary rocked her head to the side. She saw Ben wipe his hands on his overalls, fish a handkerchief out of his pocket and blow his nose then stand enjoying the breeze on his face. He still had not seen her. As she watched him, she saw a figure step from the shadow of the door behind him.

"Hello, Ben." The voice was even and quiet yet menacing.

"What brings you here?" Ben's reply was curt and unfriendly.

"Unfinished business."

"What unfinished business? We're done."

Their voices carried on the still air. Mary stood frozen to the spot, afraid to move in case she drew attention to herself. They seemed, however, to be engrossed in their discussion so she sidled round the corner of the hangar out of sight, risking a peep to try to identify the visitor. He had his back to her. She ducked back and waited then tried again. It was Charles.

"Done? …. Really? …." The silence hung heavy in the air. "Shame about the kid," Charles continued.

"Now you look here…" began Ben angrily. "That was nothing to do with me. I wasn't responsible and you know it."

Charles smiled. "I wouldn't say nothing. I would say that was your fault because you didn't think things through, didn't anticipate all possible scenarios and consequences. The way it panned out, I mean, something like that changes things, requires a bit of financial adjustment by way of compensation for mental anguish – mine – so to speak. But I'm not here to argue. I'm sure we can come to an arrangement. Think about it. You have so much to lose."

He turned on his heel and walked towards an old car that was parked a short distance away.

"Nothing to think about," called Ben after him. "We're done."

Charles sped off leaving Mary wondering what to do next. What had all that been about? She could not believe Ben had had anything to do with kidnapping Jared, he simply wouldn't. Would he? What reason could he have? If that were where his money came from, Mike would have found out and gloated by now. Anyway, it wasn't, he had had money before that.

But how did Ben know Charles?

First things first. She had to get out of this sticky spot.

"Think," she told herself. "Concentrate. I can't pretend I wasn't here because it's a long way to walk back and exposed; the chances of not being seen are slim. I could hang around for a while and pretend I've only just arrived and didn't overhear Ben and Charles talking. Then try to find out what's going on; but how? I can hardly ask Mike's help. Or I could bite the bullet and see what Ben has to say for himself."

She took a deep breath and stepped boldly round the corner and into sight.

"Hi, Ben," she called.

"Mary. What a lovely surprise. What are you doing here?" His voice was normal, no trace of tension. If he had been at all perturbed by the conversation with Charles, it did not show.

"I came to see you, of course. I was wondering if you were coming to the fete with me?"

Ben indicated that he was busy then decided that he had better come clean and admit that he did not like fetes. Not even the chance to dress up as a Victorian gentleman was enough to change his mind.

"I'll take you out some other time to make up," he bargained.

They stood looking at each other, Mary acutely conscious that it was a long way to have come to ask him if he was coming to the fete even if he was not answering his phone. She needed another reason for being there.

She thought fast. "Will you come and help me choose a car?" she blurted out.

"What now?"

"Yes…. no…. whenever…."

Ben looked at his watch and thought for a moment.

"All right, I could do with a break. Actually," he said with a wry smile: "Jack will probably be pleased to see the back of me, I'm not good with this mechanical stuff. I'm more on the executive side. There's a dealership near here; give me a few minutes to get cleaned up and I'll be with you."

When Ben returned, the overalls were gone and his hair tamed. Mary was glad not to have to walk back across the airfield and said as much.

"It's a couple of miles to the control tower from the bus stop, silly girl," Ben said.

They relapsed into silence, but Mary was still thinking about Charles. Did Ben have something to do with Jared's disappearance?

"Ben?" she said innocently. "Who was that man who was here when I came and what did he mean 'shame about the kid?'"

"Oh, that. Just some random bloke I asked to revamp the office in the corner of the hangar but his work wasn't up to standard so I fired him and he fired his apprentice. Kid couldn't get a job, got into debt and took an overdose. He says he wouldn't have had to do it if I'd paid him the full whack but why should I pay over the odds for shoddy work? I wasn't to know what the daft kid would do."

The explanation was slick but plausible.

And it would explain how Charles had ruined a young life; he had caused a suicide. But what was Mike's interest? Did he know the boy?

They drove on in silence, lost in their own thoughts until suddenly the dealership loomed in front of them. It occupied a sizeable plot adjacent to the airfield and so had plenty of room for a vast array of cars, in spite of which there were few in Mary's price range. She outlined her requirements and the salesman directed her attention to a green Mini.

"It's economical to run, it does a lot of miles to the gallon. What do you think?" he asked.

"I don't know," said Mary. "It's all right. Not very individual, though."

Ben and the salesman exchanged looks.

"Cheap to insure as well," contributed Ben.

"He should know," said a voice and there was Mike.

"Be quiet," hissed Mary.

"Thanks, I was only trying to help," said Ben.

"No, not you," she said.

"Do you have any idea what you're looking for?" inquired the salesman.

"Not really."

"That's helpful," said Mike.

"A reliable little runabout," contributed Ben.

"Isn't it time you went and minded someone else's business?" retorted Mary to Mike in a whisper.

She had not intended Ben to hear but his offended expression indicated that he had.

"Great, now look what you've done," she said out of the corner of her mouth but Mike was not in the least bit sorry.

"He's not suitable," he said. "Not *at all*."

"Can we do this some other time?" Mary's question was rhetorical.

Again, Ben heard and he looked even more offended.

"Why drag me out here for my advice if you don't want it and don't want to be here?"

"I do want your advice, Ben. I'm sorry, I'm just a bit on edge. It's a big decision."

The salesman decided it was time to step in; he had handled bickering couples before.

"How about this one," he said showing Mary a grey beetle. "Lovely little car," he observed.

"It's kind of round," said Mary.

The salesman raised his eyes to heaven. Mary gazed across the lot. Her eye alighted on a car in the far distance and grabbing Ben's hand she set off purposefully with the salesman in pursuit.

"It's adorable," she said stopping in front of a sand-coloured Suzuki soft top.

"It's a mess," objected Ben.

"I had one of those once," contributed Mike.

Mary ignored him.

"A good choice," said the salesman.

"You can't," objected Ben.

The salesman could see that Mary had taken a shine to the Vitara. He surveyed it looking sorry for itself in the parade line. "It's new in, it hasn't been valeted yet. I'm sure it will clean up very well…. or, I could perhaps knock a little off the price," he offered.

Mary continued gazing at the car affectionately. In her mind it was already hers. But winking at the salesman she allowed Ben to steer her back to the Mini.

"It's nice," she agreed. "And it's exactly what I need. I'll sleep on it."

Then, thanking the salesman for his help, she indicated to Ben that she was ready to leave. After a quick cup of tea at the airfield, Ben dropped her off at home.

"Thank you for your advice, Ben. I'm sorry about the way I behaved."

Mary kissed him and held his hands, unwilling to let him go. For a moment, they stood gazing into each other's eyes but much as Ben would have been happy to stay, he needed to return to the airfield to help Jack.

With a final hug and kiss he departed, leaving Mary to decide about the Mini. Or so he thought.

SATURDAY
DAY 56

In fact, Mary intended to ask Andrew's opinion of the Suzuki, partly because he was something of an expert on cars and partly because she felt it would be diplomatic having already asked his opinion some time ago as to what she should buy.

When Mary called him to explain that she had happened across a car she liked and wanted a second opinion, Andrew was only too happy to help.

"Can we take it out for a spin?" he asked the salesman, who gave Andrew an extremely odd look. Either he had grown a little taller and his hair a little darker since yesterday or this was not the same person Mary had been with before. He had a good memory for names and faces, he had to have in his job. It explained the bickering, though. He arranged his face into a neutral expression; the morals of his customers were not his business. Only the money they spent.

The little Vitara started at the first turn of the ignition

key; it was a bit noisy but Andrew assured her there was nothing wrong, it was just the way it sounded.

"You seem to have found yourself a real gem," he said.

They swapped places so Mary could see how the car felt to drive.

"It makes a sort of throaty roar when you start off," she remarked. "I'll call him Desert Tiger."

She would have to find a way to explain to Ben that she had been so taken with Desert Tiger that she had had to go back for him but Ben would get over it. The real problem was that Desert Tiger was perhaps not the best choice for tailing Tess; the Mini would have been less conspicuous. Never mind: Mary was not going to choose her car around Tess. Tailing Tess was a temporary activity whereas Mary and Tiger were going to be friends for a long while.

SUNDAY
DAY 57

The Sunday of the fete dawned clear and bright and according to the weather forecast it was going to be a warm afternoon.

"Thank goodness," thought Mary who had been desperately hoping it would not rain. She had put a lot of effort into the fete and so had a lot of other people so naturally she was keen that it should be a success.

Mary put on her costume and checked in the mirror; very elegant. And even though Ben had declined to come, she would not have to go on the bus in her long skirt because there was plenty of parking for Tiger.

As one of the organisers, she needed to be there early in case of last-minute hitches so perhaps it was for the best that she was going alone. As she drove over, she felt nervous. Only as recently as Friday, the scene at Lower Meadow Hall had been chaos, tents being pitched and stalls erected, awning falling down, tablecloths blowing in the breeze and bunting trailing across the grass while people scurried hither and thither looking for drawing pins and stepladders and all accompanied by a hubbub of shouted instructions. And in the middle of it all was Pete, totally in his element, sleeves rolled up, sorting out a loudspeaker system for announcements and acting as final port of call for anything and everything that anyone might think to need.

Mary parked Tiger and walked across the railway sleepers and over the grass. Relief flooded through her. This morning, all was calm. The stalls stood ready, immaculate and bright. Pete was strolling up and down the lines making last-minute checks and there was nothing for Mary to do but bring him a cup of tea and wait for the gates to open and let in the public. Then the mayor made a little speech and declared the fete open.

Mary pushed her way through the throng determined to find knick-knacks to buy and rides to go on, all in a good cause. Her only official duties now were to make sure that none of the stalls ran out of change and to cover for potty breaks. She had a go on the raffle, took her turn minding the hoop-la and threw wet sponges at Ryan. Her aim was poor and the first set of three missed so she had to buy another ticket before she finally got him but it had to be done.

By lunchtime she had visited almost every stall, chatted to Bellyache and Minty and a whole host of other people and was running out of things to do.

There was only one attraction she had not yet visited. Mary found her steps turning towards a tent with a placard outside announcing in flowery writing 'Madame Delphine: Gypsy Fortune Teller.' Should Mary have her fortune told? Yes, she should; she was responsible for Mme Delphine being there so she should see what she was like. She dithered briefly then walked up to the tent. The flap was open. Unable to knock, she peeped inside.

"Come in," called Mme Delphine. "I have been expecting you."

If Mary had an image in her mind of what a Gypsy Fortune Teller should look like then Mme Delphine was it. Her long full skirt was vibrant with colour and layers of coloured scarves almost obscured a plain, purple top. Bracelets extended halfway up her arms and she wore large, gold hoop earrings and a headdress jangling with gold coins.

"Sit down, my dear," she said, motioning Mary towards an old wooden chair beside a small square table with a tasselled cloth. Mary complied.

Mme Delphine sat opposite and took Mary's hands. Her touch was warm and light but firm, her long fingers reached to Mary's wrists. She breathed deeply, then relaxed and let the room drop away. Suddenly, Mary felt her stiffen – slightly, but the change in her grip was discernible.

"There is someone in your life who should not be there."

She looked straight into Mary's eyes. Mary sat very still and said nothing. Mme Delphine held her gaze. Mary felt Mme Delphine's eyes drilling into her; she felt she should speak but did not know what to say. She could guess exactly who Mme Delphine meant: Mike.

"I see trouble," Mme Delphine continued.

"What kind of trouble?" ventured Mary.

Mme Delphine's penetrating stare did not waver. Mary felt as though every thought and feeling she had was laid bare. The silence was unbearable. Mary made a move towards her bag – she would pay more – but Mme Delphine held her hands tightly.

Mme Delphine's face took on a far-away look. She breathed in deeply and closed her eyes.

"You are searching for…." Her eyes opened. "Jared…."

She released Mary's hands and with a flick of her wrist, she uncovered a crystal ball Mary had not noticed in the middle of the table. She took a series of deep breaths and gazed into the ball. Grey mist faded and in a clear voice Mme Delphine spoke.

"I see a coffin…. a tiny coffin…."

Horrified, Mary cried out and jerked away.

"That can't be right. It can't be!"

The ball began to glow red, tiny squares of paper whirling angrily inside it like a storm-crazed snow-globe. Mme Delphine jolted awake and flicked the cloth back over it.

"You should not have broken the connection, my dear," she admonished Mary but there was no criticism, only sympathy and understanding.

"I'm sorry, I'm so sorry."

"It is all right. You had a shock. Sadly, I cannot guarantee that you will hear what you would like to hear."

"But it can't be right." Mary thought of Mike's assurance that Jared's traffic light was yellow, that he would tell her if it changed.

"The orb does not lie."

"Of course not," agreed Mary hastily. "But it's a mistake, it has to be."

Or did it? Mike might be wrong. He and this prophecy could not both be right. Or…. or…. could the traffic light have changed colour?

Mme Delphine sat quietly watching as Mary grappled with her fears. Why would Mike lie? She had no reason to think he would. The traffic light, then. She had not seen Mike for a couple of days. It must have turned red. Meaning some misfortune had befallen Jared or was about to.

Hesitantly, Mary asked: "Is Jared dead?"

"No, my dear."

Mary slumped against the back of the chair. Jared had not passed but there was no escaping the fact that the orb foretold a threat to his life.

"Must he die? Is there no way to change it?" she demanded.

"You have time. The paper you saw in the orb was sheets from a calendar and there were many of them."

Mme Delphine got up and moved towards an old couch in the corner. "Come," she said patting the seat beside her. "Sit a while. I'll make some tea; I was about to take a break."

Mary let the warm tea flow through her veins. Her thoughts were an incoherent jumble and she felt suddenly tired. She leaned back and seemed to be floating. She almost wondered if Mme Delphine had put something in the tea.

"You need to do something about that friend of yours," advised Madame Delphine. "He plays with fire."

Mary did not have the strength to compose a reply.

"Come again to see me if you need to. Anytime," offered Mme Delphine. She handed Mary her card, an ornate tangle of swirling gold letters. "Goodbye, my dear."

Still dazed, Mary thanked her, assured her she was all right now and stumbled out into the sunshine. Cheerful music from a miniature steam organ pushed its way into her consciousness, laughing people jostled around her and reality returned.

Mary had to stay until the fete was over, so she distracted herself watching a magician and simply wandering about satisfying herself that it was all going well and everyone was having a good time. But her visit to Mme Delphine had made her uneasy and she was relieved when she was finally able to escape.

Safely back at home, Mary collapsed into a chair and fell fast asleep. It was midnight when she roused and stumbled to bed but she slept fitfully and was soon woken by a disturbance in the curtains.

"Mike?"

No answer. Blearily, she made her way to the window, putting her hand on the table to steady herself as she passed. But instead of wood, her hand encountered something soft.

"Oh, it's you, Ginge. Sorry. You're adorable but you're going to have to be adorable outside. No pets allowed."

Ginger, however, was not about to take a hint and came back every time she put him out. Mary was forced to sleep with the window closed and woke in the morning with a headache.

MONDAY
DAY 58

"Mike! Mike!" called Mary desperately. "Mike, where are you?"

"Right here," he replied popping up beside her as she was giving up and turning her attention to the hire tickets. Mary upset a mug of pens all over the floor.

"Don't do that," she hissed.

Mike stood watching as she picked them up. "You don't normally call me when you're at work."

"It's important. Come on, let's go outside."

In the distance, voices were shouting against the sound of heavy machinery but for once it was quiet near the cabin. Breathlessly, Mary began: "I went to the fete yesterday. I had my fortune told. We have to find Jared or he will die."

Mike digested this information.

"How long do we have?"

"I don't know. I …." Mary looked down at the ground. Sheepishly, she continued: "I broke the connection."

Mike did not need to lift her chin to know the sorrowful expression on her face. He put his arm around her.

"Mike, is Jared's light red?"

"It's still yellow. This Mme Delphine told you we had time. We need to step up the hunt, that's all."

"I hope so."

"Why the doubtful expression?"

"No reason. Mme Delphine seeing a coffin was a shock, that's all."

"We'll find him." Gently, Mike kissed her forehead.

Mary attempted a smile. It was a failure.

"Did Mme Delphine say something else?" asked Mike searchingly.

"Nothing that made any sense and I don't think she realised she'd said it. It's probably nothing."

"But?"

"But just before she woke from her trance, she said something that sounded like 'the Spite Brigade.'"

"What?" cried Mike.

"The Spite Brigade," repeated Mary.

"I heard you the first time."

"Mike, what's the matter?"

"They're…. that is to say I'm not saying they exist but…. Oh, darn, the cat's out of the bag now so you may as well know. The Opposition have a military-style organisation called the Minor Operations Unit, known to the rest of us as the Spite Brigade. The more experienced handle the big stuff, the Spite Brigade practise on the easier projects."

"The Opposition?" broke in Mary. "You mean…. the forces of darkness?"

233

"That's as good a name as any."

"But you said Jared's light was yellow, that there was no reason to think anyone meant him any harm, that he would be fine unless some misfortune befell him."

"Sometimes misfortune has a helping hand," observed Mike heavily.

"Oh, great! This is just great."

"It's not time to panic yet. If he were on the Task List, he would be dead already. My guess is he's a bonus, an optional extra."

"An optional extra," echoed Mary sourly.

"Well, yes. Think about it. Rachel is already feeling wretched…."

"She'll feel worse if Jared dies."

"As I was saying: Rachel is feeling wretched but find Jared and she's happy. But the kidnapper isn't – assuming we are correct in assuming that he or she wants him – so in unhappiness terms, it's a swap. Kill Jared and they are both hurting. And the net amount of misery in the world increases. And even if our initial ideas were wrong and Jared's disappearance is the mistress getting him out of the way, it will impact both Rachel and the mistress, too, if he dies; after all, out of the way is different to dead.

"However, in misery terms, other targets will produce a bigger net gain. Which brings me back to: he's a footnote to the main list. A job to be undertaken in the absence of something more satisfying."

"I can see why you call them the Spite Brigade."

"Mme Delphine's vision is a timely warning but we already knew Jared was fine unless misfortune took a hand

– with or without the help of the Spite Brigade. Don't let the Spite Brigade faze you. The only thing that has changed is we have a timescale."

"I had better be going back in," Mary said wearily.

Mike put his arm round her comfortingly. "Something will turn up. Try not to worry."

Mary took some aspirin and survived the rest of the day.

That evening, all Mary could think about was Jared. She needed to find him – urgently. Mary reviewed her list of suspects: Mike had warned her about Charles and she had seen Tess buying passports with cash. Charles had gone to the airport and tried to blackmail Ben about a 'kid.'

She could not check Ben's explanation concerning the unfortunate suicide of Charles' apprentice – if such a person ever existed – but she found it hard to believe he would get mixed up in the kidnap of a child. However, she would have to put Ben's name on the list.

Then there was Gary whose mother saw children in the garden. Again, Mary found it hard to regard him as a credible suspect but nothing was impossible.

She had already investigated Mr Danesford and the Parkers and come up with nothing.

The next step was obvious. Mary began planning her surveillance of Charles. After all, apart from being top of the list, that was urgent if he might leave the country. And in the course of investigating Charles, she might even find out where his and Mike's paths had crossed. Was Charles' apprentice real, had Mike known him or was it something else?

Rachel had said Charles was doing house extensions these days. Builders generally start around seven-thirty Mary reasoned – but if Charles was working on a domestic house, he might not be able to turn up that early, the householder might be asleep or on the school run. Then again, he could go to the builder's merchant at eight for supplies and then on to the house so she should allow time for a journey to the builder's merchant. Which suggested she should stake out Charles' house from seven or even six-thirty. Mary groaned. She would be getting up at dark o'clock (again).

TUESDAY
DAY 59

The following morning, Mary dragged herself out of bed, had a quick shower, made a flask of coffee, grabbed some chocolate, warned Pete she would be late but would make up the time and went down to find Tiger.

"Hello sweetie. Good boy," she said as he roared into life.

By this time, she was awake and feeling better. It would be some time before the novelty of owning a car wore off and this was not just any car but a Desert Tiger.

She parked a few doors down from Charles' house and waited. Deliberately, she did not think about Mike in case it alerted him to where she was or made him appear. It would not do to be found here.

"What if Ben turns up?" A wave of anxiety swept over Mary. She had not considered that but: "It's unlikely, he said his business with Charles was done."

Calm again, she turned on the radio to drown out her thoughts and in particular to drown out any thoughts of

Mike. Time went by and the only thing that Mary could safely conclude was that the Armstrong household did not like getting up in the morning. Or maybe they were on holiday or perhaps he was between jobs. Trust her to pick the one time he was not going anywhere or was not there. Just as depression was setting in at the complete waste of time that was her stake-out, Mary saw a van draw up. A man in overalls got out. He walked up the drive and knocked on the door and out came Charles. As he turned and they walked down the drive together, she saw the other man's face clearly; it was familiar but she could not place it.

"My van again, I suppose," said the man. "I doubt yours is fixed yet?"

Where had she seen him before? Never mind, it would come to her. Now for the hard bit; tailing them.

She kept well back, aware that Tiger was distinctive, but fortunately they seemed engrossed in their conversation and completely oblivious of the antics of random road users. After about seven miles they turned down a leafy street and drew up outside a private house with a partly-built extension on the side. There was a convenient side-road from which Mary could watch them but there was not much to see. Then again, all information is useful information and it was obvious that these two had been working together for a while and got on well. They worked with and around each other almost without needing to speak and they shared their breakfast break sitting on a bag of sand trading insults.

They had no sooner gone back in the house when there was a faint rustle and suddenly the seat beside her was no longer empty.

"I've been looking for you," said a voice and there was Mike. Mary jumped visibly as he continued: "What are we doing?"

"Nothing. Just…."

"Just. Clearly something we shouldn't be."

Mary looked sheepish.

He studied the situation.

"Looks to me like you're watching someone," he observed. "I'll join you."

It was a statement, not a suggestion.

"There's no need, I was about to leave."

It was true: Mary had decided there was nothing more to be learned here.

"That would be a pity." Then in a lighter tone: "I told you I once had a car like this, didn't I? Gosh this brings back memories. And I love stake-outs. Your friend Andrew put a couple of blokes to watching Mr Danesford a while back after what you told him so I tagged along. They didn't find out anything, I got on better on my own, it was really slow but I livened things up playing with their radios so Andrew overheard the odd bit of conversation that wasn't meant for his ears and vice versa."

He was as incorrigible as he was charming but Mary was not in a receptive mood. She sat on the edge of her seat, frantic. Charles might come back out at any moment. She needed to get rid of Mike.

Too late, Charles needed tools from the van.

"I thought I made myself clear. Keep away from him." Mike's tone was vaguely menacing.

"I'm not actually near him and he hasn't seen me," Mary excused herself.

Mike did not answer. Mary started the engine and set off, turning right rather than left so she would not pass the van. They drove in silence.

"Mike?" she ventured but there was no reply, he had gone.

Fair enough. In that case, she would go back and risk a brief conversation with Charles and his colleague – being careful, of course. Mary parked Tiger and walked over.

"I wonder if you could help me? I was visiting a friend who lives nearby and I saw you sitting here. My friend was thinking about having a new kitchen but she can't seem to find anyone to do it. Everyone seems to be busy. Is it the sort of thing you do?"

"Yes, miss. It wouldn't be for a couple of months but I would be happy to give your friend a quote. All work guaranteed and our prices are very reasonable." Charles handed her a business card.

"Oh, wonderful. She will be pleased."

Mary put the card in her pocket and started to walk down the path. The other two resumed their conversation.

"It's all very well buying strikers but he needs to upgrade the defence. It's no use scoring goals if you let as many in."

"Too right. We could make a better job of the team ourselves."

Mary turned.

"Actually, sorry to bother you but there is one more thing you could help me with. Can you tell me where I could get a piece of wood to match this?"

She fished the piece of painted wood she had found at Lower Meadow Hall from her bag where she had put it before she set out.

It was more than obvious from their startled reaction that both of them recognised the fragment. Charles glared at her.

"Sorry, miss, we can't help you," he said shortly.

Feigning disappointment, Mary drove away.

At work, the rest of the day passed unremarkably. Even Ryan seemed to have had both his volume control and his boisterousness turned down.

Once safely home that evening, Mary sat feeling despondent. She had found out nothing from her surveillance of Charles. She decided to go for a short walk and blow some cobwebs from her brain.

She explored streets she had not been along before and after a while she found herself at an entrance to the park she had not known existed.

"I must remember that," she thought, "It was a pleasant walk and a quick way to get here. Well, it would have been if I had come straight here."

She sat on a bench and stared out over the lake, her thoughts still wandering without structure or conclusion. Then she saw the jogger.

Mary was sure it was the same person even though the jogging clothes had given way to a grey coat and low-heeled, practical shoes. She edged nearer; as the woman moved, Mary saw that she was wearing a dark blue dress beneath the grey coat and there was a suggestion of a white collar showing at the neck. Of course! Last time Mary had lost her in the grounds of the hospital. The woman was a nurse.

This time, however, she would not be running so Mary would be able to follow. As it turned out, her quarry was about to go on duty and after a few minutes she headed into the hospital. Mary tailed her down corridor after corridor until she wondered if she would ever find her way out again until finally the nurse entered a small side-ward tucked away at the end of the building. Mary turned and retraced her steps; she did not want to arouse suspicion. But she did not go far. She found a chair by the door in a little waiting area and sat down. Sure enough, before long the nurse re-appeared and as she passed, Mary was able to read her ID badge. Nurse Jill Kendrick. She went to a store cupboard for clean sheets and returned to the little side-ward then after a while she passed Mary again, walking purposefully towards a room labelled 'New Admissions'.

Jill Kendrick was kindness itself, helping her latest charge to her bed and comforting her about how she personally knew the surgeon, how good he was, and how they would do everything to make her stay – short as it would be in such expert hands – as comfortable as possible. She unpacked the lady's belongings into a small cupboard by the side of the bed, showed her how to work the television, fluffed up her pillows and left.

"A perfect opportunity to steal a passport if there had been one," thought Mary.

It would not be often the chance presented itself because few people would carry such a thing but with a high throughput of patients, many dazed and distracted, it should be possible to come by the odd one or two. Nice little business, stealing valuables from patients.

Jill headed back to the little side-ward and as Mary turned to leave, who should she see but Mike! He, too, was heading for the side-ward.

Obviously, Mary must go there as well. Quietly, she walked to the door and peeped in. A woman lay in the bed absolutely still. A student nurse was examining a monitor while Mike hovered behind her and on the other side of the bed sat none other than Mr Danesford. Darren was crawling on the covers pushing a toy car up and down a road made from folds in the bedding. Sometimes he touched his mother's arm. Mr Danesford seemed to be encouraging him to make as much noise as possible and Mary realised he was hoping that Mrs Danesford – Anne-Marie – would hear him and wake up from her coma.

"Talk to Mummy," begged his father.

"That's not my Mummy," replied the boy. Again, Mary was struck by the husky quality of his voice.

"It's hard for the little ones to take in," said the student nurse kindly, adjusting a drip in the woman's arm under Nurse Kendrick's supervision. "She doesn't act like Mummy you see. Try not to mind."

Mary thought Mike to attract his attention. He looked up, shook himself from his reverie and joined her outside.

"What are you doing here?" he asked as they walked back to the waiting area.

"I kind of know Nurse Kendrick. How about you? Who is that lady?"

Mike confirmed what Mary had already guessed: it was Mrs Danesford. She was, indeed, in hospital as Mary had been told by Andrew. And Mr Danesford visited whenever he could although that was not very often bearing in mind that he put Darren in the works creche and worked in a factory in the daytime then handed him over to a babysitter so he could serve burgers at a fast-food outlet most evenings.

She had been in a car crash – Mary began to open her mouth but Mike silenced her – no, Mr Danesford had not attacked her and tried to kill her, she really had been in a car crash. He had dropped by the station and seen part of a police report recommending prosecution of the other driver, a teenager who had forced her off the road racing another car. As Mike described Anne-Marie's car hitting a shop-front in town, Mary thought she remembered a picture in the County Times of a mangled car with a beam that once went across the top of the shop window lying on the roof. Mrs Danesford was lucky to have got out alive.

"How long has she been like that? Will she get better?"

"They're hopeful. There's brain activity and she's breathing on her own." There was a peculiar expression on Mike's face which Mary could not interpret.

Together, Mike and Mary tiptoed back to the door and looked in. Darren now sat on Mr Danesford's lap and together the little family were listening to a tape of nursery music. Mike shivered. Mary took his arm and quietly, they left.

"How do you know Jill?" asked Mike.

"Like I said, I don't exactly know her, she's just someone I met in the park."

"Hmm…. you didn't know it was her that was Henry Parker's mistress, then?"

Carefully, he studied her reaction.

"No."

"I was surprised to see her here," he continued. "I hadn't realised she was a nurse."

"And a thief."

"Really? Did you actually see her take anything?"

Mary had not and she was not ready to tell him about Tess and the passports having only just been caught tailing Charles. They walked back to the main entrance together and Mary was glad of a guide. The place was an absolute rabbit warren.

"Are you doing anything tomorrow night?" asked Mike. "They're putting on some fireworks at the castle and I thought we might go and watch."

Washing her hair? Visiting her mother? She would have to tell him the truth, he could so easily find out what she was up to any time he liked. He was well placed to be the ultimate stalker that she would not even be able to complain to the police about because they would think she was mad.

"I'm going climbing with Ben."

"In the dark?"

"No, silly, they have a practice wall at the club. I thought I might have a go but I don't fancy ever upgrading to real mountains. Too dangerous. Ben's friend Joe was badly hurt one time. If it hadn't been for Ben, he would have died."

Mike snorted.

"Knowing there's a time limit on finding Jared, I feel bad about going out but we don't have any leads to follow at the moment."

"Your fishing expedition this morning didn't get you anywhere, then?"

"No." Mary sighed. "Why don't you escort me home? I know you like my little car."

WEDNESDAY
DAY 60

Even before Mary had pulled the heavy door to the site cabin fully open, she could tell something was going on. She stepped inside.

Bellyache had cleared the chairs and tables back at the far end of the room and appeared to be holding an impromptu dance class, a broad grin spread all over his face.

"It goes like this. Hop-skip to the left, hop-skip to the right, one-hundred-and-eighty-degree turn, raise the hand to shade the eyes and look all around then turn and face the front, little jump and…. hop-skip to the left, hop-skip to the right and so on."

"What on earth….?" inquired Mary.

"Ryan saw a rat. Scared of them, poor lad," called out Bellyache.

"Not," contradicted Ryan. "It was just the surprise. It ran out from under that palette by the fence and if I hadn't moved so fast it would have run straight over my foot."

"It's nothing to be ashamed of," said Bellyache in comforting tones. He was clearly enjoying his revenge for the Walking Speed Initiative episode. "Hop-skip, hop-skip, little jump and into the finale: the Ryan Twirl."

He was surprisingly light on his feet, thought Mary, as Bellyache spun round and took a bow.

Mary crossed to her desk and turned on her computer – except she did not because nothing happened.

"A rat probably chewed the cable," said Bellyache with a wink.

"Or the cleaner turned it off at the plug," contributed Pete flicking a switch. "Mary, there are some notes on my desk that need typing up. Bellyache, traffic duty. There's a timber delivery due in about fifteen minutes. You'll have to back him out, there won't be room to turn him in the yard."

Bellyache lumbered out, the agility he had displayed when doing the rat dance seemingly having left him, and Mary turned to her typing. Pete needed to improve his handwriting. She wrinkled her nose.

"What do you reckon that word says?" she asked Dan.

"Search me," he replied.

Mary took her best guess and carried on. Pete would have to sort it out when he came back.

* * *

After work, Mary grabbed a quick snack and went to meet Ben. The first thing she noticed as they pushed open the double doors to the climbing centre was the sweaty-foot smell reminiscent of a school gym. The second was the climbing wall.

It was not at all what Mary expected. She had envisaged a mock-up of a cliff-face with hand-holds and foot-holds of different size and spacing depending on whether the route was for beginners or the more experienced. Instead, she was amazed to see brightly coloured arches and domes splattered with what looked like lumps of play dough thrown at random by a naughty child. It was all very childish except that it was not; it looked horribly difficult. Her eyes wide, she stared at people scaling the walls, straddled across the misshapen play dough, hanging upside down from the arches. She trailed after Ben in her hard hat and climbing shoes, appalled.

"Don't worry, you'll be attached to a rope and you won't be on a route with overhangs or anything like that. It's quite safe."

Mary could not back out so she smiled at him (well, she hoped it was a smile) and followed him to one of the arches.

"I'll go up next to you and give you a few pointers if you need them. Then you can get a coffee while I scale the stalactite."

Mary's ascent must have been one of the slowest on record. The first couple of steps were all right but as she got higher up there were a couple of times when looking all round whilst trying not to look down, she could not find a lump of play dough to put her foot on and ended up clinging on for dear life stretched out like a starfish.

"Up a bit. To your left," advised Ben. "Up just a tiny.... bend your knee.... and look, we're there! Now all you have to do is get down again!"

In some ways that was harder. Mary slipped once or twice but did not fall and it was with a sense of relief that she reached the ground. Her hands were sweaty and she was shaking but: "Well done, M!" congratulated Ben.

Unsteadily, Mary made her way to the café and once he had seen her settled with a cup of hot chocolate, Ben went off to climb the stalactite.

"You'll feel better in a minute and proud of yourself, too," he said.

Calmer now, she watched him ascending like spider. She watched the other climbers, some climbing individually and others in groups. Ben paused to wave to a figure climbing an adjacent wall – a familiar figure – and suddenly it came to Mary where she had seen Charles' builder friend before: it was Alistair from the photograph that Ben's mother had shown her, Alistair that Ben knew from the army cadets, Alistair that Ben's mother did not like.

Mary's heart skipped a beat. She turned away to hide her face but fortunately, Alistair had no interest in the spectators, only the challenge of a new route. Having arrived long after Ben and Mary he was still high up on the wall when Ben once again reached the ground so to Mary's relief, Ben promised to introduce them some other time and they left.

THURSDAY
DAY 61

Back at work the following day, the backs of Mary's legs ached but sitting typing was not an option because her fingers were sore. Stiffly, she went to the bookcase.

"Announcement," boomed Pete's voice. "Gather round, I have an announcement." He waited for them to collect and he waited for silence. "I would like to congratulate everyone on the success of the fete. The numbers are in and we made seven thousand pounds which will be divided equally between the orphanage and the homeless centre in St. Mildred's Street. Any further money collected from the sale of photographs – got you there, you didn't know we hired a photographer, did you? – will go to the refurbishment of the playgroup where Minty and Bellyache have kindly volunteered to carry out minor repairs and repainting today and tomorrow instead of sitting around here all day the way they usually do."

Minty and Bellyache exchanged surprised glances; evidently this was news to them. Everyone else made for the photograph display to see how much of an idiot they been caught looking. Mary, to her relief, had managed to look elegant in all of them whether the subject of the picture or a distant figure in the background but not everyone was so lucky. There was a gratifying picture of Ryan copping a sponge in the face, another of Dan falling over backwards trying to imitate one of the acrobats and one of Pete, beer in hand and his mouth over-full with hog roast spraying crumbs over the mayor.

Seizing a radio and yellow coat: "Got to go," said Pete. "Subbies. When they're giving you their pitch, they can do everything but by the time they turn up on site they can do nothing," and he hurried out of the door.

Obviously, Mary needed the photo of Ryan amongst her keepsakes. She chose a selection showing all of the people she worked with. Her job would only last until the building was finished but this was a job she wanted to remember.

* * *

Mary sat tapping her fingers on the table. If only she had not upset the orb. Jared needed her just as Ellen had needed her. Ellen…. something touched Mary's ear. She hit at it and jumped up. Don't be silly. Spiders can't hurt you. Anyway, there's nothing there.

Mary sat back down. She had not found out anything by following Charles – no, wait, she had found a connection to Alistair but expanding her surveillance to Alistair seemed equally unlikely to yield results. And she now knew the identity of Henry's spurned mistress; it was Jill, who sold passports to Tess in the park. Stealing from patients was a far cry from kidnapping, however, and Jill would find it even harder to mix shift work with caring for Jared than Mr Danesford found caring for Darren.

She needed a new line of inquiry…. then she remembered. She had meant to do this before. Mary turned on the computer and googled Companies House. She searched for HP Property Development then sat staring at the list of directors.

She should have known: HP stood for Henry Parker! It was Henry who had owned Lower Meadow Hall, Henry and Rachel.

"Funny, Rachel didn't mention it when we were discussing the refurbishment."

Mary pondered. What was it Rachel had said? 'Terrible business.' Why? They had done well out of the fire.

She moved on to her next subject of research: Lower Meadow Hall itself. It looked to have been a beautiful building in its heyday, the classic Regency-Greek architecture set off by a landscaped park. Doric columns queued across the porch beneath a pointed canopy whilst perfectly proportioned windows peeped between them repeating across the façade. Inside, more columns marched down the vast ballroom. There were twenty-seven bedrooms and myriad reception rooms of which three had Adam fireplaces. Mary wondered how the Parkers could possibly afford a place like that but reading on, she found that the Hall had been derelict for many years and the contents looted before its purchase for conversion to a hotel and conference centre and had been auctioned for a song.

Further down the page, Mary's eye was caught by a newspaper article about the fire. Clicking it open she stared at the screen in front of her.

Julia Mallory-Quinn.

"That's where I heard the name Mallory-Quinn before!"

Mary skipped through the article refreshing her memory. A teenage girl was on a work experience placement with a local estate agent. Having visited a lot of rather ordinary properties, she had gone to Lower Meadow Hall with her mentor to see how they priced houses at the other end of the scale. She was interested in architecture and took pictures of the fireplaces and cornices on her mobile phone but she had left the phone on a windowsill and borrowed a key to go back and retrieve it after work. No-one knew how the fire had started; perhaps faulty wiring, after all, the old place had been empty for years. But Julia became trapped inside and suffered horrific burns. Mary remembered it being on the news; it was horrible to think about.

She closed the page quickly and checked over her shoulder. No-one. Not that Mary would necessarily know even if Mike were there.

Mary went over to the drawer of the Welsh dresser and fished out the piece of wood. She still could not see of what it might have been part. She picked up the bracelet and turned it over and over in her hands. It was clean now and looking at it closely, she noticed there was an inscription in tiny letters on the back of the setting of the stone by the clasp: 'JMQ from MMQ Happy 16th'.

JMQ…. MMQ…. Julia Mallory Quinn! From Mike! So, that was who Mike wanted to return it to.

Mary decided to chance another search to see if she could find any newspaper articles updating the story, in particular what had happened to Julia. Nothing. Quickly, Mary closed it down. She sat immobile, thinking.

"Penny for them," said a voice and there was Mike.

Phew. Not a moment too soon.

"Trying to decide what to have for dinner," lied Mary. "I don't fancy anything I have in the flat; let's go down to the shop. I need some air."

As they walked down the road, Mary's mind was racing. Mike must be related to Julia; the name was so unusual. And closely enough to buy her that bracelet. She would confirm as soon as she had the opportunity but Mary guessed that Julia was Mike's little sister. That would explain why he did not want to go to the fete when he found out where it was. But worse than that: Henry had received a hefty pay-out from the insurance on the Hall. Julia had been horrifically injured. Surely Mike could not be responsible for Jared's disappearance to get back at Henry Parker?

No, he would never do anything like that. And he would never team up with Charles or for that matter any of the others on her list. And he had genuinely helped her in her investigations which was more than she could say she had done for his.

But first things first – to confirm their relationship. Mary did not want to ask Mike so how could she find out for sure? Possibly from one of those sites where you can research your ancestry.

"Do I need to know his date of birth," she wondered. "Or the place?"

Casually, she inquired: "Mike, when is your birthday?"

"I don't have them anymore."

"But when you were…. I mean, before. We could still mark the occasion."

"Birthdays are supposed to be a celebration and a thank you that the person has survived another year. Especially back when times were hard and life was fragile. Hardly appropriate in my case, I'm dead."

"You're here though. Here with me. We'll just have to celebrate the anniversary of our first meeting."

Never mind, the name might be enough. Mike must be local because he knew Charles Armstrong.

A search of the obituaries in the local paper soon revealed that he was survived by a sister, Julia. No mention of parents so presumably they were dead. And that was about it; no relations and, in spite of living life in the fast lane, no scandal. Mike seemed to have been liked and respected by friends and colleagues alike.

So, what now? Everything seemed to come back to Lower Meadow Hall. Mike had a connection with Lower Meadow Hall through Julia, whatever had happened to her. Which was a good question: what had happened to her? Rachel and Henry Parker owned the Hall and now their son had disappeared. Alistair and Charles had worked on the Hall and now Charles and Tess were buying passports from Jill – what were they running from? The conversation she had overheard at the airfield suggested that Charles was blackmailing Ben: was Ben's simple explanation true or had Charles got Ben into some sort of trouble after all? Even Gary was not above suspicion what with his employment of Tess and his mother seeing children in the garden. Then there was Mr Danesford. He was being blackmailed by a woman. Mr Danesford…. he was the only one with no connection whatever to the Hall. Apparently. Perhaps his wife had some connection to Lower Meadow Hall.

Was there no one in Mary's life who was pottering along minding their own business and not doing anything criminal? She felt as though she had stumbled into a giant conspiracy but she could not see how the players were connected or where the kidnapping fitted in.

And she did not know how much time she had left. But she had better get a move on, she needed to make a difference this time.

"Keep calm," Mary told herself. "Forget the big picture for now and continue taking things one step at a time."

FRIDAY
DAY 62

Friday passed in a flash. Mary stopped walking like a robot, Minty and Bellyache painted the playgroup ('Children. All over the place. Trip hazard, Noise Assessment over the limit….' Anyone could tell Bellyache had enjoyed himself) and Pete was in his element as he ordered the subbies to dig up the floor of the plant room and start again because the electricity cable was supposed to be in a bigger and separate duct.

Mary made a final round of tea and set off early to pay the photograph money into the bank on the way home.

"Perform a U-turn when possible," instructed the satnav for the second time.

Stupid thing. It had another favourite trick, too. 'Can't see the sky' it would announce and leave her in the middle of a junction with no idea which road to take then chastise her for her choice. She turned down the nearest side-road and changed direction. Only two more miles. And then:

"Destination." She even found a parking space for Desert Tiger right outside.

The queue was not long but Mary's legs still ached; she fidgeted, wishing she could sit down. Best not to think about it. She forced her attention to her surroundings and gradually became aware that the woman queuing in the next line was familiar. Her face was partially obscured by the brim of her hat and Mary edged nearer to get a better look. She coughed softly; the woman turned then almost immediately turned away. But Mary had seen enough; it was an older version of Tess with much greyer hair. Her mother? Mary looked more closely. No, it was Tess but her make-up was dreadful, anything but flattering.

Mary's turn at her window came at the same time as Tess reached the front of her queue. Mary pushed the paying-in slip and the money through to the cashier and watched surreptitiously to see what Tess was doing. Interesting. She was opening a bank account. But wait: not in the name of Tess Armstrong. She was calling herself Vera Tomlinson and using one of the passports she had bought as ID. And she was paying in a large amount of cash.

Mary's thoughts ran in all directions. The make-up was not an accident; Vera was an old-lady name. Mary had not thought to look at the date of birth on the passport but she would be prepared to bet it belonged to a pensioner. And the money…. it must be ransom money! But would the Armstrongs really stoop so low as to kidnap Jared – their own nephew – and then collect the money and not return him? True, Mike seemed to have a very low opinion of Charles but *Tess*? Do that to her own sister? And if they had taken him, where were they hiding him?

"There you are, dear."

The cashier's voice brought Mary back to the present. She went over to a chair by the wall and sat re-arranging the contents of her handbag. And thinking. Supposing it was the money from the ransom, you can't spend that amount as cash, you can't buy a house or anything without someone asking questions. But you can't go around paying half a million pounds cash into an account without someone asking questions either. And you can't draw it out again without someone asking questions. So, how to make any use of it? Not that Tess had paid in half a million. She had paid in only a fraction of that. So, where was the rest?

Tess finished her transaction and left; naturally Mary followed. Discreetly, she tailed her and was delighted to see the hat shoved into a shopping bag, talc combed from the hair and the make-up brightened. A dark wig completed the transformation and Tess was ready for a trip to another bank. More cash was paid in and then: a transfer to Vera Tomlinson's account from her so-called daughter's. So, that's how to get a lot of cash *into* an account thought Mary, but how do you get it out and spend it? It had to go into the Armstrong's account before it would be useful for paying the mortgage and the bills.

It was time to go. She would not find out any more here.

But at least the Armstrongs were not running off abroad with Jared. Well, probably not. Not as Vera Tomlinson and David James at any rate because now Mary thought about it, a small child accompanied by grandparents with different surnames would look odd. No, the passports were for laundering money.

SATURDAY
DAY 63

Follow the money…. that was what people always said, wasn't it? Follow the money.

But follow it where? Tess had it, end of the line. Mary sat thinking hard. She must be careful not to jump to conclusions.

Firstly, how could she be sure the money she had seen Tess with was actually from the ransom? She needed a banknote from the batch Tess was paying into the bank. It wasn't likely she could get one from Tess because Tess wasn't inclined to engage with strangers and searching her bag had been nerve-racking enough let alone trying to lift a banknote…. looking back, it had been kind of exciting, though…. hmm…. how about Jill? Tess had paid Jill for the passports so Jill might have an incriminating note and it might be easier to get near her. Immediately, a plan leapt into Mary's mind.

"But I know Jill is on shift today because I saw her earlier walking through the park on her way to work." Back to Tess, then. It was a long shot but: "I could go up to Silverwood

Hall," Mary mused. Then: "No, there's no point. Gary will be running round preparing for the concert this evening. He won't let anything get in the way of that."

Mary pottered to the kitchen to make some tea, still thinking about the money. Assuming it was from the ransom, how had Tess come by it? Obviously, Charles had given it to her but Mary did not believe that Charles had the ability to plan the ransom pick-up. Think …. the person Andrew was looking for was an electronics expert who could wire a crane. And who knew about harnesses and was something of a risk-taker.… Alistair! Charles' partner Alistair with whom he had been friends for years! Ben's climbing mate Alistair! Ex-army Alistair probably knew about electronics and how to plan an operation. Ex-army Alistair that Ben's mother did not like!

It was perfect. She should tell Andrew. He could look into Charles' finances…. and that was where it all went wrong. Rachel had said Charles' business was doing better; well, if it was doing better, it was doing it without the help of ransom money because by Rachel's account the change in Charles' fortunes pre-dated the kidnapping. And the Armstrongs did not seem to be flashing the cash on a personal level. Maybe they had more sense. Because the fact was Tess had money, Mary had seen her with it. But Mary still could not believe that Tess would connive in the kidnap of Jared.

She could still suggest to Andrew that Alistair fitted the profile for the kidnapper and point out that Charles' business fortunes had improved. Or not. Put like that it sounded rather weak especially since the timing of the improvement was all wrong.

Mike had been looking into Charles' finances! She thought Mike. He floated in the air above her for just long enough to say: "Dodgy. Right dodgy," and disappeared, which was not much help.

Then again, it was a good thing he had not stayed. As sure as God made little apples, he would have said Alistair fitted the profile but so did Ben. Well, she had already put Ben on the list. If only for completeness.

How about following the money in the forward direction? Try to find out how Tess was getting it into her own account because she must be, she could not spend it otherwise. Once again, progress seemed to require making friends with Tess. About as much chance of that as fly over the moon.

She would visit Jill tomorrow. Meanwhile, she must be patient. Mary went to fetch her book but a loud 'ding' from the clock stopped her in her tracks. Mary jolted back to the real world. Gosh, was that the time? Ben was taking her to the theatre tonight.

Quickly, she showered and changed into a smart trouser suit and frilly blouse with little flowers on. A matching flower clipped in her hair completed the effect and only just in time; Ben was at the door, debonair as ever. They left straight away and Ben chatted enthusiastically about the air freight business all the way there.

Mary liked the theatre but she had not been to this particular one before. Usually, she went with her mother to the spanking new one on the other side of town because it was close to her mother's house and they would go for a meal beforehand and she would stay over and make a real event of it.

Ben and Mary walked along the rows looking for their seats which were in an aisle near the front about half way along. As yet, the row was almost empty so it was easy to sidle along. They sat looking through the programme and listening to the subdued hubbub around them. Mary gazed at the shabby red curtains, heavily looped and folded, at the ornate coat of arms centrally above them and at the dark cream painted walls with contrasting deep red rails high against the ceiling. Definitely, the place had seen better days but the harsh lighting did it no favours.

The theatre was filling up now and a middle-aged man began to make his way along the row, tripping clumsily over the feet of a lady who had done her best to angle her legs sideways out of the way and squeezed herself so far back into her seat that the handbag she clutched on her lap was wider than she was. She winced but immediately assured him it was fine, don't worry. He sat down next to Mary, spreading himself comfortably, apparently oblivious of the encroachment on Mary's space.

Ben glared at him and ever the gentlemen, changed places with her.

Straightaway, the lights began to fade and the hubbub changed to an urgent, excited whisper then silence. The seat on the other side of her remained empty. Good.

The curtains swung open to reveal a set so impressive the audience broke into applause. The play was set in the drawing room of a country house and the detail, the careful observation that had gone into its creation was truly amazing. Mary stared in admiration – mixed with a certain dawning realisation that the fireplace reminded her of something.

The colours.... the pattern.... it reminded her of the piece of painted wood she had found at Lower Meadow Hall.

Ben nudged her and whispered very quietly: "I know the bloke who did that. He has won loads of awards."

"Shh," said the middle-aged man and Ben relapsed into silence.

But Mike, who had suddenly appeared in the empty seat next to Mary, did not.

"Very nice," he said. "And I mean that. And fancy Ben knows the designer. Interested in the arts, is he?"

He knew she could not answer. Mike was just trying to needle her. And it was working; as the play progressed, he continued to comment on everything from the wardrobe to the performances to the writing and speculated as to what was probably going to happen next, punctuated with the occasional triumphant 'I told you so'.

Couldn't he shut up?

In the play, the anti-hero was leading up to a grand speech ending in threats as to what would happen to the family if his instructions were not obeyed. His final dramatic pose signalled the start of the interval and the curtains swept to a close.

"Drink?" inquired Ben and Mary gratefully accepted.

Keeping a close eye on the time and the length of the queue, they pushed their way to the bar and ordered two large glasses of wine.

"Are you enjoying the play?" asked Ben, looking at her closely.

"Fantastic," replied Mary.

"Sure? You seem a bit.... well.... distracted."

"No, really," Mary assured him looking around for Mike but he was nowhere to be seen. She elaborated just to prove she had been concentrating.

"I like that Martin Jones, he's very good, I've seen him on the television, and I reckon that girl playing the maid has a bright future. I don't think she's in luck in the play, though, I reckon that footman is just using her."

They returned to their seats and waited for the second half to begin. Mike was there waiting and he behaved no better than he had in the first half, in fact he was worse. About ten minutes in, Mary was appalled to see him up on the stage joining in with the actors. She slid down in her seat, earning a curious look from Ben. Determinedly, she pulled herself together, sat up, ignored Mike, smiled when the happy couple smiled and looked pained whenever complications arose. She squeezed Ben's hand at the final happy outcome and hung on to his arm all the way to the car.

Back at the flat, Mary complimented Ben on his choice of play; it had been very well done and kept them guessing right up to the last minute. She went to the kitchen to make a coffee, hissing 'Go away' at Mike in the process but he ignored her so all she could do was blank him while she chatted with Ben about climbing and laughingly admitted that whilst he had been bright and chipper the next day, she had walked like a zombie for a week.

Mary went over to the dresser and took out a small box wrapped in gift paper.

"For me?"

Inside was a pair of silver cuff-links shaped like aeroplanes.

Mary watched his reaction keenly.

"Do you like them?"

"I love them. Really, though, you didn't have to."

Mary thought of the times he had taken her out and of their visit to the children's hospice.

"I wanted to."

Mary had been intending to invite Ben to stay over but knowing Mike was around and in interfering mode put a stop to that. One last kiss then she made up an excuse and said a reluctant goodbye.

On arrival at her door there as a rattle and a clang and the door opposite was flung open.

"Ah, Mary, I thought I heard you. Could we have a word?"

A false smile was spread across the face of Mary's neighbour. Mary smiled weakly in return and raised her eyes to heaven. Ben beat a hasty retreat. Was it going to be the 'I'm sure it wasn't you but somebody….' or was she about to be roped into something?

"Sorry, must dash, later maybe." Mary scrabbled at her door then she was inside sighing with relief.

Closing the door, she went to find Mike and confront him about his behaviour.

"Oh, go on, you have to admit I was funny," he said and sitting in her flat without the pressure of Ben watching, she did have to admit that in retrospect yes, his antics on stage had been amusing.

"But that's not the point," she objected. "I told you before: back off. I'm not going to dump Ben to suit you. I don't know what you have against him…. you're jealous, aren't you?"

"I'm trying to protect you."

"Well, you can stop it. I don't need protecting. Anyway, I don't feel so much protected as stalked."

Mike looked wounded.

"Well?"

"All right; I admit that when we first met, I was just looking out for you but as I watched you, as I got to know you…. You're beautiful, resourceful, your heart is in the right place. I wish I had met someone like you – no, I wish I'd met you – years ago when…. before I died…. and then not died, of course."

He looked at her longingly.

"Mike, no. Don't look like that. You must realise we can never be a couple."

"Why couldn't we? Don't you love me?"

"Of course, I do. I don't know what I'd do without you. But as to being a couple, be sensible. You're not real or not alive at any rate. I would be the only person who knew you were there."

"Does it matter? So what if they think you're on your own as long as you're happy. I'm easy to have around," he wheedled. "You wouldn't even have to do my washing!"

In spite of the circumstances, Mary could not help being amused by his remark and as that strange quirky smile played around her lips, Mike felt more drawn to her than ever. But his were not the only feelings that mattered.

"It would never work. I need someone I can be seen with, who can go shopping with me, mow the lawn. I need…. Ben. We can grow old together…." She dared not say have children.

"However long we're together you will always be young to me."

There was a pause then Mike added: "We wouldn't be the first, you know. I heard some of the others gossiping about a ghost called Raphael who had a mortal lover. It would be twenty-five years ago now or thereabouts. They even had a child, a baby girl they named Destiny."

"Is that possible?" Mary was amazed.

"No. All I can think is – do you remember me saying you could see ghosts because you were born dead and that it happens occasionally? Well, Raphael left part of himself here when he died. His heart. It was taken for transplant."

"You mean anyone who donates organs…."

"I wouldn't think so. I'm guessing it's the same as with you: something that can happen occasionally."

"What happened to Raphael and his lover?"

"Raphael was never heard of again. I don't know who the mother was and I don't know what happened to Destiny, the records are sealed. The register doesn't even show if she's alive or dead."

"And you're suggesting we could be a couple. Don't you think that might be dangerous?" warned Mary.

"I haven't noticed any thunderbolts so far."

"Mike, can't you be content to be the big brother I never had? You make a very good one."

As soon as Mary said it, she realised it was far from the most sensitive thing she could have said. He had a sister – somewhere.

After a short silence Mike answered: "Big brothers look out for their little sisters. I may have fallen in love with you but that makes no difference. Speaking as your big brother, I wish you wouldn't see Ben. Whatever you may think, I have your best interests at heart."

That seemed like a good note on which to leave it.

Mary yawned. It was late.

"I can take a hint," said Mike.

"It wasn't, honestly."

"It's all right. You go to bed."

"I'm still not getting through," thought Mary as she lay staring at the ceiling. "But Mike wishes he had met me years ago. That was a lovely thing to say."

SUNDAY
DAY 64

After her usual Sunday lie-in, Mary had a quick breakfast and drove over to Jill's flat but it soon became apparent no-one was in. Jill must be on shift again. Oh well, she would go to Silverwood Hall; it might be a long shot but it was better than doing nothing.

Gary kissed her affectionately on both cheeks. Animatedly, he told her all about the re-decoration of the television room. Ever the perfectionist, he had insisted on matching the old skirting boards where damp had got in and putting side-lights that looked like candles to give an authentic touch. Most people would have cut corners to save money but Gary did it properly and excused himself that it impressed the relatives.

"Speaking of which, how is your mother?" Mary asked.

"Not too well at the moment, I'm afraid. It's nothing serious but these things wear her down at her age."

Pity. Mary had hoped to see the old lady but Gary made it clear that was out of the question. "She would love for you to come back when she's feeling better, though," he said. "She often talks about you; she says I was lucky to work with such nice people."

For her part she is lucky to have such an attentive son, thought Mary. She supposed he had always been like that at home but that they had only seen the picky, perfectionist side of him at work. It was funny how circumstance and context changed a man.

A thought struck her. Perhaps there was yet another side to Gary. Perhaps she should move him higher on her suspect list; he was spending a lot of money on Silverwood Hall. Possibly it was not a coincidence that Tess worked there. Maybe they were all in it together; whoever 'all' was.

With not being able to see Gary's mother and try to probe gently about children in the garden, it was starting to look like a wasted trip when an alarm sounded and Gary rushed off to investigate. Mary waited for him to return. And waited. And waited.

She saw an ambulance draw up at the door and wondered if she should offer her help but reasoned that she would probably be in the way. Perhaps she should go? Then again, perhaps not; what if the emergency were his mother and Gary returned to find a little note and no Mary? She would wait.

Ten more minutes and Gary returned. One of the older residents had had a fall but fortunately it was not too serious. Gary looked at Mary and dithered.

"I…. um…. I don't suppose you would help me write the report? It's just that Tess isn't here and you always were good at that sort of thing."

"Of course," Mary agreed.

She sat down at the computer in Tess's little ante-room, turned it on and waited. The screen flicked into life and the command prompt requested a password.

"Admin1," said Gary.

The report was neither long nor complicated but even so it went through four drafts before Gary was satisfied. He sighed a huge sigh and asked Mary if she would like a cup of tea.

"Yes, please," she agreed readily. She was parched.

As Gary headed out of the door, the computer flashed up a message asking if she wanted to confirm shutdown. It was too good an opportunity to miss. Quickly pulling a memory stick from her handbag, Mary went into 'Documents' and looked through the folders. Right at the top 'Accounts' caught her eye. That was what she wanted. The rest looked pretty unexciting but for completeness she also copied a folder called 'Archive.'

Gary had not yet returned from the kitchen. Back on the login screen, Mary noticed something: the computer hard drive had been partitioned into the area she had accessed to write the report and another area labelled 'Private.' She clicked the icon. The command prompt requested a password.

"Calm down," she told herself. "This is Gary we're talking about, a man of habit and little originality." She entered the password he had used at Bramwells and closing her eyes she pressed 'Enter.'

She was in. But it was not at all what she had expected. There were no secret files or incriminating emails, in fact, all Gary used the 'Private' section for was to go on dating websites. She would check 'Accounts' later but it appeared the only thing Gary was hiding was his embarrassment. Doubtless his mother would like to see him settled before she died and it must be hard for him to meet people.

Glancing over her shoulder, Mary shut down the computer and took a cheeky peep into Tess's desk. She opened the top drawer to find a sticky pot of perfume, an old sock, a chocolate bar and an assortment of pencils, ballpoint pens and tippex. Ugh! Mary shut it quickly. The bottom one was no better but in a different way; it was a mass of untidy papers that looked as though they were heading for the bin, probably dumped in a hurry one night when Tess did not have time to sort them out. Mary knew well enough from Bramwells that Gary demanded an empty desk policy. He himself was obsessively neat in his habits; the top of his desk clear and the drawers tidy to the point of being somewhat empty.

There was one interesting thing, though. On the top of the heap was a birthday card. Inside was a twenty- pound note. Quickly, Mary swapped it with one from her bag. What a stroke of luck! Against all the odds, she had one of Tess's banknotes.

"All I have to do now is establish whether it came from the ransom," she thought. "I can do that by obtaining a note from Jill and if the numbers are consecutive…. or nearly so…."

"Tea's up," Gary called cheerfully, coming through the door. By this time, Mary was sitting in the armchair looking a picture of innocence. And her heart had hardly given a flutter.

"Have you heard from Gemma and the gang?" she asked but he had not. She accepted another cup of tea and told him some anecdotes about work, knowing he would relate them to his mother and that they would make her chuckle.

It was time to go. Gary escorted her to Desert Tiger and Mary drove off still marvelling at the sense of freedom having a car gave her.

On the spur of the moment, she decided to stop by the hospital. There was a stall outside which sold fruit and flowers and as Mary paused to look, she became aware of a child standing nearby. A familiar child.

"Hello, little man," she said but he totally ignored her.

Then: "You again. I never forget a face." Clearly Mr Danesford was not pleased to see her.

"I only said 'hello'. I did not mean anything by it. You must be very proud. He's such a good-looking boy and so well-behaved. And it's a lovely age; what is he, about two?"

"Coming two-and-a-half. And yes, it is a lovely age. He was always a curious child, always into everything but now…."

Mr Danesford was the epitome of the proud father as he melted and boasted to Mary about his handsome, intelligent son and all the things he could do. They compared notes as to the best aspects of the various stages of growing up and when Mary suggested learning to sit up and play with toys on the floor, he chuckled fondly at the memory.

"They sit up then fall over sideways in slow motion. At least it gives you plenty of time to catch."

Much as Mary hated to admit that Andrew was right, it was impossible not to conclude that Mr Danesford had

274

watched Darren grow up and that he was not a recent addition to the family. Worse, Patrick Danesford seemed to be a likeable chap.

So, today had moved Gary up the list and then back down again while Mr Danesford bobbed around like a cork near the bottom. It wasn't good enough; she needed to make progress, real progress, before something terrible happened to Jared.

"Concentrate on the positive," thought Mary, "I have one of Tess's banknotes."

Mary went inside the hospital foyer and waited until she saw Mr Danesford leave. She had no need to go to the ward now in the hope of seeing them and perhaps gathering some snippet of information. The night was yet young, however, so Mary turned Tiger in the direction of her mother's. She owed Alice a visit.

"Mary, thank goodness you're here." Panic was evident in Alice's voice as she explained that the central heating had sprung a leak and there was water gushing onto the bedroom carpet.

"I just found it," she said. She had poked a tray under the pipe to catch the water but it was nowhere near enough.

"Why didn't you turn it off at the stopcock? …. Oh, never mind." Mary went delving under the sink in the kitchen while Alice found a number for an emergency plumber. And so another evening went by.

MONDAY
DAY 65

It was nice just to listen to Ryan bouncing around, thought Mary, while she instilled order into the chaos of paper that attracted itself to her desk like a magnet and to end the day with a sense of having achieved something. If only she could tidy the rest of her life so easily.

The radio made a crackling noise and went dead. Mary picked it up and increased the volume – except it was not the volume knob she turned but the one next to it that decided the channel. Oops. She was about to adjust it back to the site frequency when a voice came over: "Better get back here quick, comes Pinky and Perky." So, the subbies were communicating privately on a different frequency.

Mary giggled. She knew who they meant: Pete and Josh, the Safety Manager. Mary and Ryan rushed to the window to try to see what was going on and sure enough, Pete and Josh were striding across the muddy site, their trousers tucked into thick cream-coloured thermal socks rolled over the tops of their safety boots. Both were middle-aged and a little tubby and the addition of padded hi-vis coats only served to complete the effect. Pinky and Perky. They turned the corner out of sight.

"Wonder which one is which," mused Ryan stuffing a biscuit into his mouth.

"Wonder if they know what the subbies call them."

"Bound to. You can't keep anything secret around here."

The minutes passed and the coffee was drunk before Pete finally reappeared and as he and Josh passed the window, they heard Josh say: ".... and hanging off the b***y roof with no fall arrest system. I'll have his guts for garters when I get my hands on him."

"And I'll have those radios," added Pete.

"What's semaphore for Pinky and Perky?" Ryan asked Mary, anticipating future methods of communication if Pete took away the subbies' radios. He checked behind him before making a few suggestions. "Or Morse code?" Because there would always be an early warning system just as certainly as there would be another blitz on health and safety, starting now.

TUESDAY
DAY 66

Mary had not been at work long the next day when the phone rang. Wretched thing. She scrabbled furiously in her handbag. Miserable object would probably stop ringing before she found it. It had to be here somewhere…. Got it. It was Ben. But when Mary answered, it was not Ben's voice on the other end but a woman.

"Is that Mary Chadwick? This is Nurse Kendrick. I've been asked to call you by a friend of yours, Ben Mackay. He has had an accident."

Ten minutes later, Mary was rushing to the hospital.

She was directed to a room off one of the main wards and there was Ben, lying in bed with bandages on his hands and round his head. His body was covered with the bedding so she had no idea if there were more injuries hidden beneath it.

"Oh God! Oh no! Will he be all right?"

But even Nurse Kendrick's assurance that it looked worse

than it was did not do much to comfort Mary. She sat down quietly in a chair by the bed.

"What happened?"

"Car crash," Ben replied sleepily.

At least he seemed to possess all his faculties.

Mary sat with him as he drifted in and out of consciousness.

"Well, thank goodness you're going to be all right or so the doctors tell me. Was anyone else involved?"

"No. Well…. no." He drifted off again then briefly opened his eyes. "I could have sworn…. but that's silly."

"What?" asked Mary.

"Well…. I thought I saw a man standing in the middle of the road. He appeared out of nowhere. Right in front of me. I crashed because I swerved to avoid him. But there was no-one there."

Ben drifted back to sleep.

Mary felt helpless sitting beside him, unable even to hold his hand because of the bandages. As she watched over him, her mind was racing. A man who was not really there. Surely not? Mike wouldn't, would he? And anyway, Ben couldn't see him. Well, not usually but Mike could have chosen to make himself visible….

The room was warm and in spite of everything, Mary found she was starting to feel sleepy herself. Coffee. Yes, definitely coffee. She stumbled to the café area where a cheerful volunteer served her a large cappuccino.

When she returned to the ward, it was to see Mike bending over Ben, studying him closely. He had his back to her but something about him made her uneasy.

"Mike?"

Startled, Mike turned towards her and she was shocked by his appearance. His eyes were black pools with flecks of fire burning from deep in his skull. Everything about him seemed blacker, even his hair. He seemed tense, predatory.

"What are you doing here?"

"Oh…. I…. well…. I came to see how Ben was."

He had seemed to relax back to his old self a little when she spoke but as he turned to gaze at Ben once more, a cloud seemed to descend around him, encompassing the bed, drawing light and substance from the room to create oppression and darkness, its shadow visible over the floor around them.

Quickly, Mary called his attention.

"He'll be fine. How did you know about the accident?"

"Chance. Pure chance."

It was the kind of answer that could have been automatic, throw-away but it was not; he had had to pause and think before replying and that was enough to dispel the cloud.

Where the room had seemed to compress itself around Mike and become less substantial at the edges, now it flowed evenly and Mike disturbed it not at all. His hair and his eyes were brown again although the eyes lacked their usual warmth and the friendly smile was missing from his lips.

Mary had been intending to go but now she was reluctant to leave Ben alone. She considered asking Alice to come and sit with him but dismissed the idea; Alice could not see Mike and the nurses would likely throw her out anyway on the grounds it was not necessary for anyone to stay.

But Mary could not escape her suspicions over what might have caused the crash and what Mike was doing at the hospital. Accusingly she asked: "Ben said he saw a man standing in the road. Was that you?"

Silence.

"Did you make yourself visible? What were you trying to do? Ben could have died. Or was that what you wanted? …. Do you know anything at all about the crash? …. Mike, you have to tell me!"

Mike looked guilty and finally blurted out: "The truth is, I don't remember. I was following him but it isn't like it is for you, time and space are different and I lost him. I don't deny I was there, I wanted…. I don't know…. it's all a blur. He was in the car and I was there by the side of the road…. in the road…. I don't know. I remember him hitting the tree and them bringing him here."

"Implying you didn't do it on purpose. Why should I believe you? You were trying to harm him again just now, weren't you?"

"No!"

"It looked that way."

"No!"

Then after a pause: "He gets to me, Mary, I don't deny. Perhaps you should take me away from here in case I do something I don't mean to do."

Mary thought that was a wonderful suggestion.

"Come along," she replied. "We'll go back to my flat, there's nothing I can do here. But you have to promise to stay with me, no sneaking off."

"Promise."

He held out his arm for her to take and walked her slowly to the door. Normally, she would have leaned against him, her head on his arm, but not today.

"Bet you couldn't find your way out of here without my help anyway."

The familiar humour was returning and as she looked at his face, the old Mike seemed to be back.

Politely, she refused his offer to 'influence' the parking meter in spite of the huge charge and liberated Desert Tiger from the car park. Home at last. The flat was welcoming if a little chilly but Mary did not turn on the heater; she must not fall asleep.

She made some coffee and brought Mike some ice cream to make sure he did not run out of energy and have some kind of fade-out. She wanted him where she could see him.

"Is it because of me you don't like Ben?"

"No." His tone was patient and grave. Softly, as though in acknowledgement he was talking to himself, he added: "But I wish you wouldn't go out with him."

"We've been through this I don't know how many times. If you won't tell me why you don't like him you can't expect me to drop him." Quietly, she added: "He's nice."

Mike's expression disagreed but he said nothing.

She curled up on the sofa and wrapped her legs around him. If she should happen to doze, she wanted to feel if he tried to leave although she did not think he would. Mike was many things but he had never given Mary cause to distrust him when he had given his word.

"Stay a while."

Inevitably, Mary fell asleep.

When she roused, Mike was still there. Mary was pleased but the nervousness she had felt when they first met had returned. Was he dangerous after all? Had he tried to kill Ben? Mary stared into space. No, he couldn't be evil, he wouldn't have been allowed to return to earth, he wouldn't have been granted privileges, he would have been sent to an entirely different fate.

But he had fallen in love with her. Had he become evil since his return? One thing was for sure: he had been up to something when Ben crashed.

Mike insisted her to bed where she slept fitfully but each time she woke, he was sitting watching over her.

WEDNESDAY
DAY 67

He was still there in the morning and stayed to breakfast although he pronounced bacon sandwiches indigestible and stuck to his usual ice cream.

"Who is Ellen?" he asked.

Obviously, she had been talking in her sleep.

"A childhood friend."

Mike looked at her quizzically.

"She disappeared. It's a long time ago."

"A childhood friend," he echoed thoughtfully. "You were the other girl in the Ellen Matthews case! Poor Mary. No wonder this kidnapping is eating at you."

"It has raked up a few bad memories, I confess," Mary agreed. Then: "Mike?"

It was the perfect opportunity so why was she hesitating? Mary took the plunge. "Mike, is Ellen still alive?"

Too late, it occurred to her that he would not know off-hand and finding out was an excuse for him to leave.

"Mary, I promise I'll come straight back. You have my word."

The desperate pleading on her face when she had asked if Ellen was alive could only leave Mike highly relieved to be able to report moments later that she was.

Joy swept over Mary but was immediately tempered with regret.

"All this time. I should have gone looking."

"What could you have done? The investigation is still open and the police have not found her."

He was not wrong but it did not help.

"Help me, Mike. Find her for me."

"You know I can't. I told you already that I don't have access to information on the whereabouts of mortals. Some of the Senior Ghosts do but I don't."

"Ask them. Please."

"Mary, I can't. You don't just turn up on a Senior Ghost and ask a favour like that. The rules are there for a reason. How could I justify asking for special treatment for you? And for what purpose? Interference. No. You have my sympathy and I would expect you would have theirs but it makes no difference."

It felt like a rebuke even if it was not meant that way. Finally, she had asked the question but what had she in return? Disappointment. The only comfort was Ellen was alive. But where? And was she happy?

"Once again, I don't even know where to start looking," thought Mary. "Oh, why couldn't I have been more help at the time? And afterwards, why couldn't I remember his face?"

One day she would find Ellen but not today.

Jared, however, was another matter. The trail was not yet cold.

"Ellen's time will come. Meanwhile I *will* find Jared," Mary vowed silently to herself.

After a quick shower, Mary returned to the hospital to see Ben. Mike declined to accompany her and there was nothing she could do but let him go and hope he kept out of trouble.

Ben was still dopy but obviously improving because he was starting to fret. Someone needed to be at the airfield to process the month-end invoices and make sure the money came in, plus they were expecting a big, new contract and it was important that someone was there to answer the phone and receive their guests. Jack would deal with the practical side such as keeping the planes in the air on schedule and fuel deliveries and so on but Ben was concerned about his diplomatic skills when it came to buttering up new clients.

"You couldn't take a few days holiday and help out could you, Mary?" pleaded Ben.

"Of course," she said and it was settled.

Mary was so concerned about Ben that it did not occur to her until later that this would be a marvellous opportunity to snoop around the airfield.

She called Pete who was happy let her have a little time to visit Ben and mind the business: "But don't be away too long, you know you're the only one the printer condescends to work for."

"Come along," she said to Desert Tiger. "Nice mud and bumps and all the things you were made to enjoy."

Jack was surprised to see her because Ben had not had the energy to warn him but he was an amiable sort and welcomed her in. Truth be told, he was glad of her help. He would much rather be flying and tinkering with the planes than doing paperwork and had already shuffled it from one side of the desk to the other and back again before weighting it down with a spanner, all except for three items which were Urgent and he had therefore put aside to look at later. Much later.

The office had been created by partitioning off one end of the hangar. There was another office, a meeting room, a bathroom and a kitchen which even boasted a dishwasher. Mary got stuck into the paperwork straight away and after watching her for a few minutes, Jack sighed contentedly and went outside.

It did not take long for Mary to decide there was nothing suspicious to be found in the office. She needed to engineer an excuse to look around the other two hangars. She also needed to remain near the phone.

All afternoon it did not ring. The day was nearly over, the invoices were mostly done but still Mary could not move from the office. And she had spotted a bunch of keys hanging tantalisingly by the whiteboard. Big keys, the sort of keys that probably opened the door of a hangar for instance.

D-ring, d-ring, d-ring. Finally, the phone call Mary had been waiting for.

"Astrapoint Aviation, how may I help?"

Her tone was bright and friendly. Ben's new clients were disappointed that Ben was not there and would not be around until the end of the week but Mary assured them that there was no reason to delay their trip to inspect the facilities on offer, all the information they had asked for was prepared and Ben would come in, if only briefly, to sign the papers on

Friday if they were happy with what they saw. They would come tomorrow then, at around ten thirty. Mary knew that Jack was not going out until lunchtime and would be on hand to answer technical questions whilst she, having familiarised herself with the deal, could guide them around the portfolio and serve refreshments.

Now for a quick look in that hangar. But it was not to be. Jack came in and having apprised himself of the arrangements for the morning suggested that she could go now, he would lock up.

Desert Tiger roared obediently into life and they headed back across the airfield to civilisation. Mary called on Ben who was rather sleepy but definitely improving. He gazed at her lovingly as she assured him that everything was going fine and clumsily pressed her hand to his face.

"Thank you. For everything."

THURSDAY
DAY 68

Mary woke at her usual time. She was tempted to snuggle down for an extra ten minutes but: "Better not," she decided. Ten minutes had a habit of becoming half an hour and she did not want to be late.

Mary dropped her bag on the desk and since there was no new paperwork and Jack was nowhere to be seen, she picked up the bunch of keys and set off for the hangars. First to find the right key…. well, it was not any of those three. She was concentrating hard, squinting at the keys trying to see if there was a make on any of them that she could match to the lock when a heavy hand fell on her shoulder.

"Having trouble?"

Mary jumped in surprise. "Oh, Jack. No…. I was just wanting a look around the hangar before we show our guests the facilities available to them."

Jack took the keys from her, chose a surprisingly small and insignificant looking one and opened the door. "There you are. Totally empty. Loads of space."

The hangar was, indeed, vast and totally empty.

"How about that other one?" asked Mary.

"Mostly empty. I think they'll have enough space here, though," replied Jack starting back towards the office.

Mary stood her ground. "I'd like to see anyway if that's all right," she said. "There will be other clients after all."

"Okay," he replied easily, went over to the hangar and opened the door.

Hangar Three was a little smaller than Hangar Two but still vast and as Jack had said, it was mostly empty. No smuggled people, no drugs, no gold bullion, no rum, no cigarettes.... So much for Mike's bitchiness about how Ben and Jack really made their money. And whilst on the subject of things that could generate easy cash – no Jared.

Hangar Three was not, however, totally empty: there was a large pile of painted wood in the corner. Mary walked closer and saw a staircase and a cream and gold fireplace, both made of thin wood. There was also wallpaper, a mirror and a plywood door.

"Ben is storing it for a friend who builds stage sets," explained Jack.

Mary remembered the trip to the theatre, the fragment she had found at Lower Meadow Hall and the expressions on the faces of Charles and Alistair when she had showed it to them. Ben's friend must have stored his sets at the Hall before the Hall burned down and before Ben went into business with Jack. Strange they should react that way, though.

"I was thinking of storage as something you could offer," said Mary. "Or maybe find a furniture maker or someone like that who could have a workshop and who would need a lot of cheap space to display what he had made."

"Good idea," replied Jack. "We shall have to get you on board."

That seemed to exonerate Ben. No, wait, there was one possible hiding place left.

"Could I take a look in the old control tower?" asked Mary. "Is the equipment still in there? It must be fascinating."

"The equipment is mostly gone. And you don't want to go poking around there, it's not safe. Anyway, time to go, I should have thought."

He was right: it was time to set things out ready for their guests. Jack got the projector working while Mary put out a little buffet on the table at the end.

"Wow," observed Jack, tongue- in-cheek. "Matching cups and everything."

But really, he was nervous that today it must be him who gave the all-important talk. Sensibly, he put up Ben's slides but did not try to be Ben. Instead, he told anecdotes about his trips and directed their guests' attention to the handouts they had in front of them containing brochures about the company with photographs and testimonials and costs. It seemed to go down well. Jack and Mary chatted with them about their business over the nibbles and then they departed with cheery waves all round.

Jack, visibly relieved, went out to his precious plane. Mary cleared up and waited. Soon, she heard the engines roar into life and went outside to watch as it rose into the sky. Good. Now she could visit the control tower.

This turned out to be one occasion, however, when it would have been a good idea to listen to (Jack's) advice. The control tower was semi-derelict and very dirty. Mary held a handkerchief over her nose, coughing as the stale dust clogged her lungs. She shone her torch around but could not see much from the doorway and had to clamber over all sorts of junk in order to get far enough inside for a proper look. And having done so there was nothing to see; well, no contraband or tiny kidnap victims at any rate. Mary returned to the office wiping cobwebs out of her hair and reminding herself that finding nothing was a good thing. The downside was that she was running out of ideas about where Jared could be hidden.

Mary left early to visit Ben. He was looking much better and could even wiggle his fingers. "See. The signature might be wonky but I'll sign that contract tomorrow, no trouble."

FRIDAY
DAY 69

Mary waited what seemed like an age for the doctor to do his rounds and discharge Ben from hospital. She took him to his house to bathe and change then on to work to meet the new clients to sign the deal. Running on adrenaline, he livened up considerably for the duration of their visit but it was obvious to Mary he was still far from well.

Business concluded, she insisted him into Tiger and took him home.

"Could we stop at the garage?" he asked.

"No," replied Mary. "Your car will be ready when it's ready. You can't drive it yet anyway."

Mary bustled round cooking a meal – 'the first decent food I've had in three days' – and stayed until evening by which time Ben was growing sleepy.

"I don't mind staying. I can make up a bed on the sofa," she offered but accepted Ben's protestations that it was not necessary. Now that Ben was on the mend, she had time to worry about what Mike was doing and she felt uneasy.

Mary checked that Ben had taken his pills and that the phone was beside the bed, kissed him tenderly and let herself out.

She should call her on mother. Or not. Alice would understand Mary was busy what with Ben's accident. Mary went home.

Although Mike was so much in her thoughts, he did not appear. Deliberately, she called him but with no result. Unable to rest she turned on the television hoping for distraction and fell asleep in front of a gripping tale of…. something or other… still wondering about Mike.

Mary need not have worried; Mike had his own problems. He had been about to set off on one of his regular visits to the hospital when he felt himself being pulled in another direction. Not just pulled but tugged and hard. When Mary called him, for instance, there was a gentle feeling of wafting through the air and he could resist and ignore her if he wanted to. This, however, was like being propelled through treacle; he felt his features distorting and he was powerless to resist.

Then it was over. Mike counted his arms and legs and found he was intact and sitting in a comfortable armchair in a shabby room cluttered with furniture. A woman sat opposite.

"And how are you, young man?" she asked looking straight at Mike. He looked confused.

"Yes, you. I can see you…. the question is: what to do about you. Time for some answers, I think. What have you been up to?" It was Mme Delphine.

Silence.

"Now that will not help you at all," she scolded. "You would be better to cooperate. I do not sense any real evil in you but there is something…. powerful emotion – but then you would not be here otherwise…. recklessness, yes recklessness and…. wait – grief." She looked deep into his eyes and her gaze was almost painful. "Revenge."

She stood up and went over to poke the fire. Mike sat rooted to the chair, unable to move. He was glad she was not staring at him anymore but he still felt peculiar. Mme Delphine pushed an old kettle onto the hotplate and prepared some herbal tea.

"Drink that," she ordered. "You will feel better. And then I advise you to do some thinking. If you carry on like this it will not end well. A little repentance might be in order."

Mike found his voice. "I don't know what you mean."

"Yes, you do. You are skating on thin ice. You do not have sufficient control of your emotions. You desire to protect but your desire grows tentacles that reach outward to threaten and to possess."

Her face took on a wistful expression. "I remember another such as you. He was handsome and clever. He, too, allowed himself to love…. and to hate."

A young man with a shock of black, curly hair and black eyes hung in the air next to them but only for a moment.

Mike started. Cautiously, he inquired: "What happened to him?"

"He was cast out," replied Mme Delphine.

"But I just saw him," objected Mike.

"You saw a shadow," said Mme Delphine sadly. She shook herself.

"You know the rules. Once you have passed you cannot return except as an observer. You may not change the future. Be careful your interpretation of this rule is not too creative.

"And a word of warning concerning another rule you seem to be having trouble with: No information about the Other Realm is to be communicated to mortals – including and especially you may not confirm its existence. If you draw Mary too far into your world she must stay there. You know this."

"You know about the Other Realm. You're still here."

"I was born this way. It is my destiny."

"It could be hers."

"Perhaps, but it would be unwise to test that theory. What will be will be but only in its own good time."

Mme Delphine gave the fire another poke.

"Already you have given Mary a glimpse of the other side. You risk her life."

"She could see ghosts when she was a child. I didn't do it."

"She was persuaded it was imagination. You tell her otherwise. You help her in her quest by giving her information."

"Fate might intervene to render it inaccurate or unhelpful. It isn't proof. And what about you? You foretell the future."

"And there are many who call me a charlatan."

"So, how are we different?"

"You talk of registers. You talk of Raphael and of my daughter."

Mike began to panic. "Then how come Mary hasn't passed?"

"Clearly, she has not finished playing her part in the mortal world."

Mike shuddered. "I shouldn't have told Mary the things I did. I have to make it right."

But there was a part of him that would prefer to say nothing and let events run their course.

Mme Delphine nodded knowingly.

That was it. All over. Mme Delphine had said what she wanted to say and now she was letting him go.

The journey back was not as bad as the outward one but Mike still felt vaguely odd and had to rest for a week.

SATURDAY
DAY 70

Usually, Mary would get up late on a Saturday but today she had things to do. First, she sent Ben a message asking how he was and promising to call later but 'Much better. No need to fuss' came back straight away. That was a relief: having told Charles she had a friend who wanted a new kitchen that day when she had gone out spying on him and Alistair, Mary had arranged for them to come to her own flat to quote for the 'work' at their earliest opportunity and she was reluctant to cancel. Who knew when they would next be free?

However, knowing Charles and Alistair would recognise her, Mary needed someone else to play host. Mary had not seen Gemma since the wedding. Now that she was back from honeymoon, Mary could not wait to hear all about it and Gemma could not wait to tell her. Sun-drenched islands were not Mary's cup of tea but when they had spoken on the phone, Gemma had described the scenery as 'knock-out' and the rainforest as 'amazing,' although she had, of course, found plenty of time to lie on the beach. Mary had seen films on the television and she wished that one day she might see the rainforest herself. If Gemma was impressed then that only made her wish harder; it must be worth it.

Mary's plan was that shortly before Charles and Alistair were due, Mary would receive a call to say that her mother had had a minor fall. Unable to contact Charles, she would ask Gemma to let him in for her. Meanwhile, unbeknownst to Gemma, Mary would lurk around outside the window and listen to the conversation in the hope of finding out more about Charles' character and motivations, similarly Alistair.

"I'm surprised at the landlord leaving it all to you," observed Gemma.

"The builders have a strict brief. There's no need for him to be present whilst collecting initial quotes. He'll short-list the favourites and take it from there himself," explained Mary.

The plan started well. Charles measured up for new doors and worktops as instructed but sucked his teeth over the supporting frames. He would do what he was asked to do but he wouldn't want the client wasting money and really, complete replacements would be better. They would build them from scratch, much cheaper than going to a kitchen shop and twice as good.

"Perhaps you could quote for both options," suggested Gemma.

It was time for Alistair to play his part.

"Do you mind if I use your loo?" he asked.

"Go ahead," replied Gemma, directing him to the bathroom. She hoped Mary would not mind.

Alistair soon returned. "If Miss could find a little more money, it would make a big difference if we were to put a slightly longer window in there," he suggested. "Apart from making it brighter, you would be able to use the window sill for bottles of shampoo and so on. Think about it."

Gemma began to say it was not up to her but interrupted by a crash from outside the window, she stopped. Charles looked outside: oops. Mary might have prevented Gemma from saying the wrong thing but she was not quite fast enough sprinting round the corner.

Her mind was racing. The best thing to do, she decided, was to turn up on the doorstep. After all, this was her friend's flat, her friend that wanted a new kitchen so why shouldn't she visit?

Gemma opened the door but before she had a chance to speak, Mary beat her to it.

"Hi, Gemma. I just fell over some kid's ride-on tractor someone left outside the kitchen window. Ouch." She hobbled inside rubbing her shin. "I need to sit down."

Mary made for the living room leaving Gemma to show Charles and Alistair out, maintaining the impression it was she and not Mary who lived in the flat. On the way past, Charles glared at her; clearly, he had not forgotten her since their last meeting, had not forgotten about her producing the piece of wood from Lower Meadow Hall. Equally clearly, he was not the type to forgive and forget. Mary watched as he stamped off. She could not help thinking it was a rather strong reaction. Why did it matter that Ben's friend had been storing his stage sets at the Hall?

Gemma returned bearing cups of tea.

"You were quick. Is your mother all right?"

"False alarm," replied the now magically recovered Mary. She clicked her tongue. "Those two, I don't know. Talk about maximising the job. There's nothing wrong with the frames of the cupboards that I can see and as to the bathroom window…."

But it was the look that Charles had given her that really struck her. What had she ever done to him except show him a little piece of painted wood?

SUNDAY
DAY 71

Did Jill work every weekend? Mary exhaled her frustration and drove back to her flat but she did not go in; instead, she sat drumming her fingers on the steering wheel. She could not confirm her theory about the ransom money like this but Charles was definitely freaked out about something. He had ruined a young life but what had he done? Was he a danger to Jared (assuming he knew where he was)?

And how much longer did Mary have to find the boy? It was two weeks since she had upset the orb; surely it must be safe by now to consult it again?

She took out the card Mme Delphine had given her and programmed the address into her satnav.

Mme Delphine's house was easy to spot. The quaint old timber-framed cottage with a gypsy caravan in the garden could have come from a picture in a story book.

"Hello, my dear." Mme Delphine ushered Mary into the front room.

Dark oak furniture and heavy velvet curtains made the room even dimmer than the low ceilings dictated whilst the lamps that were dotted around failed to dent the shadows and black cats weaved their way through books and ornaments on every surface.

"Do not mind my little ones." Mme Delphine indicated a chair by the table in the middle of the room. "Come. Sit."

She collected her crystal and placed it in the centre of the table.

"You want to know how much time you have."

Mme Delphine took Mary's hands and held them over the orb then she placed them on the table.

"Concentrate."

Obediently, Mary stared into the crystal.... and saw nothing. Automatically, she leaned forward, willing something to appear.

"Do not touch," Mme Delphine warned.

Then: "One hundred! I see the number one hundred!" exclaimed Mary excitedly.

She continued to gaze into the crystal ball. All of a sudden, a spider appeared. It grew bigger and bigger until it filled the whole orb. Its eyes shone with a brilliant red light and it clawed at the glass trying to get out, fangs outstretched.

"No!" screamed Mary and recoiled, shaking.

Mme Delphine waved her own hands over the orb and the vision faded.

As they shared a pot of Mme Delphine's herbal tea, one of the cats came over and sat on Mary's lap. She stroked it absent-mindedly.

"Until I broke the connection when I consulted Mme Delphine at the fete," reasoned Mary to herself, "the orb was showing the pages of a calendar falling and there were a lot of them whirling round inside. Now it tells me 'one hundred'. It must mean one hundred days, it must."

"Does that help you, my dear?" inquired Mme Delphine.

"Oh yes. Thank you."

She continued to stroke the cat.

"I have one hundred days to save Jared, presumably starting from the day he was snatched," she whispered quietly in its ear. "I wonder why one hundred. Is it significant in some way?"

Mary nearly fell off her chair in surprise as the cat replied: "Only that as things stand there is space in the Spite Brigade's diary. And it has a certain ring to it, don't you think?"

MONDAY
DAY 72

Mary's thoughts were far from work as she entered the site cabin the following day.

"One hundred," she muttered under her breath. "That leaves twenty-eight."

"Twenty-eight what?" asked Dan, moving aside so Mary could join them at the window.

"Oh, nothing."

Mary peered out but could see nothing unusual.

"The groundworkers were getting behind so their boss has come to show them how it's done," Dan explained. Mary was no wiser.

Pete chimed in.

"See that one there, in the middle, slightly stooping? Notice anything?"

Mary did not.

"He's eighty-one!" continued Pete triumphantly. "He believes in leading by example. By the end of the day, he'll be fresh as a daisy having done a hard day's work and the young-uns will be flat on their backs from keeping up with him. You see."

Outside, the hours passed and work was progressing nicely but: "I can't see him. Where is he?" asked Pete.

"Gone for the dumper," replied Ryan.

"He doesn't have a card to drive it," said Pete. "Too stubborn to get one, which means he isn't allowed to drive it on site."

"It's his dumper and he has probably been driving it for the last fifty years," observed Minty.

"Doesn't matter. We can't risk an accident and him with no card." The speaker was Josh.

"Are you going to tell him, or shall I?" Pete's question was rhetorical. They both reached for their coats; there was safety in numbers.

"It's not really a problem," Dan told Mary when they had gone. "The old man is formidable but very polite and well-mannered and he knows the rules."

"It's a shame though," said Mary. "Poor chap."

They went back to what they were doing and waited for Pete's words to come true, which they did. By the end of the day the lads looked crashed but not so the stooping figure making for the gate at a controlled run ahead of them.

* * *

Mary felt bad for neglecting Ben over the weekend but he had not seemed to mind. 'It's good for you to see Gemma, you don't need to hang around an old crock like me all the time' he had said. Mary's trip to Mme Delphine having upset her mood, she had made an excuse for not calling on Sunday but: "I must go tonight," she resolved.

To Mary's surprise, Ben's once more immaculate sports car stood outside his house and Ben himself seemed considerably improved.

"I shall return to work tomorrow," he announced.

"Don't overdo it," Mary warned.

"I'll be fine. I had a good rest over the weekend."

They spent the evening cuddled on the sofa. It was the most relaxed Ben had seen Mary for some time although he could not know that the reason was Mike's continued absence.

TUESDAY
DAY 73

Of course, Mike's absence was a mixed blessing. It was good that he was not getting in the way and had not tried to harm Ben again but Mary would have liked to know what he was doing. At work she wondered, and where normally she would have concentrated harder in case that caused him to appear, now she made no effort to discipline her thoughts. At home she called him but still he did not come.

Ben, however, did. Mary opened the door to see a large bunch of beautiful flowers then Ben's face appeared from behind them.

"A thank you gift," he explained. "You did a wonderful job, M, in fact Jack is still singing your praises. You took a lot of strain off him and impressed him with your business acumen to boot. He said I was a lucky man."

Mary invited him in but: "Just for a moment," he said. "I can't stop but there was something I wanted to ask you. I was thinking of taking a little trip to Rome and I thought we might go together."

Mary gasped. Her lips parted and her eyes widened. How wonderful. Then she looked doubtful.

She had only twenty-seven days left to find Jared. How could she relax? How could she excuse a vacation?

Then there was the fact she had only just taken time off to fill in for Ben at Astrapoint. And there was the problem that Mike's jealousy was likely to be aroused by a scheme like this.

"You have lots of holiday left," Ben encouraged her.

"But it's such short notice. And I've only just had time off."

"Pull a sickie for once in your life. I'm only talking about a long weekend. It would be good for both of us. Call it recuperation for me and a well-deserved rest for you."

Mary considered. She didn't like to pull a sickie but Rome was very tempting. Mike seemed to be away and even if he appeared, Ben would be with her and therefore safe.

But what about Jared? Twenty-seven days was quite a long time…. wasn't it? Or was it? She must not let Jared down. He must not become another Ellen.

Nor did she want to upset Ben, who was still standing there looking pleadingly at her.

"Come on, M, say 'yes'."

"Could I let you know?" Mary threw herself into his arms. "Don't think I'm not grateful, it's a lovely idea but…. I'll let you know, all right?"

* * *

In bed that night, Mary thought about Jared. Before Ben's accident, she had formed a plan to see whether Jill had any banknotes from the ransom. The plan must be put into practise – now. Right now. That is to say, tomorrow.

After that, Mary would decide what to do next. Then she would decide about Rome.

Not taking into account Mike's opinion. Mind you, thinking about it, it was over a week since their argument. Had he got the point? Was he backing off?

Mary thought of their last conversation. This Destiny girl sounded intriguing. Perhaps she had special powers. If so, she might be able to help find Jared; she would certainly be a useful person to know. But finding her would be as big a challenge as finding Jared himself.

"Oh no, you don't." As Mary drifted into sleep, Mike, who had been standing by the wall watching her, read her thoughts. He stepped over to the bed and placed his fingers on her forehead, probing, searching.

Ah, here it was, the memory of his account of Raphael and his love. Mike screwed his eyes shut and transmitted a pulse of energy down through his fingers and into Mary's mind. It travelled to its target like a lighted fuse and the memory burned up in a brilliant silver flash.

He should wipe the Spite Brigade, too. Again, Mike probed her mind but drew back. It was too soon: Mary needed that memory. And it was not self-contained. He must trust her and hope his superiors would do the same.

WEDNESDAY
DAY 74

Time to visit Jill.

"Please don't be on duty this evening," Mary prayed. "Not again."

Good; her luck was in. The curtains were open and she could see Jill moving around in the corner maisonette. Mary took a deep breath, walked up the path and knocked on the door. When Jill opened it, she was already holding up a picture of a cat she had downloaded from the internet and beginning her speech. She stopped.

"Gosh, hello, I didn't realise it was you."

It took Jill a moment to place Mary as Ben's visitor at the hospital but Mary had thought it wise to make the introduction up front rather than have Jill gradually realise as the charade went on.

"You've lost your cat you say?"

"Yes. I've been out looking most evenings and today I saw her run into the garden here and I wondered if I might have a look around."

"Of course. I'll come and help."

Not surprisingly, for all their poking under bushes and calling, Muffin did not appear. Mary looked suitably downcast.

"Come on in and have a cup of tea," invited Jill and soon Mary was sitting in a comfortable chair in Jill's living room. Her eyes darted all round until she fixed on an ornate box on the sideboard. Next to it was a photograph that had been laid flat so the image was not visible. She tip-toed across the room and looked into the kitchen; Jill was pouring boiling water into a teapot.

Quickly, Mary went over to the sideboard. The photograph was of Jill and Henry. She picked up the box. It was one of those puzzle boxes with a secret mechanism to open it. Fortunately, Mary had helped out in an antique shop as a Saturday job when she was a teenager so she had it open in a trice.

Inside was a pile of notes and underneath, a collection of gold rings and assorted jewellery. Hastily, Mary took the top two banknotes and replaced them with notes from her pocket. It only took a moment but Mary's heart was hammering. Wait, there was something else: a piece of folded paper had been tucked into the felt that lined the lid. Deftly, Mary extracted it. It was a cutting from a newspaper report in the County Times: 'Tragic Crash in Castle Street.' It was about Anne-Marie Danesford's accident – Mary recognised the picture of the mangled car immediately – and on the back was scrawled a telephone number. Time was pressing and Mary's hands were shaking as she hurriedly memorised the number and replaced the cutting.

A voice from the doorway said: "What do you think you are doing?" and Mary jumped out of her skin. She turned guiltily towards Jill, the box in her hands.

"I was just looking at your box. It's lovely. My mother had one just like it when I was little. It's a musical box, isn't it? What tune does it play?"

Jill put the tea-tray on the table and took the box from her.

"It doesn't. It's not a musical box. There, you pour. Help yourself to biscuits."

The box was a safe hiding place that Mary could not possibly have worked out in so short a time (if ever) but even so, Jill turned her back so that Mary could not see what she was doing and checked it over. It was exactly as it should be; there were no signs of anyone having fiddled with it. The contents were all there undisturbed. Still a little wary, Jill sat down.

Mary was still fussing about her cat. Apparently. In fact, her thoughts were elsewhere. She would have liked to ask about Henry but with the photograph turned over she could not think of a lead-in.

There was a lull in the conversation.

"How is your friend who had the accident?" asked Jill politely.

"Ben? Oh, he's fine now, thank you. It seems he bounces where others damage."

"Like his mate, then. I remember him visiting an army pal after a climbing accident and he was lucky to be alive, too. They all came visiting, it was quite the army re-union. It's nice, that sort of thing."

So, Jill knew Ben and the army crowd. It must be through Alistair that she had met Tess; after all, it was not likely that Henry had introduced them. No sane man would introduce his mistress to his wife's sister. But even if she were unaware of the connection, Tess was not the friendly type and Mary could not imagine them striking up a conversation. An introduction by Alistair to Tess would stop right there, she felt. 'This is Tess.' 'Pleased to meet you.' End of subject. She could, however, imagine Charles and Alistair sitting outside some house extension somewhere, Alistair pressuring Charles over helping him with the ransom money and Charles saying it was not easy, Tess had an idea but they would need ID. In her mind's eye, Mary saw Alistair immediately thinking of Jill and Charles sucking his teeth and asking whether Alistair was sure Jill could be trusted. Then, once introduced, she could easily imagine Charles and Jill forming a bond based on their shared resentment of Henry and the scheme progressing from there.

Mary left to continue her search for Muffin, ducked round the corner, jumped into Tiger and returned to her flat. The numbers on the banknotes turned out to be consecutive and similar to the number on the note she had taken from Tess. It may only be circumstantial but it was evidence they were from the same batch and therefore likely to have come from the ransom.

It was good to have proved her theory but it did not advance Mary's investigation.

The newspaper cutting, however, was another matter. Mary would not mind betting that the telephone number belonged to the Danesfords. Hiding her number, she called it. And recognised Patrick Danesford's as the voice that answered. Hmm. Jill had no legitimate reason for needing Danesford's private number so it seemed reasonable to conclude that it had, indeed, been her that blackmailed him to collect the money from the second ransom. But where did Mrs Danesford's accident fit in?

It would come to her. First, there was one little problem Mary needed to attend to before she could draw a line under Muffin and matters arising and that was replacing the original banknotes in Jill's box. Mary reasoned that it would look odd when Andrew finally recovered the notes if all but two came from the ransom.

"I'll never con my way in there again," she thought. "I'll have to burgle the place." The very thought made her shiver. She might be getting blasé about following suspects or tricking them into answering her questions but burglary?

"Mike! Mike! I need you."

He appeared quite quickly but to Mary it seemed an age.

"Do I deduce I'm forgiven?"

Mary did not reply.

"What happened to "How are you, long time no see…."

But she had no idea he had been ill or even that such a thing was possible so why should she be concerned?

"I need you to do a little job for me."

The nervousness she once again felt in his presence since Ben's accident was completely subsumed by the need to put matters in order.

It was not difficult for Mike to swap the banknotes and also the one she had taken from Tess, setting Mary's mind at rest.

"See? I told you we would make a great team," he told her, blowing her a kiss as he departed. She stared exasperatedly after him.

THURSDAY
DAY 75

The moment Mary opened the door to Andrew, she knew something was wrong. It was not just that he did not usually call in the morning, it was the way he shuffled his feet, the look in his eyes.

"You'd better come in."

He sat tense and straight, holding an envelope. "There's something you need to see. We're keeping a lid on it but the media have a way of getting hold of information. I'd hate you to find out that way."

Mary did not take her eyes off his face as she took the envelope from him. Her hands shook as she drew out a series of photographs. They were of Jared – and he was dead. He lay on a wooden floor, his pallid face in sharp contrast to his bright jumper and the warm brown of the floor. Mary stared in shock. He couldn't be dead, it wasn't time, his light was yellow, there were twenty-five days left.

"No!" Then: "Have you told Rachel?"

"I've told her that we have reason to believe Jared is dead."

"Is she all right?"

"In denial. She said she'd know, that mothers can sense these things. She's not ready to accept it so I thought it best not to go into why we think so just yet."

Mary put the photographs back in the envelope.

Andrew watched her, concerned. "Is there anything I can do? Is there anyone I can call?"

Mary waved Andrew away. "I'd like to be alone."

She lay on the sofa staring into space. Mme Delphine's one hundred days had not been a prediction of the day Jared would die. It had been a maximum window within which he must be found. But the traffic light – did not matter. Something had gone wrong. The Spite Brigade. They must have changed their plans, perhaps filled up Day 100 with Tasks then seized a chance to fit Jared in earlier. So much for optional or 'Day 100' having a certain ring to it.

Mary wanted to be sick. She had let Jared down. Just when she thought she was getting somewhere. She rolled over and picked up her phone. She did not need to pull a sickie now; she really was sick. Pete advised she take Friday off as well and Mary was in no mood to resist.

"Mike! Mike!" This was a fine time to ignore her. "Mike!"

No response. Did he know about Jared? Could he find out what had happened?

"Mike!"

Mary went back to staring at the ceiling.

She called Rachel. No answer. Perhaps it was just as well; she did not know what to say.

She ought to call Ben. Mary consulted the clock. It would wait. No, it wouldn't. She should have let him know her decision before now.

"Ben. I've been thinking and if that trip is still on offer, I'd like to go." Well, why not? She couldn't help Jared now and it might do her good to get away.

"Although when I come back, I will find whoever did this," she vowed. "And when I do, he or she will wish they had never been born."

FRIDAY
DAY 76

Mary was not really in the right mood for a weekend away but having decided to go, she must pretend as well as she could in fairness to Ben and once there, there would be plenty in Rome to take her mind off Jared.

The first thing Mary noticed at the airfield was a smart new plane on the runway. It was like a proper plane but in miniature and it was brilliant white with no logo on it. Ben stowed her case and escorted her aboard: today he was a passenger and for once Jack was not their pilot; he had weekend collections to make for the business.

"Where did you get this? Is it yours?"

"No, it belongs to a friend…. I might get one, though," Ben said thoughtfully.

The flight was short and uneventful. The plane taxied to a halt, the door opened and as Mary reached the top of the steps to descend to the tarmac, she was hit by the smell of pizza. It seemed to be an ingredient of the warm air and if she had not been feeling so wretched, Mary would have laughed in delight. Then they made their way through customs to a waiting mini-bus and were driven straight to their hotel. Ben had planned everything.

Outside, the hotel looked decayed with its ancient light beige stonework and paint peeling in the sun but inside it was bright and modern. The ceilings were high and the arched windows seemed to reach for the sky. There were panels of travertine marble on the walls and pictures of old Rome. Ben had booked a suite with a sitting area and balcony.

Pushing away images of Jared, Mary went to unpack but it was not long before she was rushing to the balcony and saying excitedly to Ben: "Come and see the bathroom, it's amazing. The sink is so big you could have a bath in it!"

So keen was she to share her discovery that she forgot that the t-shirt she had pulled on in place of her travelling clothes, although decent, only just reached to her bottom. Her shapely legs were on full view below. Ben moved towards her as though pulled on an invisible string and cupped her face in his hands. The child-like wonder in her eyes, that funny crooked smile.... he bent forward. Passionately, they kissed.

They shared some wine on the balcony before deciding to venture out for a walk. Ben produced a tourist map and they headed for the Trevi Fountain. Mary could not fail to be impressed as she stood staring up at the statues and at the huge façade behind them.

"Now you must take a coin in your right hand and throw it over your left shoulder into the water to ensure your return to Rome one day," Ben advised Mary. "Says so here," he added.

Already she knew she would love to come back so she did as he said.

Evening was approaching so they decided to head back to the hotel. Mary smiled up at Ben…. and then she saw him. It couldn't be, could it? It could.

"Hello," said Mike. He took her arm. "I do so love an evening stroll and in such a beautiful city."

Mary groaned.

"Stone in my shoe," she explained to Ben. "Hang on." She pretended to empty it out. "That's better."

All the way to the hotel she ignored Mike until finally she was 'alone' in her bedroom.

"What are you up to?" she demanded.

"Well, that's nice. Why must I be up to something? I'm having a holiday."

"Here. What a coincidence."

"Isn't it?" he replied.

"Since you are here, why didn't you tell me Jared was dead? Why didn't you come when I called?"

"What are you talking about? Jared is not dead."

"Don't lie to me, I've seen the photos. Possibly your precious register is wrong."

Doubt in Mary's mind on that score might not be a bad thing in view of what Mme Delphine had said. Nonetheless, Mike could not let her think Jared had died and give up looking for him. If she did that and then he did die, it would destroy her.

"I don't know what you've seen but Jared is still alive."

"Then why would someone pretend he was dead?"

"I don't know. To shut down you and Andrew, stop you investigating, perhaps? To end the media attention – after a

322

flurry of interest immediately following the announcement, of course. All in all, I should say faking a few photos would be a good move on the part of whoever has him. He'll drop out of the news, the police will move the case down in priority and start looking for a body not a child."

Could he be telling the truth? Mary looked at him keenly. Was it possible the photographs were faked? There had been no directions as to where to find the body. Hope flooded through her. One hundred days had not passed: the light was yellow: Jared was alive.

She must continue her search as soon as she got back to England. Ben – and everyone else – would have to take a back seat. For the first time since she arrived in Rome, Mary's smile was more than a re-shaping of her mouth; it lit up her eyes, her cheeks, it extended all the way to her toes. Mike took an involuntary half-step towards her and checked himself.

"I need to get changed for dinner."

Mike did not move.

"How about a little privacy?" suggested Mary.

"Oh, yes of course. See you around."

Lovely as everything was, Mary was on edge throughout dinner which upset Ben's good humour although he tried not to show it. Mike, however, was nowhere to be seen.

SATURDAY
DAY 77

The next day, Ben and Mary left early and headed for the Vatican City. To start with, their walk was uneventful and by the time they reached the Tiber, Mary's grip on Ben's hand had loosened to its normal light pressure. Ben pointed up river to the Pont Sant'Angelo and 'that sweet little castle' as Mary put it, squinting into the distance. Ben smiled indulgently.

"Not if you knew anything about its history," he said.

Her gaze adjusted nearer and she gave a start: a man was walking across the river. Walking on the water. It might be a holy place but that was ridiculous. She looked again and realised the awful truth; it was not so much a case of a man walking on the water as a ghost dancing across it. It was Mike.

"What are you looking at?" asked Ben.

"Nothing," she replied.

They continued on their way to the Vatican and although Mike stayed away Ben continued to look less than amused.

"Think how many people must be here when it's packed

for the Papal Mass at Christmas," they agreed as together they contemplated the vastness of St Peter's Square. They crossed to St Peter's itself where Mary found it hard to know where to look first and yet for all the columns and statues and the inlaid marble, the thing she would remember most was the candles surrounding the steps leading down to St Peter's tomb.

They moved on to the Sistine Chapel to marvel at the brightly painted ceiling and listen to the tour guides talking about Michelangelo.

Once out of the chapel, though, things started to go downhill. Mary thought the Vatican Museums were fascinating and even Ben's eyes went out on stalks at the sight of 'Nero's bathtub', a massive dish of red porphyry worth billions in modern money, although Mary was not sure whether it was the object or the cost that transfixed him. Then Mary noticed Mike. How could she not? He was floating about peering over the side of the dish and pretending to bathe, singing as (fully dressed) he lathered his armpits with imaginary soap.

She hurried Ben away.

"What's the matter?" he asked.

"Nothing. I'm just getting tired. We've walked a long way, one way and another."

It did not quite ring true. It was a very sudden onset of tiredness but some refreshment would be welcome so Ben steered her towards the exit. As they walked, Mary gave mixed messages, still trying to listen in to the tour guides and yet seeming keen to leave. Slow progress and foot-dragging, the more usual symptoms of tiredness, were noticeably absent. Even so, Ben hailed a taxi and soon they were back at the hotel.

They had been so engrossed in their sightseeing neither had realised how late it was, so rather than grab a cup of tea they booked an early dinner on the roof terrace and went to their room to change. Ben held out his arms for Mary to fasten his cufflinks in place as a finishing touch and looked in the mirror.

"Very smart. Thank you again."

The view across Rome was stunning but Mary's admiring comments were cut short when Mike started posing on the parapet. But there was no escape; he joined them at the table. When Ben took her hand, Mike held the other one; when Ben asked what she would like to eat, he turned the menu to blank pages; when Ben chatted amiably, he talked over him so Mary ended up distracted and confused. It was a relief to go to bed.

"Better luck tomorrow," thought Mary but more in hope than expectation.

Nor was it a peaceful night. It had been a little while since Mary had had a nightmare but since the timing could hardly be worse, tonight was obviously the night. As the spider walked across her face she woke, aware she was screaming out loud. Where was Ellen.... and where was Jared? She should not be enjoying herself, she had work to do.

Her screams startled Ben into consciousness.

"Nightmare," she muttered by way of explanation. "Go back to sleep. It was only a nightmare."

Ben reached out for her and put his arms around her. He stroked her face gently.

"Come here. Tell me about it…. Or not," he added seeing the expression in her eyes.

"Not," Mary replied.

"Come here and have a cuddle. There, that's better." He kissed her and held her close. Closer.

"Dream still seem real?"

"No, I think you have driven it away," she replied and fell asleep in his arms.

SUNDAY
DAY 78

The first thing Mary did when they went out the next day was to buy a little model of the Colosseum from one of the many street vendors selling souvenirs.

"We should go there," she said and they set off in the general direction, stopping on the way at churches that seemed to have fallen into a bucket of gold.

"To think that those frescos had to be finished in a day before the plaster set," marvelled Mary in yet another church, gazing at paintings that occupied entire walls.

But it was not all sightseeing; there were shop windows to be inspected also, shop windows full of clothes and jewellery that made Mary's eyes pop. Suddenly, she felt someone hit her arm and turned to see a beggar with his hand outstretched; she had stood staring so long inadvertently ignoring him that he decided to push the point. Ben shooed him away.

They walked on and rounding a corner they came upon a wide street thronged with people. Flowers spilled from window boxes on the balconies of the houses, baskets of flowers hung by the doors and more flowers grew in tubs in the centre of the street. There seemed to be some kind of festival going on. As they looked more closely, they realised that the crowd was broken into groups each listening to a musician or watching a play being performed by a handful of young people standing on boxes.

Ben and Mary moved through the crowd watching one entertainment after another. They paused to look at a living statue dressed as in ancient Rome and covered from head to foot in white powder as though made of stone. She did not stir as tourists stood beside her and took photographs.

They moved on and Mary was about to say 'Look, there's another' when a certain familiarity struck her. The 'living' statue in top hat and tails and brightly coloured waistcoat was…. Mike. She glanced at Ben; he was looking straight at Mike. Mike swept off his hat and bowed low…. but Ben remained oblivious; he could not see him. He could, however, see Mary's reaction; yet again she was staring at nothing with a strange expression on her face.

They pushed on through the busy street and made for the Colosseum. As they passed groups of tourists, fascinating snippets of information fell from the lips of their tour guides about how the walls used to be thicker but the stone had been plundered in later centuries and how it had had a roof which could be put on and off if it rained. But the queues were long and Ben and Mary decided not to go inside.

All around there were ice cream sellers. The day was warm and ice cream was a welcome idea but afraid it would attract Mike, Mary resisted. She checked all around but could not see him.

"Actually, yes, that would be nice," she agreed after all.

Ben went to fetch it and it *was* nice and even better, Mike did not come begging for a spoonful but Mary remained nervous until it was all gone.

Suddenly he appeared, making her jump. "Don't worry, had some earlier so you needn't feel guilty." Then he was gone.

By now Ben was having trouble disguising his impatience and suggested they go back to the hotel.

"Early start tomorrow," he said. One last, quiet dinner and the holiday was over.

MONDAY
DAY 79

Both were quiet on the plane on the way home, too. Finally, Ben broke the silence.

"Mary, I don't know how to say this…. I think it's best just to say it…. what I mean is, it's not working, is it? Us, I mean."

His words came as a bolt form the blue. They got on well together, he must know she…. liked him. She stared at him but no words came.

"The thing is, whenever I'm with you, you seem distracted. I've even tried taking you right away from things, just the two of us, in the hope we could forget the world for a while but it doesn't seem to make any difference. It's as though a part of you is always somewhere else, not with me."

She wanted to say he was wrong, that things would be different from now on but she could not. Mike clearly had no intention of leaving them alone.

"If there's someone else, I'd rather you told me."

"Ben, no. Please.... I mean.... you should know I wouldn't do that." Shocked into hardly realising what she was saying, Mary babbled: "I met someone around the same time as you...."

Was it possible he looked both triumphant and pained at the same time?

".... but we could never be together because he isn't real."

"You're not making sense. What do you mean 'not real'? Look, Mary, you're fun, kind, clever and I really like you but you need to sort yourself out."

The 'I know' that escaped her was hardly a whisper.

"Couldn't we try again and if it doesn't work out.... I've had a lot on my mind.... the kidnapping.... you remember I told you I saw the little boy...."

"The kidnapping is not your problem. For your own good you must let it go."

"I can't. You see, years ago...." Mary stopped. Her own experience was buried deep and if their relationship was not secure then she would not let him in. She should have told him when she had the nightmare, she did not know why she had not but it was too late now.

"You need counselling. I really do like you but you need help. Half the time you're not quite here and now it's people who aren't real and what's all this business about spiders?"

There was a pause then, deeply offended, Mary said: "If that's your attitude you might be right. Maybe it would be better if we stopped seeing each other."

As Ben looked into her eyes, he saw layers of emotion from anger at the top to sadness and fear deep down. Somewhere in the mix there was a reflection of her standing there in that ridiculous t-shirt. Desire softened his expression and that is how she would remember him, tender and loving, but Mary was not about to forgive what he had just said. Counselling, indeed. She turned on her heel and walked away, knowing that he was staring after her.

TUESDAY
DAY 80

The best thing to do next was to throw herself into work. Mary went in early to a cheery greeting from Pete but as the hours passed, he noticed she was not her usual self.

"Are you sure you're all right, Mary? It's all right for you to take a bit longer if you're not all right yet."

She assured him she was fine but they all started giving her a wide berth anyway just in case they caught something. Mary was relieved not to have to make conversation.

At home that evening she was pondering whether, if she did take a few more days off, she could make good use of them in her hunt for Jared, when Mike walked in.

"Ben has gone," said Mary accusingly.

Mike did not try to hide his pleasure but at least he did not gloat.

"He wasn't suitable," he said shorty.

"It was none of your business," returned Mary. "We discussed this."

They sat in silence, Mike showing no sign of leaving. His presence was like sandpaper against the rawness of her feelings. She had loved Ben and if it had to end, she would not have chosen for it to do so on such bad terms.

"You should go away and leave me alone."

"It isn't time for me to go."

"I didn't mean your concerns whatever they are and I will honour my part of our bargain if you'll only tell me what to do. What I meant was that with Ben gone, you don't need to 'protect' me anymore."

Patiently, Mike replied: "If that's what you want, I can guarantee you won't see me again."

Mary could have screamed. That was not the same as him going away and not being there. It was pointless.

"No," she replied slowly. "It isn't. Not really."

Because it was not.

Again, they sat in silence.

"Just for curiosity," Mary began. "If you wanted to split us up, why didn't you just scare Ben away? Why focus on me and make me look a fool?"

"Oh, Mary, it wasn't like that at all. What are you suggesting I should have done – drape a sheet over myself and go 'woo'? Play poltergeists? I don't think Ben is the type to freak out easily and why would he connect it with you unless I only messed him about when you were there? If he got the point even then. And anyway, I didn't want to risk getting too close to him; you saw what happened when he crashed his car."

Once again, they lapsed into silence.

"How is your sleuthing coming on?" Mike asked trying to change the subject.

A hint of panic was detectable in Mary's voice as she replied: "I only have twenty days left to save Jared. Oh Mike, you can't go, not yet. I need all the help I can get."

"Tell me."

Mary contemplated. Before her trip to Rome, she had found Jill in possession of banknotes which were almost certainly from the ransom. They had come from Tess which meant Charles (acting together with Alistair and Jill) was still her top suspect. Mike, however, had told her to keep away from Charles. Mary sat silent.

"For what it's worth, Henry Parker's finances appear to be in good order," contributed Mike.

No motive there, then.

Of course, the main objective was not to find the kidnapper, important as that was, but to find Jared.

Mary broke the silence. "Since we last compared notes, I searched the airfield. Jared wasn't there."

"I already knew that."

"Why didn't you say?"

"You didn't ask."

"Is he at Silverwood Hall?"

"No, you're wasting your time there."

"Mike, do you know where he is?"

"No, Mary, I don't."

Each reverted to their own thoughts until interrupted by a siren screaming past. Mary went to the window to see a fire engine disappearing round the corner at speed. Soon it was followed by another and in the distance, she saw a plume of smoke rising against the cloudless sky. She pulled excitedly on Mike's arm.

"Look, see up there where the smoke is. There's nothing up there except Silverwood Hall."

She rushed to get her coat and jumped into Tiger. Mike jumped in too.

The Hall was silhouetted against the grey sky, one corner illuminated by brilliant yellow flames which curled out of one of the windows and licked at the floor above. As they approached, Mary could feel the heat. She saw ash float down, fragile as snow and settle on the grass. The smell of burning filled the air. There would not be much left of Gary's office but to everyone's relief the fire had not spread to the residential part of the building.

Mary soon spotted Gary, distraught, pacing backwards and forwards in front of the hectic scene as the firemen aimed water at the blaze.

"Mary, thank goodness. I can't find Mother; they won't let me through." Panic was obvious in his voice. "Mary, I can't find her. She wasn't in her flat when the alarms went off."

Mike had left before he completed the sentence.

All the other residents were accounted for, all except Violet. It was an anxious few minutes before Mike was able to report that there was definitely no-one in the building and Mary would have loved to be able to pass this information to Gary but she could not. Mike flitted off again for what seemed like an age before finally he re-appeared to say that he had found her.

"She's sitting on a bench in the walled garden talking to the roses," he said.

"Move away, there's nothing you can do here," instructed a fireman.

Mary steered Gary across the lawn. Fortunately, he was in too much of a state to wonder where they were going then, the moment they reached the archway to the garden, he spotted Violet and broke into a run.

"Gary, dear, I'm so sorry, it's all my fault." She seemed short of breath and started to cough.

"Shh…. it's all right. Everything is going to be fine."

There was an ambulance on the driveway so Mary went to call them over and soon Violet was on her way to hospital with Gary in attendance. Mary went home to grab some sleep, pausing only to summon Mike and thank him. She knew it must have been difficult for him after what had happened to Julia at Lower Meadow Hall.

Mary's idea of grabbing some sleep did not, however, go according to plan. She was tired and slept deeply for a while then half-woke with the image in front of her eyes of the Hall on fire. Thoughts raced through her mind, thoughts about fires, about Mike …. and about Julia. Henry had done well out of the fire at Lower Meadow Hall and Julia had been badly burned, killed for all Mary knew. Maybe Mike was involved in Jared's disappearance after all.

She remembered the way he had looked in the hospital with Ben. Had he driven a wedge between her and Ben out of concern for her welfare because he knew something about Ben that he would not tell her or had he done it to separate her from her closest friend?

And then he went and played hero at Silverwood Hall. Typical.

Confused she fell asleep, unsure what was real and what was some strange waking dream.

WEDNESDAY
DAY 81

The next day, Mary was surprised to find she was not as tired as she expected after such a bad night. It was just as well; she needed to finish work early to visit Violet who had been kept in for observation. She would take some flowers but did she need to stop at the cashpoint? Mary rummaged in her handbag.... no, she had enough money but where were her keys? She would not be able to drive far without those. Wondering once again how things can hide so successfully in such a small space, she rummaged deeper and came across something hard.... it was the memory stick with the information she had copied from Gary's computer. She had forgotten all about it what with everything that had happened.

Visiting time at the hospital was not for another hour so Mary could allow herself a little peep. She plugged the memory stick into the computer and flicked through 'Accounts.' It did not mean a thing to her. She tried 'Archive' and found it was equally boring and inscrutable.... no, wait.... there was another copy of the accounts but this one was different. This one had more residents living in the Home, paying more for accommodation and showed more money going out for Gary's improvements and updates. Funnily enough, the extra money going in was exactly balanced by the additional expenses, so although revenues and costs had changed the final bottom-line figures for overheads and profit were the same.

Mary closed down the computer and sat thinking. So, that was how it was done. The extra residents were the likes of Vera Tomlinson; Tess paid cash into their bank accounts and then paid out care bills. Mary would not mind betting the 'extra work' on the Home was done by Charles thereby getting 'legitimate' money into the firm's account. Neat. Gary and the auditors would see only the first set of accounts whilst the other set was nothing but a tracker for Tess. Provided Tess took it slowly and nobody trawled through the Silverwood bank account counting residents (who were by their nature a fluctuating population) all would be well. For all his perfectionism, Gary's interests lay elsewhere and Tess might expect to survive the occasional audit with a bit of smoke and mirrors.

"Gosh, look at the time!" Mary jumped up and made for the door. "'Bye everyone, see you tomorrow."

Thank goodness for Tiger, she never would have made it on the bus.

Gary took the flowers she brought and fussed around wrapping a wet cloth around the stems. "I won't put them in a vase because we're going soon, we're just waiting for the doctor to sign the discharge," he said.

"But we can't go yet," piped up Violet. "I have a visitor."

They looked up and saw Andrew. He sat down beside the bed and introduced himself to the old lady.

"Are you feeling better?" he asked.

"Oh yes. And I'm so glad you've come, dear," she answered. "There's something I want to tell you. You see, it was all my fault. I told my son and he wouldn't listen – about that Lucy, you know – I told him 'She cheated Mr Howard and she is cheating you' but he wouldn't listen and he let her keep coming."

Gary signalled to Andrew to say nothing. "They think I don't know what I'm talking about but I do. So, I fetched my candle…."

Gary raised his eyes to heaven. She would revert to the ways of her childhood.

"…. and I went to the office to see what she'd been up to. But I tripped and I dropped the candle and the papers on the desk caught fire…."

Gary winced. There should not have been any papers on the desk. Tess was innately untidy for all his admonitions.

Her voice trembled. "…. and I couldn't put it out and there was a lot of smoke and I went for help but I'm slow on my feet these days…."

"It's all right, Mum," Gary comforted her. "No harm done, no-one was hurt, it was an accident, we'll get it all put right, you'll see. Look, here's the doctor. You have a little talk with the doctor, we'll wait outside."

Safely outside, Gary turned to Andrew.

"Take no notice. It's just the ramblings of an old lady. Lucy was a home-help who worked for an old gentleman in the village when Mother was younger. She was small and dark-haired like Tess who does my accounts. Mother got confused and got it into her head that Tess was cheating me, doing clever things with 'that computer.'"

"She wasn't far wrong," muttered Mary.

Andrew gave her a curious look.

"Later," she mouthed.

The doctor had finished now, so they all went back to Violet.

"He said I can take you home now, Mum," Gary told her.

"But what about my visitors?" asked Violet, looking first at Andrew then Mary then back to Andrew.

"They'll come up to the Hall another day when you've had some rest and you can serve them tea and have a chat in comfort."

"Of course, we will." Mary gave Violet a hug.

"Goodbye, see you soon," said Andrew and they left. He turned to Mary.

"What was all that about?"

"Violet gets confused but she's not daft and when she said Lucy meaning Tess was cheating Gary…. you see, I was up at the Hall helping Gary with something – we're old friends – and I sort of downloaded the accounts from the computer…."

Andrew refrained from pointing out that you can download something or not download something but you cannot sort of download it and waited.

"The thing is, Tess has been using Silverwood to launder money without Gary knowing." A sudden thought crossed her mind: "He'll be appalled when he finds out."

"So, your sort of download wasn't entirely a sort of accident? Or do you make a habit of prying into other people's finances? I think you had better start at the beginning."

".... I was coming to see you Andrew, honestly, I've only just looked through the accounts myself," Mary finished. "And it's just as well I have it all on the memory stick in view of the fire at the Hall," she pleaded. Once again, she rummaged in her bag. "Here."

* * *

Mary took the long way home. Coincidently, this took her past the airfield. It was not that she had any interest in what Ben was doing. She just fancied taking Tiger for a little trip.

As Mary drove through the village, she saw Ben's sports car parked outside the pub. She parked nearby, fluffed up her hair and re-applied her fading make-up.

The pub was warm and welcoming. Mary's eyes darted around checking the guests. No Ben. She ordered a bar-snack and as she ate, every time the door opened or shut, Mary craned to see who had passed through. A tidy stream of people but no Ben.

It was, of course, a relief not to see him. She would not have known what to say to him anyway. With her sensible hat on, Mary knew that until Mike was good and ready to leave, she could not see Ben again. Even if he would see her. And the fact that his phone was permanently on answerphone suggested he would not. She could not blame him, she had had no right to be offended by what he had said and when it came right down to it, she had deserved to be dumped.

So why when he appeared out of nowhere and walked past her heading for the door did Mary get butterflies in her stomach? He half turned and in spite of herself, Mary was about to call out when a girl walked briskly up to join him. He smiled, the girl took his arm and they left together.

Mary's stomach churned.

"Ben can have any girl he likes so what did I expect?" she asked herself crossly.

She finished her meal and walked slowly back to Tiger.

THURSDAY
DAY 82

A phone call from Andrew always made Mary nervous: after all, Mike could not check the register constantly.

"It won't bite," heckled Ryan as she gingerly picked up the ringing mobile.

"Of course not. Phones don't bite. Rats bite," called out Bellyache. He turned to Minty. "Had a really good dinner last night," he said loudly enough for the whole room to hear. "Ratatouille and a nice big steak."

"Hope you went for a walk afterwards," advised Ryan. "Not too fast, mind."

Smiling, Mary left them to their banter and put the phone to her ear.

"I called to say that when you were hunting for that memory stick yesterday and you unpacked your bag, you dropped your purse. I didn't notice in time to call out to you but I have it here."

"Gosh, thanks, Andrew. I hadn't even missed it but I was

intending to call at the supermarket on the way home and it would have been embarrassing to get to the checkout and find it wasn't there. Could I call by and collect it?"

Some hours later, Mary arrived at the police station to find that Andrew had been busy since the previous day. Charles had indeed been working at Silverwood Hall and receiving payment for work (and imaginary work) done there. Not believing Charles capable of organising the ransom pick-up and working on the assumption that it was ransom money that was being laundered, Andrew had followed up with an investigation of Charles' partner Alistair. A search of Alistair's bank account having revealed deposits of money at the same time as money went in to Charles' account for the 'work' done at the Hall, Alistair had admitted that it was he who had collected the ransom but he insisted that he had not taken Jared. He had merely reasoned that Jared was missing, Mr Parker was rich and that he, Alistair, could send a ransom demand and pick up a nice little sum, thank you very much.

Andrew continued: "But Alistair needed a wingman, someone on the ground who would keep a surreptitious eye on the escape route and be ready with a car. And he needed to launder the money when he had it. Which is where Charles and Tess came in. Charles would be the get-away driver and Tess would take charge of the cash. Alistair would collect his share in the form of a bonus in his pay packet whilst Charles and Tess would retain their cut.

"Henry had a mistress…"

"Jill Kendrick," Mary butted in.

"How did you know that?"

"Little bird told me. Do carry on."

"Jill Kendrick supplied passports for use as ID in exchange for a share of the money because she felt rejected and owed; Henry had promised to leave his wife for her but the time was never right. First, he couldn't leave because of breaking up the family, then it was because Rachel needed him after Jared disappeared. Finding out that he had other mistresses and never meant a word of it was the last straw."

So, the ransom demand was all Alistair's idea. Not Charles' but Alistair's. Most of the rest, however, Mary had already worked out. Not that she would let on to Andrew; she would have far too much explaining to do.

"Hmm…." was all she said.

"All of which is fine as far as it goes," remarked Andrew to Mary. "But I get the distinct feeling that little lot (he gestured in the direction of the interview rooms were Charles and Tess and Alistair were being held) are feeling relieved, as though in spite of my discovery of who organised the ransom and what happened to the money, there's something I still don't know." He looked thoughtful. "I wonder how Alistair talked Charles and Tess into it. I wonder if he has some leverage. After all, their business was already picking up. Maybe it wasn't a crime of opportunity, maybe they did have something to do with it."

For now, though, the only thing was to let them go pending further action being taken.

As luck would have it, Charles and Tess entered the corridor from adjacent rooms just as Mary and Andrew were finishing their conversation at one end of it and Rachel and Henry were arriving at the other. Tess ran to Rachel, grabbed hold of her arm and clung to her.

"Please, you must believe me, whatever they start telling you about Charles and me taking money we didn't have anything to do with Jared's disappearance. Rachel, I'm so sorry, Rachel please look at me, say you believe me."

Sergeant Rivers pulled Tess away. Andrew nodded to him and Mary realised it had not been luck that had put them all in the corridor together, Andrew had planned that little scene to see what would happen. Tess was practically on her knees. She was either a good actress or she was telling the truth when she said she and Charles had had nothing to do with the kidnapping. And Rachel and Henry…. Mary swung round to look at Andrew – she could see in his eyes he was testing them, too – Rachel did not know where to put herself. She seemed at once embarrassed by Tess's behaviour and totally taken aback. If Andrew had thought she had some part in Jared's disappearance, perhaps because of having found out about Henry's affairs and wanting to get back at him, show him what was important, then now was a good time to think again. As for Henry himself, he stood stern and impassive as ever but automatically his arm went around Rachel swinging her round so her face was buried in his jacket and her pain was not visible to the world.

Sergeant Rivers showed Rachel and Henry to Andrew's office and the others made for the door.

As they went, Mary heard Charles say to Tess: "You know who that is?"

He was talking about her.

"Gary's friend," she replied innocently.

"No, Ben's girl. Or Ben's interfering little bitch might be more accurate."

Did he know it was her evidence that had brought him there? Had he somehow found out that she had been snooping at the airfield? Mary had no way of knowing.

FRIDAY
DAY 83

Peace and quiet at last. Well quiet, anyway. Mary was still feeling on edge so she would have to settle for quiet without the peace. That evening, she sat down to think but straight away her gaze lit upon the yellow chrysanthemum on the mantelpiece and she could not help noticing it was looking peaky. She jumped up and fetched some water. No sooner had she settled back down again than Mike appeared.

In typical Mike fashion he observed: "You know why that plant doesn't thrive? You don't water it."

"Do so too. It's wet, go and see."

"It's only wet because you just did it. I saw you."

Smarticus.

"Do you want something or are you just visiting?"

He sat beside her and put his arm around her. Mary neither responded nor moved away.

"Keeping in touch. What have you been up to?"

Mary told him all about Andrew arresting Alistair and fellow conspirators over the first ransom demand.

"Well done," he applauded. "A word of warning, though: if Charles Armstrong thinks you had something to do with the fact they got caught, you had better watch your step. I have said it before and I will say it again: he's dangerous."

At that moment, there was a rustle and a clatter at the door. Mary went over to find her neighbour on the doorstep holding a thick envelope.

"This came for you earlier."

Mary thanked her and went back inside. She sliced the envelope open and sat smiling faintly, lips parted, examining each of the wedding photographs in detail before handing them to Mike to admire.

She moved the plant and put them on the mantelpiece in a row, her favourite in the middle.

"There," she said, visibly cheered.

"Now, where were we? Andrew is satisfied that the first ransom demand was Alistair taking advantage of the kidnapping to make some money but he never had Jared. And we know the second demand wasn't sent by the same person as the first. I reckon Jill sent it."

"Because?"

"She copied down Danesford's phone number. She wouldn't need to do that to call from the hospital about Anne-Marie. Assuming it was Jill you heard pressuring Danesford to pick up the money, it explains Danesford countering: 'I'm not going to do it. I know about you and him, don't pretend it doesn't suit you the way things are.' Danesford must have found out Jill was Henry's mistress.

"Presumably the threat in the note 'You betrayed me and now you will pay' referred to the money. It was never a threat against Jared's life."

"It fits," agreed Mike.

"Mike?" ventured Mary. "What colour is Jared's light?"

"Yellow. Stop panicking. We have seventeen days."

They lapsed into silence, staring straight ahead. Then suddenly, Mary jumped out of her chair and leapt across to the mantelpiece.

"Look. Look at Max and Oliver." She handed her favourite photo to Mike. "Don't you see?"

"See what?"

"They're brothers. Max and Oliver look similar because they're brothers and they both look just like their father. They could be twins; you could even mistake them for the same person. I did."

"Yes…. and?"

"That's it. Darren and Jared are brothers! That's why I thought Darren was Jared."

Mike digested this information. "You're saying Rachel had an affair with Patrick Danesford?"

"Must have. Although it does seem un-Rachel-like and where on earth would they meet? Then Danesford has another child with Anne-Marie who is the spitting image of Jared. Of course, they're only half-brothers unlike Max and Oliver, but they're little yet so even if they grow to look different later, it's possible they could look the same now. Unless, unless…. I've got it! Henry had an affair with Anne-Marie – we know he's a serial cheat – then Anne-Marie had a baby at roughly the same time as Rachel and they look

352

similar because they share a father. And I remember Andrew saying that Jared said 'Mum' to photos of both Rachel and Anne-Marie because there is a resemblance there, too."

Mary was getting in to this. "Or Anne-Marie had twins – that would explain how they could be so alike – and gave up one of them because they simply could not afford it and the Parkers adopted the baby."

"Okay. I don't see where any of this is getting us, though. You're still short of a child," said Mike reasonably.

He was right; even if Darren was Jared that just reduced the question to 'Where is Darren?' rather than 'Where is Jared?' It was a bit of hole in her argument, Mary had to admit. Quite a lot of a hole.

SATURDAY
DAY 84

Only two weeks left to find Jared. It was all very well concluding Jill sent the second note but if she did not have Jared, it did not help. So, what now?

Mary tried to call Rachel but the network was unavailable.

"Pity," she thought. "It's about time I invited her over and I could have seen if she knows Patrick Danesford."

Gary's mother was not yet receiving visitors. Mary re-read the account of the fire at Lower Meadow Hall and wondered yet again what, if anything, was its connection to the kidnapping. She asked herself the same question regarding Mrs Danesford's accident in view of the newspaper cutting she had found at Jill's flat.

Mary went round and round the same thought processes without result.

"Why couldn't the crystal ball have given me a clue as to where he is or what sort of danger he's in, instead of showing me spiders?" she wondered in frustration.

Mary went for a walk in the park; the Danesford family were not there. She drove past the Parker's house; the car was gone and the lights were off. By the time night came, it was inevitable that Mary should toss and turn and dream of Ellen.

The two of them were running through the long grass in the field wearing necklaces made of daisy chains, they were heading for the stile, panting, laughing…. Suddenly, there was a man. He grabbed them both by the arm and propelled them to the gate. Ellen screamed and struggled, Mary too, but he held tight, so tight their arms were bruised. He pulled them behind him across two more fields, not caring they could hardly keep up, yanking them to their feet when they tripped over tussocks of grass. They arrived at the shed and roughly, he pushed Mary inside. She saw Ellen bite him. She saw him hit her. Then he tucked Ellen under his arm where she hung limp like a rag doll and slammed the door of the shed shut.

Darkness. The earthy smell of damp sacking. A huge spider with red eyes. Thank goodness it was contained in a glass orb…. but the orb was rolling, faster, faster. What if it collided with something and smashed? The spider would escape.

Mary sprang to catch it – and woke lying across the bed with her hand outstretched.

SUNDAY
DAY 85

Mary was feeling stressed. Saturday had passed into history with no progress in the hunt for Jared and to cap it all, tomorrow she had to go to Head Office in London for training in document control. She had looked up the train times and ironed her shirt and put everything ready for the following morning but the idea of being alone in London was daunting and worse was the fact she hated travelling.

Mary sat down to read a book by way of distraction but could not concentrate. She got up and paced the room. She picked up her phone to call Gemma and put it down again. Roll on tomorrow.

MONDAY
DAY 86

Mary set out early the following morning in order to be absolutely sure of not missing the train and as a result, having nothing to do but stand and wait did not help at all. The station was busy and everyone else seemed to know exactly where they were going whereas Mary kept checking the platform guide and straining to hear the announcements, terrified that somehow, in spite of everything, she was on the wrong platform and would end up running to somewhere else and arriving all hot and bothered if she caught the train at all.

It was nearly departure time and the already crowded platform was swelling with new arrivals. Mary thought she saw Mike and she was about to wave when a commuter with a briefcase walked in front of him. So, he had come to see her off after all. The man walked on and once again Mary had a clear view of Mike – except that he was not there. She looked all round but could not see him. Disappointed,

Mary made her way towards the edge of the platform to be sure of getting on the train. She could only hope she would be near a door. She heard a gentle clanking and looked along the line to see the train coming slowly towards her, its headlights on, the driver sitting stiffly in the cab. Then as it drew level, she felt a forceful push and lurched forward, her foot slipping – she was standing on nothing, she would fall onto the line. The gentle clanking carried on. The train was almost upon her and in that moment of panic she was sure she would die.

And then it was over. She was blown backwards as air rushed before her and she fell heavily back onto the platform striking her head as she did so.

* * *

Slowly, Mary came to. She was in hospital and a doctor was shining a light in her eyes.

"You've been a lucky girl," he remarked. "Can you tell me what happened?"

Mary stared back at him, wild-eyed and silent. Her eyes darted around the room.

"I don't know." She tried to concentrate and a picture came into her mind: "Falling…. I'm falling…." There was panic in her voice as she rose from the pillow.

"Shh…." said the doctor, gently settling her back. "It's all right. You're safe now."

He looked across at her mother. "Maybe later," he said. "She's confused. It's not unusual after a blow to the head but don't worry, there's no lasting damage."

Alice stayed for a while chatting about the neighbours and giving Mary an update on the plumbing.

"I'll have to do some re-decorating, you can help me choose the wallpaper," she told Mary but it was clear that her attempts to amuse her daughter were wasted. Mary was glassy-eyed and apt to lose track of what her mother was saying. Alice kissed her on the cheek and left, promising to come back tomorrow. On the way out, she stopped to speak to the doctor who again assured her that Mary's behaviour was perfectly normal under the circumstances and that everything was fine.

TUESDAY
DAY 87

"I brought a newspaper," she told Mary the next day then went through it reading out loud the headlines and sundry amusing stories because Mary could not be bothered to read it herself. It was too much effort. Most things were too much effort come to that and yet Alice was pleased to see that Mary was looking brighter. Obviously, the doctors thought so too because visitors were no longer restricted to family and Alice was relieved when Pete and Ryan walked in because with the best will in the world, she had run out of anything to say. Mary actually laughed to see Ryan trying to sit tidily and not bounce around or talk too loudly.

Visiting time over, the nurses came round handing out warm drinks then round again to adjust the bed ends so that the patients were no longer propped up but settled comfortably for the night. Mary weakly smiled her gratitude then lay staring at the ceiling. Eventually, drowsiness began to overtake her but as she slipped into a doze, Jared's face appeared, merged into Ellen's and back to his own.

"I shouldn't be lying here: I should be searching for Jared."

Mary stood up – and immediately fell backwards, her head swimming. This was ridiculous. She sat up, swung her feet back to the floor and tried again. This time, she made it to the chair. It was no good. She would have to crawl back to bed and see what tomorrow brought.

WEDNESDAY
DAY 88

Mary woke to realise that her headache had almost gone and as she sat in bed waiting for the doctor, the frustration of being cooped up in hospital and the enforced rest made her feel she had energy to burn. If she had been able to don gym clothes and go for a run, she would have found that she wore out quickly but that was not the point; Mary was filled with a desire to wave her arms and jump up and down.

She would go to the loo. Mary put on her dressing gown and walked up the ward to speak to the nurse at the desk then headed out of the door. Looking along the corridor, she could see a little garden through the glass in the door at the end so now she made for that; they would realise where she had gone, they wouldn't mind, surely.

In order to reach the garden, Mary had to pass a number of little ante-rooms some of which being used as examination rooms or closets but not all. As she reached a quiet room near the end, Mary stopped in her tracks. A girl lay motionless in bed but what caught Mary's attention was that she had a visitor and that visitor was: Mike.

Mary's mind was racing. It was not Anne-Marie. There were no new suspects for him to tail so this had to be to do with whatever else he did. It had to be Julia. Quietly, she tiptoed past the door so as not to intrude on their privacy.

The question now was how long to hang around in the garden. She had no idea how long Mike had been there or when he would leave but she could not stay away too long in case they missed her on the ward. She would have to go back. At least slippers were quiet. But in the event, Mary need not have worried; when she passed the little room, Mike was no longer there.

Mary looked around to make sure no-one was watching then entered the room and closed the door behind her. A clipboard on the end of the bed confirmed her suspicions: Julia Mallory-Quinn. Her face was badly scarred and her arms bore the tell-tale marks of skin grafts but she was alive. Mary studied her. She must have been absolutely beautiful before the fire. Not that she was ugly now but the poor girl would have some adjusting to do.

Back outside, Mary met an orderly.

"The girl there, Julia, does anyone ever visit?" she asked.

"Not any more. There was a brother used to come but he stopped."

"He stopped because he died," Mary thought. It was so sad. And so hard for Mike to see Julia lying there in a coma like that.

Mary wandered thoughtfully back to the ward.

"Good news," said the nurse cheerfully. "The doctor says

you can leave as long as there's someone to look after you for a day or two."

"I can go to my mother's."

She packed her bag and phoned Alice who turned up with a taxi and Mary was free.

But not free to do as she liked. First, she would have to convince her mother that, in spite of what the hospital had said, she did not need minding.

THURSDAY
DAY 89

Mary slept late and when she finally woke, it was to realise she was hungry. She pulled on her cosy old dressing gown and went downstairs to see what was in the fridge.

Alice appeared almost immediately out of nowhere to take the sausages from Mary's hand saying: "You go and sit down, I'll do that."

Mary complied. "Are you going to have some with me?"

Her mother had not been intending to but Mary forced an admission that she had not had breakfast and persuaded her to join her pleading: "You can't let me eat alone."

It was pleasant sitting in the kitchen together eating sausage sandwiches. It was good just being out of hospital.

Now for a nice bath. Mary been able to take showers at the hospital but tailing down the corridor with her washbag, looking around for somewhere to hang her clothes and her towel, digging around for her clean underwear in the bag she had left on the plastic chair when she was ready to get dressed again, it was not relaxing.

Mary lay there, her body floating in the hot water, her mind drifting somewhere above. Mmm.

There was a soft tap at the door.

"Are you all right in there? You've been a long time."

"Fine, thank you, Mum."

She had better get out. Mary kept a few clothes at her mother's. She chose a thick check shirt and a pair of old, soft trousers and went downstairs to see what Alice was doing. Alice had been filling the bird feeder and was about to take it outside.

Automatically she began: "Ah, Mary dear, would you mind…." then her voice tailed off. "No, I'll do it."

She positively sprang to the door before Mary could say anything.

"There now, I'll make a nice cup of tea and we can watch the birds. Here, lean forward and I'll plump up that cushion for you."

"Mum, you don't need to fuss, it was only a little bump on the head."

Alice snorted. "You bumped your head a couple of times when you were little but I don't remember you landing up in hospital for days."

"All right, all right. But I'm fine now, honestly."

It was true she did feel fine, ready to go back to work, even.

"Oh no, young lady. The doctor said a few days complete rest and that is what you are going to have."

Mary sighed. She knew of old it was dangerous letting her mother speak to doctors. There was an up-side however.

Alice screened visitors at the door and mostly conveyed their good wishes without letting them in, for which Mary was grateful. She was more tired than she had thought.

Somehow, the next few hours passed. Alice pottered about dusting and tidying and making frequent trips to check on Mary and ply her with cups of tea.

Then: "Three o'clock. We're on duty," cried Alice making for the front room.

"What?"

"Neighbourhood Watch. It's my turn to keep an eye on Mrs Evans' dustbin. Someone keeps putting whisky bottles in it and she finds it embarrassing since she's teetotal. What must the dustmen think!"

Mary raised her eyebrows and went to sit in the bay window with Alice. There was a long list of things she could not do such as watching television (it will give you a headache in your condition) or reading a book (the print is far too small; it can't be good for you to strain over that at a time like this) but apparently, observing dustbins was not one of them.

A signal from number nineteen released them at four after an uneventful shift. Alice fetched the paper and read the crossword clues to Mary who began well but soon started to fade.

"Early dinner and into bed for you," insisted Alice and Mary was not inclined to argue, much as she wanted to leave and resume the hunt for Jared. Another good night's sleep should do the trick and then…. then…. surely the break she needed would come.

Mary slept soundly for about three hours then woke to see Mike sitting in the chair by the window.

"Just seeing how you were," he explained.

"I'm all right. Mum is driving me crazy but to be fair she has a point; I still seem to get tired easily."

"Yes, I've seen her."

They lapsed into silence. Mike gazed fondly at Mary. She was studying him quietly, wondering whether to ask about Julia or rather how to approach the subject when the air in the corner of the room began to ripple and take form, capturing both their attention. Slowly, a presence emerged.

"You were summoned. You did not come."

Mike trembled.

"I have important matters to attend to. I have a bargain to honour."

"You were summoned. We were indulgent. Still, you did not come."

"I need more time."

Mary could hear the anguish in his voice. He reached out for her but with their fingertips only inches apart both he and his escort evaporated before her eyes.

Mary stared uncomprehendingly at the place where they had been. What had just happened? She sank onto the bed and lay staring at the ceiling. Mike was in trouble, that much was clear.

And it was all her fault. If only she hadn't gone out with Ben. He had always been jealous and he had looked so threatening in the hospital.... Or was it something else? Did he have a hand in the kidnapping after all? If he blamed Henry for what had happened to Julia, was he right? Had Henry set the fire for the insurance pay-out? And where was Jared?

She must try not to think about it, it made her head hurt. That stupid accident. Yes, the accident. Why hadn't he helped, where had he got to when she needed him…. Another thought forced its way in, uninvited, unwanted…. could it have been Mike who pushed her? He was the only person there that she knew.

No, it was not possible. She remembered how she and Mike had met, how he always said the right thing, how funny he was and how patient. Right up to the last time she had seen him which was only a day or so ago. Tears flowed freely down her cheeks.

In that moment Mary knew she could not hide anymore; she loved him and not as a brother.

FRIDAY
DAY 90

By morning, Mary's eyes were red-rimmed and watery with black rings underneath them. She had not slept a wink. Alice took one look at her and headed for the telephone to call Dr Tanner but Mary stopped her.

"I don't need a doctor. I'm not ill, I just had a bad night."

"Huh," thought Alice but she did not say anything. Instead, she made some breakfast and suggested Mary try to have some rest.

"You could always lie on the sofa if you don't want to go back to bed."

Tentatively, her mother asked: "I know you broke up but would you like me to get in touch with Ben?"

"No," stated Mary flatly, although it started her thinking all over again. Ben had been her fault, too. He was gone because she could not shut Mike out. Mary crossed to the window where the rain was running down the glass like tears against the background of a miserable, grey sky. The weather reflected exactly how she felt.

In another mood she would have loved the way the sunlight turned the edges of the droplets to silver and watched them racing each other to the bottom, sometimes joining together, sometimes moving sideways, sometimes petering out and she would have played the game she had played so often as a child – pick two and guess which one would win. But not today.

Alice beat a hasty retreat. Her mention of Ben had started Mary off again so it was probably best if she gave her a few minutes to dry her eyes then brought some nice warm croissants and coffee and kept her company. Mary should not be left alone to brood.

Mary herself, however, had other plans. She had resolved to consult Mme Delphine and she had no intention of explaining to her mother where she was going and why, let alone the whole history of events leading up to the present situation. She must announce her immediate return to her own flat which meant she must convince her mother she was better. After breakfast, she would have (or pretend to have) a little sleep, wake up cheerful, and explain that she had been letting things get on top of her. Her appearance was nothing a bit of effort and makeup would not cure: job done.

But no sooner was breakfast over than the doorbell rang. It was Andrew. In a loud stage whisper Alice explained that Mary looked awful, that she was still fragile after the accident and that she was taking the break-up with Ben badly.

Goodness she could be annoying. Alice had an unrivalled talent for taking two and two and making five and did not even have the decency to keep her conclusions to herself.

Andrew entered the room and closed the door behind him. Mary directed him to a chair by the window; she knew her mother would be listening at the door and by greeting him quietly she set the tone for the conversation.

"Have you turned up something further about the kidnapping?" she asked, worried that time was passing and there were only ten days left to find Jared.

"I haven't come about that, Mary. Although, of course, we're still looking into it even though…. circumstances have changed." Diplomatically, he avoided saying 'even though we have evidence Jared is dead.' "No, I have a few questions about your accident at the station. Tell me everything you can remember."

But although Mary's memory was clear now, she could not remember much.

"I was concentrating on the train, checking the number on the front, making absolutely sure I wasn't getting on the wrong one. I moved nearer to the platform edge with the other passengers to make sure I got on. People were crowding all around me. Then I felt propelled forward – pushed – and then and blown backwards again, presumably by the draught from the train."

"I hate to have to ask this," said Andrew sounding at the same time genuinely apologetic and business-like: "But I have a statement from the train driver saying he thought you were trying to commit suicide but changed your mind."

Mary was shocked. "That's ridiculous. You can't think that, you can't. I've told you what happened. I wasn't depressed, I was going on a training course, it was a good opportunity, it would have increased my chances of another contract when this job is over. I might have got a pay rise, even a new career. I was looking forward to it."

Then another thought hit her. "Don't whatever you do repeat that to my mother. Please Andrew. She's bad enough already. She would never let me out of her sight."

"What about the break-up with Ben? Your mother said you were taking it hard."

Mary was dismissive. "Everybody breaks up with boyfriends. Anyone I bring home, my mother hears wedding bells. It was no big deal."

"You do understand I had to ask. Perhaps there will be something on the CCTV. The driver sees only a narrow angle and we didn't get much from eye-witnesses on the platform; they were all more concerned with what they were doing."

"Andrew, about that suicide suggestion again. Promise me you won't say anything to my mother."

"Of course, I won't."

"Thanks. Now let's talk about something else."

Alice came in to find them chatting quietly about how Mary's precious Tiger was running and trivia like that. To all intents and purposes, Andrew's had been a social call. He stood up and took his leave.

"Look after yourself, Mary. See you again soon."

Now it was time for Mary to put her plan into action. Alice was not keen to let her go but there was nothing she could do about it so she had to content herself with pressing some sandwiches into Mary's hand by way of lunch and extracting a promise that she would phone that evening.

* * *

Mary headed straight for Mme Delphine's.

"Something has happened."

"Yes," said Mary. "I had an accident and Mike was there and then he wasn't and he came to see me but…." Briefly she told Mme Delphine the story.

"And you think perhaps someone pushed you but you did not see anyone."

Mary nodded.

"And you say this 'presence' took Mike away?"

"Yes."

"Oh dear." She rocked gently and started to hum.

Mme Delphine took out her crystal ball from the cupboard and sat at her little table staring into it in a trance. All Mary could see was swirling mist but Madame Delphine seemed to see events and people in the shifting shadows.

"I see him…. and you, Mary. I see a train…. but you ask about Mike. The shadows are changing…. I see a road flanked with trees…. I see a young man in a car…. the car is swerving…." She shivered and the spell was broken.

"Your Mike must return for judgement over events that night. Direct interference in the life of a mortal is not permitted."

Mary nodded.

Mme Delphine continued. "It was not his place to determine what should be and what should not. Emergency intervention was required."

"It's serious, isn't it? How serious? What will happen to him?"

"That will depend on whether there was malice in his heart."

The fear in Mary's eyes deepened.

"Who was the young man in the car?" inquired Mme Delphine.

"Ben," Mary replied slowly. "He was involved in a crash. He thought he saw…." Her voice tailed off.

"I see," said Mme Delphine.

"Maybe Ben was wrong."

"Maybe."

SATURDAY
DAY 91

"There's bad timing and there's bad timing," Mary thought. "If I had to have an accident, why now? Andrew thinks Jared is dead and as to Mike, assuming he isn't involved, I could do with some help and where is he? Gone."

But help to do what? The fact was, Mary did not know where to go from here. She sat thinking. There were no witnesses to the kidnapping, there had been two ransom demands but the first was not connected with Jared's disappearance and there was no evidence the second was either.

What was Jill Kendrick – because Mary was sure it was her – holding over Mr Danesford?

Why did it bother Charles that she had found that piece of wood at Lower Meadow Hall? She went over to the drawer and took it out and turned it over and over in her hands.

"Something will turn up," she told herself. "It has to."

Mary threw away all the food that had gone out of date

while she was away and cleaned out the fridge. Then she went shopping to top it all up again and buy something nice to eat that night.

On the way home, she saw a pretty shirt in a shop window and on reflection she decided that yes, she did deserve it after all she had been through and also, it was about time she wore something different to work. She entered the shop. The assistant had her back to Mary; she was chatting happily with a colleague as they put price tickets on the new stock. She laughed…. and her laugh pierced Mary's heart like a knife.

It was Ellen.

Mary hurried over.

"Ellen?"

The assistant turned.

She was too young, her nose was the wrong shape, her eyes were the wrong colour.

"I'm sorry, I thought you were someone else." Mary cast her eyes to the floor and ran for cover behind the clothes rack. Tears were close.

She blew her nose. This was not the time to let things get to her. She picked up the pretty shirt and went to ask the girl if she could try it on.

Back at home once again, she finished her meal then settled down in the chair to phone her mother. She told Alice all about the shirt and how she might buy some new trousers, too. She did her best to sound upbeat and forward-looking. If she called but kept out of the way, she should be able to convince her mother she had got over the accident and that she had got over Ben as well whilst Alice would not be able to examine her critically and conclude that she looked pale.

DAY 92

Mary had never known a day pass so slowly. She was worried about Jared; there were only eight days left and she did not know what to do.

She was worried about Mike but she had been to see Mme Delphine only the day before yesterday.

She picked up her book and put it down again. She found a film to watch on the television but could not concentrate.

It might be cheeky to go back to Mme Delphine so soon but inevitably, Mary decided to go after work the next day. For now, she would have a rest and make sure that she was ready for whatever the coming week might throw at her.

MONDAY
DAY 93

On Monday, Mary bounced in to work with a big smile and slightly more make-up than usual in order that the accident would be forgotten there, too, as soon as possible. She did not want people asking how she was, she wanted things to be normal and the truth was she was also somewhat embarrassed about it all.

Mary was surprised how the building had progressed in the few days she had been not been there.

"It always speeds up at the end," they said. "And come over here and have a look at this!"

Their next project was already well through the pre-construction phase and the designers had brought a virtual reality view of the building as it would be when finished.

"You don't get motion sickness, do you?" asked Pete but although Mary did, the kit was only there for one day and she was not going to pass up the chance of touring the college before a spade had been put in the ground. Josh was doubtful about letting Mary have a go but she was well enough to be signed off and back at work so there was little he could say.

She sat down and Josh put a headset on her then as she turned round, she saw paths and trees and people. She turned back and Josh, who was at the controls, took her down a wide path to the entrance.

"Wait until we go through a door," he said gleefully and Mary soon discovered that he meant exactly that; they went through closed doors without opening them so that they sort of hit you in the face and were not there. "You can go through ceilings, too," he said demonstrating.

"Now I know how Mike must feel," thought Mary. It was an odd sensation. Oh, Mike.

They walked down corridors and into laboratories and lecture theatres.

"Let's go downstairs," said Josh and Mary, who was already feeling strange, found herself gripping the arms of the chair. All in all, she was not sorry she had insisted on having a go but she was glad she did not have to jump up and walk a straight line when it was over.

"Good?" asked Pete.

"Yes."

"All right, then. Because you'll be coming with us as part of the team if you would like to."

Mary would have jumped for joy if she had not been feeling so wonky.

"We'll set up that course again, too," he promised.

At the end of the day Mary, who had considered asking to leave early and could contain herself no longer, headed straight for Mme Delphine's. However, even before she reached the house, she noticed that the gypsy caravan had gone. Mary walked up the path and rang the doorbell. No answer, just a distant echo. She peeped through a gap in the curtains. Everything looked as normal but there was a kind of emptiness; the cats that usually roamed the house and sat on the bookshelves were not there.

"Vadoma's away," called a voice and Mary turned to see the neighbour standing by the hedge. "She usually goes down to the coast for a day or two this time of year. She does a bit of fortune telling while she's there but it still makes a break. 'There's nothing like a bit of sea air' that's what Vadoma says."

Mary walked slowly back up the path dragging her feet, climbed into Tiger and went home.

TUESDAY
DAY 94

Mary drove home past Mme Delphine's just in case but the gypsy caravan was not there. She supposed it would be a few days before Mme Delphine returned. She kicked off her shoes and was about to turn on the television when there was a knock at the door.

"Andrew! Come in."

Andrew followed her to the living room, sat down and cleared his throat.

"I've come about the incident on the station…. we've examined the CCTV footage and it seems you *were* pushed. By Charles Armstrong. We have pictures of him coming down the steps to the platform, joining the crowd, then when you went to the platform edge ready to get on the train, he can clearly be seen putting his hand to the centre of your back very carefully so you wouldn't feel the contact then pushing you. We're absolutely sure it was him because he made the mistake of removing the bobble hat he was wearing before he left the station and we have that on camera, too."

A range of emotions crossed Mary's face. Incredulity, then almost instantly realisation – after all, Mike had warned her he was dangerous – and finally relief.

"So, you don't think I was trying to commit suicide anymore?"

"No, of course not, I never really did. But I had to ask," Andrew excused himself.

"It's all right. I'm just glad it's all cleared up now."

Andrew lapsed back into official mode. "Do you have any idea why Charles might want to kill you?"

"No. He must have worked out the Silverwood accounts came from me, I suppose. And I saw Tess in the park when I visited Gary and I saw her in the bank and she saw me, too. It seems a bit extreme, though."

There was also the conversation between Charles and Ben at the airfield but Charles had not seen her as far as she knew and Mary still did not know what to make of their exchange. Ben would not harm a child. Quite the opposite: he gave money to the hospice.

"Nothing else? You're sure?"

"Nothing else. Unless.... now I think about it there's something I ought to give you. It probably is not important but I found this at Lower Meadow Hall when we went over to make some preparations for the works fete."

Mary produced the piece of wood. Strictly speaking, she should give him the bracelet as well but Mike had been keen for it to be returned to its owner and she could never carry out his wish if it was shut in an evidence locker.

"I think it comes from a stage set. I'm guessing the chap who designs them used to store them there. But the funny thing is, when I showed it to Charles Armstrong, he seemed rattled I was asking about it."

"You showed it to Charles Armstrong?"

Sheepishly, Mary said: "I saw him doing some building work and we got talking." Talking was a stretch, Charles was even less friendly and conversational than his wife but never mind. "Anyway, I thought you ought to have it."

Andrew fished out a bag and Mary dropped it in.

Then: "Have you arrested him?" ventured Mary.

"The Armstrongs are away on holiday, due back early tomorrow morning. We'll pick them up straight away. You're quite safe," he assured her.

"And Alistair?"

"We don't want to pick him up until we can pick up Charles and Tess as well, in case we have to release him before Charles and Tess return. It would give him a chance to warn them."

Andrew looked at his watch.

"Do you have to be somewhere?" asked Mary.

"No," he replied. "Actually, my shift is finishing in five, four, three, two, one…. done."

"In that case, would you stay a little while?"

Andrew having indicated that he was not busy, Mary went to put the kettle on. She felt in need of company.

WEDNESDAY
DAY 95

Mary could not, however, block out her thoughts for ever. Charles had pushed her. Not Mike but Charles. The truth dawned. Mike, her self-appointed guardian, had followed her to the station. He saw the train coming towards her and he saw her standing on air, about to fall. All he had to do was let events take their course and they would be together, forever. But she had a right to a life. In an instant, he had vanished from the crowd and reappeared on the track. He blew, hard, and Mary fell backwards onto the platform. Logically, she had always known it could not have been the draught from the train because the train was moving far too slowly by that time.

Mary was late for work and had difficulty concentrating. Only five days left. With Mike gone, Mary could not ask about the traffic light but it did not matter; she knew she was nearly out of time.

They were finishing early today and as the clock struck four: "What's the matter, chair electrified?" inquired Ryan but Mary simply shot out of the door leaving a somewhat rushed 'goodbye' hanging in the air behind her. If she left straight away, she could get to the coast and have a couple of hours there and still be back before it got late.

The resort mentioned by Mme Delphine's neighbour was not large but even so there were a lot of stalls along the promenade. Mary walked past amusement arcades, hot-dog stands and fish and chip sellers, past piles of brightly coloured beach towels and balls and buckets and spades, past stands of sunglasses and all kinds of knick-knacks. The last of the stalls was in sight and Mme Delphine was nowhere to be seen.

Sighing deeply, Mary turned and went down some steps leading to the beach. She would at least go for a stroll along the sand and dip her toes in the sea having come this far. As she paddled in the soothing water, shoes in hand, she turned to look back at the town with its hotels and restaurants, at the houses lining the sea front, at the car park and adjoining fields – and then she saw it. The gypsy caravan was parked in a quiet spot where the cars petered out and a path led to the headland. If she had carried on to the very last stall, she would have seen it.

Ignoring the sand in her toes, she shoved her feet into her shoes and hurried back to the promenade. The stalls were closing as Mary hurried past to arrive somewhat out of breath at the caravan.

Mme Delphine welcomed her in. It was immediately obvious that Mary was upset.

"I know the truth about what happened on the station and I know Mike didn't try to push me, he saved me. I'm sorry I doubted him." She stared sadly at her clasped fingers then looked up at Mme Delphine. "I love him."

"There, there," comforted Mme Delphine.

"Please, can't you see what is happening to him?"

The silence seemed to last forever before Mme Delphine, silently imploring forgiveness, replied: "The crystal is dark. You were on my mind and I consulted it before you came. I saw nothing."

THURSDAY
DAY 96

After an uneventful day at work, Mary arrived back home to find Andrew on the doorstep. He had spent the intervening days continuing his investigation of Charles' accounts and fruitful it was too; he had discovered a whole new scam going on and solved a cold case to boot. Andrew was positively rubbing his hands in glee and needed someone to tell. Mary was all ears.

"Continuing from where we left off, Charles didn't need to get involved in the ransom, he was forced in to it," Andrew explained: "But I'll return to that later. His business was in trouble but then his fortunes turned round completely and all as a result of a job he did at Lower Meadow Hall."

Mary waited in silence.

"Basically, it was a refurbishment that never happened. And we have got the mastermind behind it all, some bloke named Ben MacKay."

"Ben!" Mary was incredulous.

"You know him?"

"Kind of. I used to. Or I thought I did." She mumbled a brief half-explanation; after all, it was none of his business.

"I'm sorry, Mary, but the real reason MacKay left his job at the insurance company when he went to join you at Bramwells was to draw a line under that chapter of his life; files closed, Ben Mackay gone, all over, no-one would look at any of it again. He was a young man in a hurry, you see. He sat at his desk on his not very generous salary and saw all these people getting insurance pay-outs for whiplash injuries they didn't have because it was easier for the insurance companies to pay up than fight the claim. So, he decided to get a piece of the action. It started out with him easing the path of accident claims for a cash-for-crash gang and taking a cut. But he couldn't do too many. He cut his ties with them and moved to a different department where he started plotting the Big One.

"That's where Charles came in. They met through Alistair when Alistair and Charles did some work on Ben's house. Charles was excited about his next project – Lower Meadow Hall – which was much bigger and more exciting than house extensions. But he was also resentful at the amount of money it would make for Henry. Which is where they discovered an interest in common, as you might say.

"But this time, MacKay wanted to be in control. He had found the cash-for-crash too haphazard. The gangs on the ground could easily have simply not given him his share and there wouldn't have been a thing he could do about it. MacKay taking control was fine by Charles; he was happy to let him sort out the details because planning wasn't his strong point. I don't know whether you know that Ben MacKay loves the theatre…."

"Yes," interrupted Mary. "We went one time. It was good."

"And he knows a famous set designer," continued Andrew.

"Yes. He stores his sets at the airfield these days. And?"

"They cooked up a scheme whereby instead of actually doing the refurbishment, Charles would simply install a stage set created by MacKay's mate. They would use the fact that these things look realistic from a distance to fool Henry into thinking the work had been done because Henry was happy to take a hands-off approach and monitor the job via progress photographs sent by Charles to show how they were getting on. Henry could cavort with his mistress and take an interest at the end when it was all finished. Then, before Henry could actually visit the Hall, they would set fire to it to cover their tracks and MacKay would nod the paperwork through and that would be that."

"But I don't see how Charles made a lot of money. All right, he was paid for work done…. and I don't see how Ben got any money at all," objected Mary. "The insurance pay-out went to Henry."

"Yes, it did. But Charles was reimbursed for some very expensive materials he hadn't bought, for example Adam fireplaces which were nothing but plywood. Which is why Charles wanted you dead, why he was not at all pleased to see that piece of wood you found. Henry wanted the place restored as faithfully as possible to how it had once been. Wonderful what careful examination of accounts can tell you. And no need to feel guilty about Henry and Rachel if Tess was thinking of it because the insurance pay-out meant they didn't lose.

"Meanwhile, Ben MacKay just happened to own the subcontractor company that did the structural repairs – and of course, no-one could tell after the fire that the work hadn't been done. Nothing but mastic and plenty of noise and 'Danger Keep Out' notices to fool any snoopers and more photographs for Henry. Another pretence with fake invoices to back it up. Your Ben had his own independent source of insurance money just in case Charles didn't cough up his fee for planning it all and felt more secure than with his previous schemes and made more money.

"Speaking of which, we've only just started looking into Mr MacKay's finances but he does seem to live rather well so I wouldn't be surprised to find more going on that we don't know about yet."

"How could I be so stupid? How could I fall for someone like that even a little bit?" wondered Mary and as though he could tell what she was thinking, Andrew comforted her: "He's a sociopath, they take everybody in."

In the back of her mind, Mary was still thinking about what Charles had said at the airfield that day. 'Shame about the kid.' Alistair had taken advantage of Jared's disappearance to send the ransom note but was it possible that Ben had organised the kidnapping? And never sent a note himself because something had gone wrong, something that Charles knew about because he was part of the plot? No, Tess would not allow it – but maybe Tess did not know.

"What about Jared?" she demanded.

"Charles swore he would never hurt Jared and that he had no idea what had happened to him and I believe him.

Apart from that, we're no nearer I'm afraid. The ransom was our only real lead. Follow the money. As regards the ransom, Alistair really was just taking advantage of the situation because he worked on the Hall – obviously, Charles couldn't do everything himself – soon realised what the rest of them were up to then when Jared was taken, he saw a chance to even things up a bit moneywise and Charles and Tess could hardly refuse to help. All sweetened with a suitable cut for Charles, of course."

Mary pottered to the kitchen and returned with hot coffee and chocolate biscuits.

"Most welcome," said Andrew.

"Mmm…. helps me think. Did you find out anything further about the second ransom demand?"

"Oh, didn't I say? That was the nurse, Jill Kendrick. After she helped Alistair in his little scheme by supplying the passports to get back at Henry for not leaving his wife, it occurred to her that she could put in a demand of her own."

Mary nodded. "How did she explain the fact the money wasn't picked up?"

"Simply that she changed her mind. She said she realised it was a nasty thing to do, adding more stress and misery to the Parkers and that she wished she had never sent it."

"Well," thought Mary. "She could hardly tell the truth without getting herself in more trouble."

Nor could Mary tell Andrew that Jill had not been prepared to risk picking up the money herself and instead had been blackmailing Mr Danesford to collect it for her because there was no way she could know something like that in the absence of Mike and she could not suggest a reason why Jill might be blackmailing Mr Danesford because she did not know one. Possibly, it had something to do with Mrs Danesford but again, Mary did not know what and could not tell Andrew she had been snooping at Jill's flat and found the newspaper cutting.

"Would you like to stay a while? I was about to order pizza."

Andrew would like to stay. Business over (except he could not help keep going back to it, this was such a coup) he was happy to enjoy Mary's company for a couple of hours before off home to bed and an early start tomorrow. They would be going to pick up Ben and although Andrew assumed that being his own boss, Ben would work gentleman's hours so around ten should be about right, he, Andrew, had a task force to organise.

"Can I come?" asked Mary.

"Sorry, no, this is a police operation."

Not to worry, Mary knew the time and the place and she would ensure that she and Tiger were in position at the airfield in plenty of time the next day.

FRIDAY
DAY 97

The problem was: how to traverse the vast open space between the entrance to the airfield and the hangars without being seen. Now that she and Ben had split up, Mary had no reason to be there and an excuse would probably come over as exactly that. Early was the best way, she concluded; early and pray.

Mary drove up to the entrance and took out some binoculars. Ben's sports car was parked in its usual place outside Hanger One. There were no planes on the runway so Jack was not sitting in some cockpit with a birds-eye view of the whole airfield. There were no mechanics milling about – they must still be in the hangar completing last-minute checks.

Mary put Tiger into gear and bumped across the old, disused runway to the back of Hangar Three. No-one would see her car there. She waited. No-one appeared demanding to know what she was doing there. So far, so good. Mary slid down in her seat.

Time passed and Mary thought she saw movement in the lane. The police were getting into position. She got out of her car and shut the door, conscious of the noise it made in the tense silence. For a few moments, Mary stood absolutely still then she ran the short distance to Hangar One, her feet clacking on the concrete. She pressed herself up against the night-cooled metal. She was short of breath, not from running but for fear she had been heard. She stood recovering then crept to the far corner of the hangar listening for voices. Nothing.

No, wait. Andrew was at the hangar door. In the distance, police cars were on the airfield ready to converge at his signal. Briefly, he entered the hangar then emerged shading his eyes to look across the runway.

Not many yards from Mary's vantage point, Jack was fussing round his precious plane. The smell of fuel was heavy in the air. Ben appeared from behind one of the wheels. Jack began to walk away and as Ben's eyes followed him, he saw Andrew.

Ben summed up the situation in a heartbeat. He climbed into the cockpit and started up the engines. Andrew unclipped a radio from his belt and began to give orders. Police cars sped out of nowhere from three different directions and started to close in.

They were too far away; they would never make it.

Ben could not be allowed to escape, not after the way he had fooled her with his agreeable manners and his charity work, not after he said he loved her and made her feel wretched for failing to give him her full attention, not after the injuries caused to Mike's sister.

On impulse, Mary ran over and climbed aboard. Her heart was in her mouth as she took the seat next to him. They taxied down the runway, swerving to avoid a police car and rose into the air. Ben turned to her and Mary was afraid he was going to push her out; probably to her death since they were already airborne. She thought of all the things she would leave unfinished – Jared, Ellen – and of the people she had not said 'goodbye' to. It must not end here.

Instead, Ben motioned to the headset.

"Good of you to join me. Does that mean you want to give our relationship another go?"

Was he serious? The arrogance.

"Ben, this is crazy. You have to give yourself up. Where will you go?"

"I have property abroad and money in off-shore accounts in case of need. No-one should underestimate Ben MacKay."

"Turn the plane around Ben, please. Think of your parents."

"I'll invite them to join us. We could have quite the life, M. All you have to do is see that therapist and we'll be very happy. I still love that girl I met at Bramwells; I never stopped."

As the fields below gave way to coastline he started to hum. Where should they go? Georgia perhaps. For now. He was going through the possibilities in his head, thinking aloud for Mary's benefit, when the plane gave a jolt. Odd. It was a beautiful calm day, no turbulence at all.

What he had not noticed was that while he was dreaming, Mary had squashed herself as far as possible against the door leaving well over half of her seat empty.

The plane did it again. It seemed to be developing a mind of its own. It was turning! Frantically, Ben pushed buttons and pulled levers but nothing seemed to make any difference. Now he was panicking, hands running all over the instrument panel randomly trying anything.

Mary smiled in amusement. She had to crane uncomfortably round Mike, who was sitting in the other half of her seat, to get a good view of what was happening but it was worth it. Mary did not know anything about flying but it was obvious to her that Mike was a skilled pilot and thank goodness he was. Unseen by Ben, he sat beside him anticipating and thwarting every move. Appalled and uncomprehending, Ben gave up trying to influence this clearly eccentric piece of hardware of which Jack was so fond as they executed a wide circle and turned back towards the airfield.

Ben knew where the plane was headed and that he would be arrested on arrival. There should be a parachute…. but as he moved to look for it, he found himself pushed back and pinned to the seat.

"Stay there…."

Mary could see that Mike took quiet satisfaction in seeing the real fear in Ben's eyes as he looked wildly around the cockpit to see who had spoken.

Back at the airfield, Jack had watched as his beloved plane turned to a speck in the sky and disappeared. He could have wept.

For his part, Andrew looked on in frustration as his quarry flew over their heads and away, the happiness he had felt the previous evening gone in a flash, his mind full of pictures of his colleagues weaving their way down the corridor, arms outstretched, pretending to be aeroplanes....

Wearily, the task force was preparing to leave.

Jack was the first to hear the engine.

"It is. It can't be. It is." Jack would know his baby anywhere. He strained his eyes towards the sky, searching excitedly.

Then with a shout of 'Look, there' one of the policemen alerted them to the returning plane. The dot he pointed at grew bigger; it really was coming back.

"Well, I never. Why would he come back? Well, I never." Andrew was dumbfounded. But the reason did not matter, only the fact. He shook himself, took charge and started giving orders.

As the plane taxied to a halt, Jack ran to meet it. There was no point telling him to keep back, it was not going to happen. Police personnel converged on Ben as he came down the steps and he was taken into custody. Immediately they dispersed, Andrew paused only to mouth a hurried 'See you later' to Mary before he joined them in their dash to the police station to get Ben locked up as soon as possible.

Good, they were gone. Now Mary could turn her attention to the tall figure standing alone on the runway looking very happy.

"That was wonderful," he shouted, Mary hardly able to hear him against the rising wind. She was not sure if he meant flying again or the sight of Ben being taken away in handcuffs.

Mary took few steps towards him.

"Mike. What on earth are you doing here? How...." her voice tailed off as he looked as though he was about to say something, shivered and was gone.

And no matter how much she thought him he did not come back.

* * *

Andrew called that evening.

"Well done you," he congratulated her. "I didn't know you could fly a plane."

"Nor did I," observed Mary.

"That MacKay fellow says it flew itself."

"Amazing. The wonders of modern technology."

"Well, I think you deserve a medal."

Mary hated taking the credit for something she had not done but she could hardly say 'It wasn't me; it was Mike.'

"Actually, I rather enjoyed it. I mean, there were a few scary moments, of course, but all in all, it was fun."

She pictured Ryan's reaction on her return to work. There would be no keeping her exploits secret because it was about to be in all the papers. It would be good publicity for the launch of her new career, though, now that finally she knew what she wanted to do. She would gradually slide into detective work of some sort.

Mary knew what her first case would be, too. She would find Ellen.

DAY 98

The next day, Mary could not discipline her thoughts. She had, of course, called on Mme Delphine but there was no reply. Ideas (or maybe they would be more accurately described as fears) floated through her mind. Should she have told Andrew what Charles had said at the airfield? 'Shame about the kid….' Then it hit her. Charles had not been referring to Jared at all, he had been referring to Julia.

Poor Julia. What a price to pay for a simple 'wrong place, wrong time.' Mary could visualise her going back to Lower Meadow Hall for her phone, delaying to admire the proportions of the entrance hall, imagining how it must have been in its heyday – dances, dresses – wishing she could gain entrance to the almost completed State Rooms of which she had only seen pictures…. just a little peep through the keyhole…. wow.

And then suddenly the whole Hall was on fire. By now Mary had looked up the report and she remembered clearly what it had said. It had concluded that the fire may (or may not) have been the result of a faulty connection in the electrical distribution board combined with a lack of fire protection to the fuse cupboard ceiling. Rumours persisted that there was more to it but in the absence of evidence to the contrary, there was little that could be said.

Apparently, the fire had quickly spread out of control throughout the whole building because adaptations to the Hall over the years to add amenities had produced hidden voids including perhaps some that were not documented because of the loss of building plans and records.

Now, of course, more information had come to light: the fire was arson. According to Ben and Charles, the plan had been to destroy the State Rooms and the part where the so-called structural work had been done and to make it look like an accident but the fire intensified engulfing the whole building and forcing Charles and Alistair to run for their lives. Obviously, they denied knowing Julia was there. Mary imagined Julia stumbling about, coughing, trying to get out.

She imagined poor Mike grieving for the injured Julia first in life and then in death, unable to rest until he knew whether it was really an accident or whether she had seen too much and if it was attempted murder, who was responsible.

Naturally, Mike's initial investigations would have focussed on Henry who had profited hugely from the fire but once he realised how much trust Henry had placed in Charles and how vital the fire had been to Charles' change of fortune, the focus had changed to Charles. Realising that Charles was no criminal mastermind and digging deeper had brought Mike to Ben and to Bramwells.

It was so clear now that it was not just jealousy that made him try to separate her and Ben who was undeniably responsible for the whole idea, the brains behind it all, even if he did not actually strike the match.

All of which explained Mike's return, his 'research.'

And as Mike looked for answers, consumed by grief, what should he find but Mary walking straight into Ben's arms. Then, as he learned more about Ben and his embryonic criminal empire, so he became more protective of Mary and his hatred grew.

Her thoughts darted out of control in all directions. How could she ever have even contemplated the idea that Mike had meant her harm? When Mme Delphine said there was someone in her life who should not be there, why had she assumed she meant Mike? She could equally well have meant Ben.

"Mike, I have been so wrong about everything. I'm so sorry," she whispered to the room in general.

Oh Mike. If only she could speak to him one more time.

SUNDAY
DAY 99

Day ninety-nine. Only one day left.

"I must pull myself together and try to salvage the only thing it might still be possible to salvage out of this whole episode. I must find Jared." The thought filled Mary's mind. It took up so much space, she could hardly think. And yet, think she must.

Accepting that neither Charles, Tess, Alistair, Ben nor Jill had taken Jared whatever else they might have done left only Gary, Mr Danesford or the Parkers themselves.

Mary stood looking out of the window.... and saw Rachel coming down the path. Oh, my goodness, she had totally forgotten that she had invited her.

"What a charming little flat," Rachel cried as soon as she walked in. "I love your choice of curtains."

"Sadly, I can't take any credit for them, they came with the flat."

"No matter, you chose the flat, curtains included and you have the whole place looking lovely."

Mary waved Rachel to a chair. She scrutinised her carefully. Was she being determinedly cheerful to hide her grief or did she not accept Andrew's assertion that Jared was dead? Had he shown her the photographs?

Hastily, Mary pushed some sandwiches together and tipped doughnuts onto a plate while she made some tea. Rachel sat waiting for her to return and looking around the room, her eye was caught by the wedding pictures on the mantelpiece.

"May I?"

Mary handed them to her. Unnoticed, she slipped an extra photograph onto the bottom of the pile.

"You do look nice, Mary. Is that your boyfriend?" She pointed to Ben.

"Used to be. It's all over now."

Rachel noted her pained expression.

"Poor Mary." She turned back to the photographs, changing the subject. "And it's such a lovely setting. Who is the bride?"

"Someone from where I used to work. We keep in touch, though."

"And who is this?" Rachel had reached the final photograph. It was of Mr Danesford, taken in the park with Mary's camera on zoom. Mary studied her and detected nothing but innocent inquiry. Obviously, they did not know each other, still less had had an affair.

"It's my cousin," she lied.

Thinking hard, she offered Rachel a sandwich. That seemed to kill the idea that Jared and Darren were brothers with Rachel as the mother of both (which Mary had never really found credible) but it still left the scenario where

Henry was the father and Mary had to know. She had so few ideas left and so little time.

Mary risked continuing. She took the photos and started arranging them on the mantelpiece again.

"It was a lovely wedding. I wonder if we'll hear the patter of tiny feet soon."

Rachel winced.

"I'm sorry, I shouldn't have said that."

"Don't be silly, it's a perfectly natural thing to say. Just because we had trouble…."

Then the floodgates opened; Rachel seemed to want to talk. "We tried and tried for years, it was so disheartening and then when we went for tests it turned out Henry was sterile."

Mary started in surprise. She had not seen that coming. If Rachel was not the mother of both and Henry was not the father that would mean that Jared and Darren could not be brothers….

Before Mary could expand the thought further, Rachel continued: "He took it badly; it was a blow to his masculinity and he felt he'd let me down because he knew how much I wanted a baby."

Rachel was clearly upset by the memory but although Mary tried to change the subject she carried on.

"So, I went for IVF. It didn't work and it didn't work and I felt ill and Henry didn't know whether to keep paying for more – I was so lucky we could afford it – or to ban any more attempts because of my health but they said we were too old to adopt and I cried so much…. then after all the years of heartache, finally we had Jared and we were so happy…." In spite of Rachel's best efforts, a quiet sob escaped. "And now he's gone…."

Rachel sat quietly for a while lost in her own thoughts while Mary's mind worked overtime.

"Jared should have been going to the hospital next week," offered Rachel.

"Was he ill?"

This was worrying. Any health problems should have been made public right from the start. However, even at this late stage, if there were something, it might give Mary a clue as to what sort of danger Jared was in, what sort of misfortune might befall him. Especially if it were something the Spite Brigade could capitalise on. Eagerly, she waited for Rachel to continue.

But: "He wasn't ill. He was booked in for a hearing test. The nurse at the clinic seemed to think it was a good idea just as a precaution. She said there was a flatness about his speech then she whispered and shook some little beads in a ball and he didn't respond. She called him more loudly, though, and he turned round. Children do ignore what doesn't interest them, though, don't they?"

The question was rhetorical.

The sandwiches being finished, Mary offered Rachel a doughnut. Not only, in Mary's opinion, did chocolate cheer up most situations but cake and doughnuts did likewise. Between mouthfuls, Mary got the conversation going again and they found themselves reminiscing about the holiday.

"Maybe we should go away for a girls' weekend some time," suggested Rachel and Mary found the idea welcome.

And so it was that she was smiling as she showed Rachel out.

"It is good to see you looking so much better, Mary my dear," said a voice and Mme Delphine stepped into the hallway.

"Oh, well, I…."

"There is no need to explain."

"Come in."

Mary told Mme Delphine about Ben's arrest.

"I saw Mike. Then he was gone again."

"Mike was shown leniency because it was accepted that he did not plan the accident and in saving your life on the station, he displayed selflessness and true love. He was sent into solitary confinement for a period of quiet contemplation. You saw him at the airfield only because he was allowed out to help apprehend Ben.

"But before he returned, he was able to give me a message. It is very brief I am afraid. He said to tell you 'Wear stout shoes and take a fish slice.'"

"Was that it? What does it mean?"

Mme Delphine shrugged.

"I thought perhaps you might know."

* * *

Alone again, Mary sat brooding. Rachel had said that Henry was sterile and Jared was the result of IVF. That was a revelation. And it gave Mary an idea.

She had better speak to Andrew. But first she had something she needed to look up.

Mary went to the computer. First, she brought up a copy of the newspaper cutting she had seen in Jill's flat and read carefully through it. She was moving on to research the Danesford family tree when the internet crashed.

Great. Mary crawled behind the sofa, located the box and turned it off and on again. The light was red. She tried again. Still red.

Mary stood up – and out of the window, she a man fiddling in a box at the side of the road. Mary went out and spoke to him.

"What's the problem?"

"Not working."

"I can see that," said Mary impatiently. "What's wrong with it?"

"Could be a connection somewhere. Could be water getting in. I won't know until I do some more tests."

"How long will that take?"

The man sucked his teeth. "Maybe an hour." He whistled cheerfully. "Could be here all night."

Mary returned to her flat. Now what? She was running out of time.

The article having given the name of the town where the accident happened, Mary had searched the electoral role for Danesford's old address and she was glad she had. She would go there just in case the connection was not restored. If it was, she could still dial in when she got back.

Mary looked at her watch. It was a three-hour drive. Everyone would be in bed by the time she arrived.

"Perhaps luck will be on my side," she told herself as she jumped into Tiger.

Looking along the deserted street, Mary's heart sank. She slumped over the steering wheel, head lying on her arms and breathed deeply. All she wanted to do was confirm her theory. Was it so much to ask?

A knock on the window brought her back to her surroundings.

"Are you all right?" The man in the yellow coat was clearly concerned.

Mary got out of the car.

"Yes, yes. Sorry. I've had a long drive and now I'm here it seems it was all for nothing. I came to see Patrick Danesford but his flat is empty. He's an old friend. Do you know him?"

"I know him. He couldn't bear to stay here after what happened. Tragic, it was," replied the man. Briefly he recounted the story.

"How awful." It wasn't just words; Mary was truly appalled.

She was also right, if not quite in the way she had expected.

The man continued on his way to work and Mary drove home. Dawn was breaking by the time she arrived. She had been up all night but she did not care. She woke up the computer and tried the internet again. It was working!

She checked the records. Her suspicions (and the man's story) were confirmed.

MONDAY
DAY 100

Andrew should be arriving at the police station any time now.

"I only hope it's soon enough," thought Mary desperately. Today, Jared would die. With or without the help of the Spite Brigade. And she still had no idea what to look out for, only that she must prevent it from happening.

There were two more things to do before Mary left the flat. She went to the hall cupboard and took out her stout winter shoes then went to the kitchen for the fish slice. She rammed it into her handbag leaving the zip slightly open because the end of the handle stuck out and set off for the police station.

Andrew, as usual, had a desk full of work. Even so, he was very aware the kidnapping case was not closed. They had caught Ben and Charles and Tess and Alistair and Jill. They were in the process of recovering the ransom money and of course, the nagging doubts surrounding the Lower Meadow Hall case were now put to rest. But, like Ellen's family before them, the Parkers needed closure and it was his responsibility to see they had it.

Sergeant Rivers alerted him to Mary's visit. She stood quietly at the door, waiting.

"Young lady wants a word; she says it won't take long."

Andrew motioned her in. Her presence made him think of Jared and as he sat tapping the desk with his pencil, he spoke his thoughts aloud.

"We'll carry on looking for Jared's…. er…. for Jared. We won't give up."

"He is not dead. And I know where he is," said Mary. "Patrick Danesford has him."

"Now Mary…."

"No, really." Excitedly she pulled out the photo from Gemma's wedding. "See here, look."

Andrew looked baffled. "I don't see Danesford."

"No, this is a photo from a wedding I just went to." Mary sounded impatient. "Look at these two people." She pointed.

"They're twins," observed Andrew.

"No, they're not," replied Mary triumphantly. "They're brothers, there's a two-year age gap. But see how similar they look."

"Yes…." agreed Andrew. "But I don't see the point."

"I was staring at the photo and it came to me: Jared and Darren are brothers! Like Max and Oliver in the photo here they look so similar they could be twins. So, I engineered a little chat with Rachel Parker…." Andrew raised his eyebrows, "…. I mean I didn't really think Rachel would have an affair…. and it turns out Jared was the result of IVF. Henry Parker is sterile."

Andrew took in the information.

"You think Patrick Danesford was the sperm donor."

"Yes. That has to be it, the boys are practically identical. I can't prove it, of course, but I'm sure you could. You and your lab."

"And I suppose the sightings of near-identical children reported after the reward was offered would be sisters." Andrew sounded thoughtful. "The important question is: does Danesford have Darren or Jared and where is the other one?"

"He has Jared, I told you already. Darren is dead. I checked the account of Mrs Danesford's accident in the paper because it occurred to me that Darren might have died in the crash…."

"He didn't," interrupted Andrew. "I read the report."

"No, but I went to Danesford's old address and a neighbour told me that a few days after Darren came home from hospital, Danesford went to his room and found him dead. A blood clot on the brain. A delayed consequence of the accident. It can happen. So, when I got home, I checked death certificates to make sure."

"And that's what Jill Kendrick was blackmailing Patrick Danesford with," she muttered under her breath. As to why she had not, even anonymously, told the police that Danesford had Jared and not Darren, Mary could only speculate that she had not wanted to risk him retaliating that she been blackmailing him since an investigation would immediately have revealed that she had been Henry's (betrayed) mistress and that it was she who had sent the second note. Her career would be over. Now, of course, the police had discovered all that anyway.

"And then Danesford saw Jared on the bus…."

"That must have been a shock, no wonder he looked like he'd seen a ghost," interrupted Mary.

"And he took him as a replacement for Darren."

"Because he desperately didn't want Darren to be gone and because he thought Jared might rouse Anne-Marie from her coma."

"We'll pick him up. Sergeant!" called Andrew.

Mary looked at her watch. "It's his day off. He'll be at the hospital visiting his wife. I want to go to the hospital, perhaps I could hitch a ride?"

"Certainly."

"Oh, and by the way, I found out something else. Mrs Parker was waiting for a hearing test for Jared."

"So, the kid is deaf. I wish she'd thought to mention that before."

"No, he's not, he just doesn't have the annoyingly sharp little ears they usually have. I suppose she didn't mention it because she doesn't quite believe it. He's her first so she had no comparison and if she's always close to him and he's used to her voice it might take a while for the penny to drop. She told me herself he was her world."

"Which explains why the child in the park ignored me when I called him," thought Mary ruefully. "I couldn't shout so he didn't hear. It explains why his speech isn't clear as well."

And come to think of it, it might explain his potential misfortune, too: Jared was to be run over.

Mary's relief that they were going to get him was immense but she wanted to be on her way. She wanted to be with him, looking out for him. If only she could warn Andrew.

Mary hopped from foot to foot as she waited for him to put on his coat. For his part, as Mary turned to the door, Andrew noticed the handle of the fish slice sticking out of her handbag and did a double-take. Best not to ask, he decided.

Once at the hospital, it was with a mounting sense of relief that Mary guided Andrew and Sergeant Rivers to Mrs Danesford's room. They arrived to see Patrick Danesford sitting beside Anne-Marie's bed reading to Jared who began an enthusiastic if tuneless rendition of 'Old MacDonald had a farm' and was squealing like a pig and mooing like a cow in all the right places.

Thank goodness. They had arrived in time. Jared was alive, Andrew was about to arrest Mr Danesford and Jared would soon be safely back with Rachel who was not likely to let him out of her sight – or her arms – for some time. The tension flowed out of Mary: she felt more relaxed than she had felt for months.

Mr MacDonald's farm having acquired a full set of animals, Patrick Danesford closed the book. Jared looked at him expectantly – there were other books in the shopping bag – but Patrick Danesford's eyes were glued to the screen on the monitor beside Anne-Marie's bed. It was beeping and a graph was jumping on the screen. As they stood in the doorway, they saw her stir.

"Narna," said Jared.

"Yes, all right," Patrick Danesford replied absent-mindedly.

Jared crawled over to a shopping bag on the bed and took out a banana. He settled down happily to peel it.

Mary, like Patrick Danesford, was looking at the screen when: "Mary! Look out!" It was Mike's voice. "Can't stop," he added urgently and was gone.

Mary turned towards the origin of the cry. Out of the corner of her eye she detected movement. A large brown spider was crawling out of the shopping bag and heading straight for Jared. Instantly Mary saw it, she recognised it as a banana spider, one of the most poisonous spiders in the world.

Mary froze. Her mouth went dry, her throat constricted. It was huge. She began to feel dizzy. She was about to faint.

Worse still, it had all been for nothing. She had been desperate to find Jared because of Ellen. She had been determined to find him by the hundredth day so that tiny coffin would remain empty.

So much for car accidents. The Spite Brigade had chosen the perfect weapon; they knew she was terrified of spiders, that even if she arrived in time, she would stand here like this, watching, paralysed, as the spider crawled onto Jared's hand. Any moment, it would bite. She would have failed again. And she would have a new nightmare to add to the old one, the nightmare of watching Jared die and knowing that this time, she really could have changed history.

Meanwhile, the Spite Brigade would be taking pleasure in having carried out their mission in such a way as to further increase the misery.

"Pull yourself together. He needs you."

This time it was not Mike speaking but the little voice in her head.

Mary jolted from her trance and operating entirely on autopilot, she yanked the fish slice from her bag and flicked the spider onto the floor. She screwed her eyes shut and down came her foot.

Crunch.

She shuddered, and turning to Andrew, she buried her face in his shoulder, whimpering.

"Ugh! Ugh!"

He looked surprised but put his arms around her and patted her back.

"There, there. It's all right."

Mary raised her head a little and looked at him.

"Is it dead?"

"Oh, yes. Some zoologist type probably wanted that."

Again, Mary raised her head and looked at him.

"Tough," she whispered and buried her face in the folds of his jacket. Gently, Andrew extricated himself.

By now, Mr Danesford had become aware of their presence. He looked from Andrew to the sergeant and back again, his expression betraying that he knew why they were there. He handed Darren to the nurse, asking her to take the little boy outside so he could have a quiet moment with his wife. Gently, he kissed her. She opened her eyes fully and touched his arm.

"I thought I heard Darren."

Andrew, watching, shook his head.

"All in good time, darling. You've been very ill. The doctor is on his way." He looked up at Andrew, his eyes full of tears and patted her hand. "All in good time."

How could he tell her, and yet he would have to, but not now. For now, it was best she thought she would see Darren all in good time, whereas the fact was that all in good time she would learn the painful truth.

Sergeant Rivers took hold of Patrick Danesford's arm.

"Before you go," Andrew broke in. "How did you arrange to get the photos of Jared playing dead?"

"I got him to help me make some biscuits. We had a great time. While we were doing it, I 'accidently' dropped the pat of butter into the bowl of flour. The flour went up in the air and all over the place. He was covered." Patrick Danesford chuckled at memory. "I dusted it off his jumper and out of his hair and I wiped his face – or so he thought, but actually I was rubbing the flour in. We finished the biscuits and he was so tired he fell asleep on the floor. I put a bluish cloth over the lamp and took the photos before I moved him to bed. Simple."

Sergeant Rivers escorted Patrick Danesford away. Andrew suggested a cup of tea. He and Mary made their way to the volunteers' station where they sat in silence, each lost in their own thoughts.

"What a mess," mused Mary. "And it's all my fault. Well, sort of. Oh, I don't know."

She shook her head and muttered regretfully to herself: "And I should have listened when Mike tried to warn me about Ben…."

"Who is Mike?" asked Andrew.

"Just someone."

"It's not your fault, anyway. You didn't kidnap Jared or invent money-making schemes. Any damage arising is down to those who did."

"Speaking of which, what will happen to Mr Danesford?"

"That's for the court to decide. Danesford's lawyer will doubtless argue that he wasn't thinking straight in his emotional state, that he didn't mean any harm, that his only intention was to get Darren back for Anne-Marie."

Business concluded, Andrew was ready to leave but not Mary who reminded him she had asked to hitch a ride because she wanted to go to the hospital irrespective of Andrew's arrest of Mr Danesford.

Andrew took her hand and inquired: "Anything I can do?"

"No, you go."

"Catch you later, then." He gave her hand a squeeze and departed.

Mary got up slowly and made her way to Julia's room, but here she was in for another surprise.

* * *

When Mary entered the room, she saw Mike sitting by the bed but something about him stopped her in her tracks. She stood silently by the door. The hand that was holding Julia's seemed strangely translucent, in fact, Mike looked altogether less substantial. Even his thick, dark hair had a see-through quality to it. She must have stood unnoticed watching them for ten minutes and during that time, Mike seemed to grow steadily paler. She wanted to go to him but knew she should not.

The only sound was the regular beep of Julia's monitor. That is, until the beep changed to a continuous monotone and Mary realised that Julia had died. In a daze, she walked over and pulled the cord by the bed to summon help. It seemed like hours before the nurses came running and bundled her out of the room but of course it was not.

Alone in the corridor, she replayed the scene over and over in her mind. Mike had seemed to fade and disappear to be replaced by a polyhedron of light dancing in the air. Dancing with another polyhedron that was Julia. The Mike polyhedron came over and hovered in front of her then returned to its place. And then they flew through the window and were gone.

Mary waited for the nurses to come and speak to her but she knew what they had to say. She stumbled from the hospital crying, not just for Julia but because she knew that this time, Mike was gone for ever.

EPILOGUE

Slowly, Mary made her way home, her footsteps the only sound in the empty street. She let herself in and took off her coat. The flat had grown larger and emptier since she left it that morning and full of irrelevance. Irrelevant letters waiting for her to deal with them, irrelevant reminders pinned to the wall in order of pointlessness. She made herself a cup of coffee and sat staring into space. Time passed and the coffee had gone cold when she became aware of movement at the window.

"Come on, Ginge," she said spying her little friend outside. "Come on in, I could do with a cuddle."

The cat did not need telling twice. He walked straight in as though he owned the place and jumped onto the sofa. Mary gathered him into her arms and he purred like an express train as she stroked the top of his head. They watched television together then she found him a piece of chicken in the fridge and he curled up on the rug and went to sleep.

Mary went to bed. In the morning, still lying in bed, she phoned in sick; she needed a day or two before she could face her workmates. Eventually she got up, moped around in her dressing gown and made beans on toast. The next day was pretty much the same except she had a bath and phoned for a pizza. The next day too. And the next. And the next.

With a new week beginning, she returned to work where Dan and Ryan provided plenty of distraction in their usual inimitable way and the days passed – mechanically – but they passed.

Mary considered going to stay with her mother for a while but it was a long way from work so she made do with frequent visits. One such visit found her mother particularly chirpy as she ushered Mary in.

"Look who I've found," and there sat Andrew wearing a somewhat boyish grin. At least someone was happy.

Conscious that she was being churlish, Mary congratulated Andrew on his now confirmed imminent promotion. She felt Alice's eyes boring into her back, heard a sigh escape and imagined the clasped hands and the little smile as he invited her for a champagne dinner by way of celebration and although Mary was not ready to feel as enthusiastic as she might, she accepted the invitation gracefully.

But much as Alice might erroneously think that with Ben gone – and what a disappointment he had turned out to be – that the mature and reliable Andrew was the ideal choice as replacement, Mary did not need another man in her life. Her track record in that area was iffy to say the least. She was enjoying the simplicity of being alone.

She turned to look at Andrew as he talked to her mother. True, he had not criticised her stubborn refusal to let the kidnapping go. He was good with people. Through the window, the sun shone across his face accentuating the warmth in his eyes. He was not at all like either Ben or Mike but he had a certain something she could not place.

Life might be simpler but the truth was Mary felt lonely with both Ben and Mike gone.

She went over to join them.

* * *

Mary had worked it all out now: Mike had come back because of Julia. He needed answers before he could rest. She should have realised that something (or someone) had drawn him to the office. Logic should have quickly narrowed the list of suspects if she had been thinking about it the right way; he had appeared at the same time as Ben.

Clearly, he had been allowed to return one last time to escort Julia to the Other Realm but with her death, his link to the mortal world was broken and he had to leave for good.

So, it was with amazement that she arrived home one night to find Mike sitting in her chair.

"But how come…." she began.

"What happened to 'Nice to see you, how are you?'" teased Mike.

"Well, yes of course, but how come…. I mean I thought…."

"After a period of contemplation, it was agreed I was suitable for rehabilitation. Which is where I have been. With the guilty facing the music and Julia…. passed over…. that should have been the end of the matter. But you wouldn't stop calling me."

"I wasn't calling, I was just worried and I couldn't get you out of my thoughts." She gave him a hug. "Not that it isn't great to have you back."

"Good to be here."

"I got your message. Thank you for the happy ending."

Mike chuckled.

"I heard what happened. My brave girl, eyes tight shut…. one of those rare instances where the murderer wasn't the last to see the victim alive."

"Oh, shut up. You're no better than you ever were, period of contemplation or no period of contemplation." She smiled indulgently at him and Mike smiled back.

"I should have known. The spider in the crystal ball…."

"It's not surprising you discounted it as nothing but a manifestation of your fears. Are you over the spider phobia now?"

"Yes…. No…. Yes…. I don't have to like them, do I?"

"I think you can be excused a certain lack of enthusiasm."

Thoughtfully, Mary said: "There is something bothering me, though. We made a bargain. I said I needed supernatural help and I did although not in the way I thought – stout shoes and a fish slice, indeed! But you never said what it was you wanted me to do for you. I owe you my half of the bargain."

"You don't. You did it without me asking. I wanted Ben and his co-conspirators parcelled up and delivered to Andrew tied up with a big red bow. All that time ago, I couldn't give you the documents from the insurance company that proved Ben's guilt…."

Mary nodded. She remembered him telling her that would be interference too far. That he was still investigating Charles and Alistair. And that it would be wrong to ask her anyway.

"Because, at the time, I loved Ben."

"But you approached the problem from the other end. I watched as all by yourself, you found evidence against Charles and Alistair that led back to Ben."

In the comfortable silence that followed, Mary sat looking affectionately at Mike. She sighed. There was something else she had to know.

Hesitantly she asked: "Is this it? Will I ever see you again?"

"Gosh, I don't know. If you carry on yelling the way you have been, I expect you will. Otherwise, none of us will get any peace."

Mary smiled a wide, happy smile.

"Stay a while. I have ice cream."

"Who could resist an invitation like that?"